Derek's Revenge

Derek has not had much success getting his first great novel started - in fact, the research it requires has nearly cost him his marriage and ruined several pairs of his wife's tights. All he needs is a better topic, maybe he should be writing non-fiction, he is a journalist, after all…
As is normal for Derek, things go pretty rapidly and hilariously downhill from there!

I0667088

Mac Black

Current occupation: a writer of humorous fiction. Previous working background: shipbuilding on the River Clyde, tyre manufacturing in Dundee and working in the food industry in Fife (in jobs that didn't make his hands too dirty).

He was born in Glasgow and lived there for about half a life before moving to Carnoustie and then to Cupar, his present home.

He has been married for a long time.

Current titles by Mac Black

Please... Call Me Derek
Derek's in Trouble
Derek's Revenge
Derek's Good Relations (2013)

Why not check the publisher's website www.uppublications.ltd.uk or follow Mac on www.macblack.info

First published in Great Britain in 2012 by U P Publications Ltd
Head Office: 25 Bedford Street, Peterborough, UK. PE1 4DN

Cover design copyright © Mike Peers 2012

A CIP Catalogue record of this book is available from the British Library

ISBN 978-1908135124

9 3 5 7 0 8 6 4 2 1

Also published for Kindle by U P Publications under ISBN 978-1908135131

FIRST PAPERBACK EDITION

Published by U P Publications - Printed in England by The Lightning Source Group

www.uppublications.ltd.uk
www.macblack.info

DEREK'S REVENGE

Mac Black

U P Publications
2012

1

Derek Toozlethwaite was unhappy. There he sat, alone in the cottage with his thoughts...

For those who may not have known him before, this is a bloke who used to be known as 'Sweaty', not a particularly attractive name as I'm sure you will readily agree, and one which gave him pain to hear, over ...and over ...and...

Being stuck with Sweaty for such a long time, he thought things would never change, but they did. During the last twelve months, he determined to make people call him by his real name, Swea... Sorry (habit dies hard) by his real name, Derek, and at long last he could claim he was winning. It had been an emotional journey and one where maybe he could be accused of treating the problem too emotionally; he lost his temper every so often, but it worked!

One by one, his friends and relations resisted successfully the temptation to continue with the silly nickname, but although he was delighted about that, at this very moment he was feeling bad, nothing to do with his name – he was lacking a mother.

It wasn't true depression, obviously, or something to visit the doctor about. No-one else needed to know. It was a very private thing, but he was suffering. His was a severe case of mumlessness. Yes, you say, but at the age he has reached, surely he has developed some immunity, but he hasn't.

Today it is hitting him hard.

He had never known her presence, or even what she looked like. You can imagine his frustration – no photographs seemed to exist. He wasn't aware if she was still alive, though he had no reason to believe that she was not, and the possibility that she was out there somewhere and he was simply being ignored, bugged him.

Of course, with Derek, this was only one of many things bugging him, but the fact that today he felt motherless pushed this to the top of his 'bugging-me' list. He was almost thirty-two and married with a lovely wife and, though he had grown up being cared for lovingly by his grandparents for nearly thirty of his developing years, he just couldn't help it, this motherless feeling was niggling away. It was odd though, he'd been ok yesterday...

At least he had a birth certificate to look at. That showed his mother named as Millicent, Millicent Smith and he had a father called James Toozlethwaite. He had a daddy – he wasn't a little bastard – and knowing that should have satisfied Derek. Admittedly they were with him for a short spell, but realistically it was a very short spell – when he'd been too young to know. They both vanished over the horizon soon after he was born. Surely, being the age he was then, he could feel reassured that it was nothing that he did personally. He couldn't have said or even done anything to have caused their departure, being so ridiculously young and, though 'blame' was a word he knew very well, it couldn't have been his fault then.

Granny and Grandad Smith being lumbered with a smelly little kid – as he surely must have been – were always magnanimous about it all. They certainly never grumbled at him for existing – maybe for many of the other things that he did wrongly later in life, but not just for existing. He realised he could have finished up in an orphanage, or been fostered out, so he did appreciate the amount of work he must have caused his elderly grandparents. There was no question – they must have loved him. He probably hadn't said it to them often enough in the past, he knew, and now he was a grown man it was difficult to say it aloud but ...he loved them back.

They must have already gone through the difficult bringing-up process with his mother. Doing it once was probably hard enough, and yet, they did it again – for him. Why, he asked himself? Did they bring it on themselves perhaps? Had they maybe failed with her?

Derek was an experienced journalist now and one with

considerable expertise when it came to encouraging people he interviewed to talk freely. He should have been capable of wheedling the full story out of his grandparents – but no. Over the years, he'd failed to prise it from them, the reasons for his mum's departure. It remained a big secret.

Of course, his mother's leaving could have been acrimonious, therefore too painful for his grandparents to talk about and it could be that they decided it would be best just to forget. As Gran often told him, 'You can't change what's passed, Derek.' Whatever it was, it too remained a secret kept from him.

What they knew, and were not disclosing, could probably be likened to laws for State Secrets. Eventually the facts would become available and the knowledge made public after all concerned had probably kicked the bucket – including him. How pessimistic he was becoming. Now, he was regretting having started to think about it!

He tried searching the extensive amount of information available on internet. The means was available, and he made the time to look, but he found absolutely nothing that helped. All and sundry seemed to be managing to trace their family trees. Why couldn't he? Worse still, their family trees had lots of lovely branches on them and roots too. Why did he get only zilch when he tried? He just wanted to locate his mother. That wasn't too much to ask, surely?

In a moment of sad reflection, it occurred to him ...maybe he should just accept she did not want to know him. It was her choice to go and she'd made no attempt to return for him. It was so unfair. She left him behind, and...

He felt like curling up in a corner and sucking his thumb, but he couldn't do that – he was a man. Men don't do that but, he reflected, at least there was something in life he could be thankful for – at long last, fewer people were calling him Sweaty.

2

About thirty years earlier, on the other side of the huge Atlantic Ocean, in another room far away from Newingsworth, a lonely young woman was finding it hard work, after he had left her on her own with the baby.

He may have stopped making contact but she knew he was out there, she knew where he was. She couldn't possibly miss reading about him – and the others, in fact it was unavoidable reading if you glanced at almost any newspaper. When they played, they hit the headlines, enjoying very little privacy. Their lives were always in the public eye, weeks before a concert, and weeks after. The time in between kept them busy too, with interviews and photographic sessions for newspapers and magazines, or the albums, and of course, they never stopped working on new ideas, pushing the music forward.

The newspaper lying open on the table was full of it as usual, telling how wonderful they were in achieving yet again another sell-out concert. The Detroit News loved them, always had and never printed a bad word about them in all five years of their professional musical life in the States. Some newspapers in other cities were not quite as kind and generous with their comments, but the band hadn't received negative criticism from any. The life they were pursuing was a fantastic roller coaster, and she had been part of it.

Ever since they began, universally, the critics had heaped praise in plenty on their shoulders, but other writers lacked the obvious affection that the music critic for The Detroit News seemed to have for the group, and especially for her. The headline he'd used this time was as good as ever. This was the first concert they'd done since splitting but she was delighted to see that this guy hadn't forgotten, although she did think it read remarkably like an obituary...

MILLIE – WE MISSED YOU.

'Rabid Revenge'– they have done it again – it was rocking all over the country – and for sure no-one in this city could possibly dodge hearing them at the volume the music was played. They have a new girl, Sadie Truman. She is good, very good, and she is showing great promise, but not yet nearly to the high standards set by the lovely recently-departed Millie. Their new lead singer has a lot to live up to. Millie's voice had a 'not to be missed quality' to it, with a rough and aggressive edge, almost as if there was no need for the mike; and with her overpowering personality – wow – she could have bullied me into submission any time she wanted.'

What had the guy meant when he typed that last comment, she wondered, "...bullied me into...?" Oh, of course, he's talking about the line from 'Down boy': 'If I use my whip, will you submit, or fight me for the power?' I suppose he knows I wrote that one – he's been a fan for a while, knows everything about me. Wonder if he really means it...?

'When she sang, she sang for me and me alone, and she was not only a voice in a million, Millie was a looker too – those legs, and that body, and the smile... You can tell I was a number one fan of that young lady, but now, she's gone – sad, sad, sad. Sadie's voice is less strident, though I'm sure it will develop, and to be fair, she looks good too, but I still yearn for Millie. The band, as well as singing hits from their previous four albums, 'Dark nights get darker,' 'Pressure under decompression,' 'Nail the Lid down tight Baby,' and 'She hadn't cut her nails,' played new stuff from their latest recording, not yet on sale but due for release next week. Rush to your local record store on Tuesday for 'Cross eyes don't please me.' It'll go quickly. We particularly liked the track 'Baby, it is dark and lonely down here,' with the solo played by Sailor, which made it sound good to be

buried alive. Bonzo, as usual, drove the females in the audience wild, moving his body exactly in the manner they were there to see. He knows what his fans like. It was a great concert, really great, but... We mean it sincerely when we say – we love you all, Sadie, Bonzo, Growler, Twister, and Sailor, (and we are heartbroken that you are not part of it now, Millie). Stay as good as you all are, for America's sake, and 'Rabid Revenge,' we'll love you – forever...'

Oh... how she missed the excitement of a live gig, the adrenalin surge just before going onstage, the joy of seeing all these faces staring up – hard to believe that they are there to see her – and the hypnotic effect of thousands of arms waving in time as they sang along, every single person out there knowing all the lyrics, just as well as she did.

She'd been the only female in a group of hard-rocking males, and the composer of a lot of the material too. She was the kingpin, she told herself, no, the Queenpin, if such a word exists. If it doesn't, it should, because that was what she was... For herself, these were thoughts of consolation – for someone who had been replaced. It was difficult to accept, but they were coping without her – not as well as before, according to the Detroit critic who had adored her – but they were coping all the same, and no doubt would continue to do so.

It had not been totally her choice, but in the circumstances she must accept that the logic rang true; she wasn't reliable during the latter stages of the pregnancy. It was unacceptable – the show had to go on: so much pressure. Mountainous loads of dollars were involved in the setting up and breaking down of each of these gigs, and her not performing could not be contemplated. There was always a lot at stake in the music business, with the reputations of a great many people hanging on every note, and dollar. She knew that for certain, particularly aware of all those shadowy figures in the background. These were the people who had enormous influence within the business. They demanded blood. These men in the background, and they were usually men, were the ones who could make a band a big success, or kill it off...

For almost five years, since they'd started playing for big money, living out of a suitcase was their life. She reckoned she'd stayed in hotel bedrooms in all the major cities in the States, during that time. Working hard had been the rule, and probably working overly hard. When starting out, there wasn't really any choice, then the momentum took over and they couldn't stop. They'd been fresh and new and spectacular even then, backed by a small record company, one that was determined to be bigger. Together they made it happen and everyone smelled of roses.

Buying this place had been wise. She stood looking out at the view – magnificent. It might not be the penthouse that she dreamed of a few years back, and having a child hadn't been intended then, but she was comfortably off and there was no chance of starving. The little one would be well cared for, so what else mattered? Some things are meant to be, and her five exciting years at the top were not easily forgotten. There probably would be regrets in the future, about how it came about; her stupidity again, she thought sadly. There were already many other things she regretted in her life. She'd had to make choices, major choices at times and, on reflection, many were the wrong ones.

Becoming pregnant that first time hadn't been intentional. Back then, he wanted her to be rid of it, and that riled her. They were young and just left school. She refused to contemplate a termination but, after having the child, she faced a choice, a difficult choice. One possibility was an adventurous fun-filled career as a singer in a rock band, a band with ambitions to be world famous. The alternative seemed less attractive – she could be a stay-at-home mum, looking after a baby. Which should it be?

The baby lost out!

Someone else looked after it and the episode became a thing of the past. It happened before the big-time began: best forgotten ...but every now and again she wondered.

The original five expected to stay together and being young meant taking chances back then. When they started out they did well and became favourites as a rock band, succeeding, even during their last years at school, until Steven pulled out and mussed up the whole plan. He left after the first contract was signed. It caused an incredible fuss, especially as the ink had hardly dried on the paper. He flew back home on his own – and then there were four.

Luckily for everyone, the record company had another instrumentalist on their books, one who fitted the bill nicely. They had a commitment to him but lacked the correct match until the four from Britain came along with a need, a gap in the line-up. In fact, although Steven's departure caused such a rumpus, it helped the company out of a hole by giving this new guy a home. That's how Bonzo started with them.

The school friendship... Her idle thoughts took her back to Steven Thwaite; he'd fancied her during the previous school year but never acted on it. He was keen on her, she could see that clearly and had he shown more fervour she might have encouraged him but he hung back and she didn't. Probably, on reflection, she could have been happy with him. A lot changed, of course, when he found out she was having the baby. He backed off very quickly. His attitude to her altered completely and she couldn't blame him – he wasn't the father.

She wasn't sure that his reason for leaving had been totally due to her though. He had always been less enthusiastic than the others about going full-time professional. The others, and that certainly included her, were dedicated to the music, and the writing, and to performing their own material – they loved everything associated with the band's business.

Bonzo took Steven's place. Bonzo was quite a character. You couldn't help but like him immediately. A great guitar player and he could double as vocalist, sang his own compositions too. It had been similar with Steven but whereas Steven's songs had been good, Bonzo's were great. The transition was remarkably successful. Bonzo fitted in fast – he was that sort of person, and, as they settled down, playing and socialising together in the new format, the style of the band gradually developed to become a different and even more successful sound than their earlier days.

That was when their reputation and the demand for tickets for their performances took off, but all was now past for her. Financially she was ok, with lots of cash in the old bank account, accumulated, even in the short time she'd tasted success. She wouldn't stop working, not altogether, but there was no need to unless she chose. If she considered work in the future, it would be something completely different. There was no rush: plenty of time to think about it. Maybe in ten, fifteen years time with a grown-up child, she would carve out a new career – prove to everyone, herself especially, that there is more to this gal than just a voice and an attractive body.

"I can live without 'Rabid Revenge'," she suddenly spoke aloud, looking down at the baby lying there, gurgling and kicking. Coping without the baby's father would be difficult. It was to be a new life for her, a totally new experience.

'Rabid Revenge' was now in her past, and he had cut loose, so he was in the past too. Clearly, she would have to get used to it, even though she knew already that she would miss him and knew she would think of him often in the future. Eventually, she would be able to regard life more rationally. There would still be memories and sad thoughts, but one thing was certain, he would, by then, be in a pigeonhole clearly identified as another of her wrong decisions.

3

Hammy, in the cottage as a temporary lodger, was beginning to get on his nerves. Derek liked Hammy, but the sooner the work on the farmhouse was completed, the sooner normality could return to Toozlethwaite Manor. 'Sex' had become a very naughty word in the house. Since their lodger arrived, rejection was the norm for Derek if he even suggested a cuddle to Sally. "Certainly not – Hamish is in the other room," was her curt response to each failed request. Hammy was always there. Well, always at the wrong times.

However, Derek's prospects for some canoodling were looking considerably brighter, thanks to Hammy's suggestion – a plan to take up residence in a caravan. He knew the very one; an old one admittedly, but it would become his temporary home. Someone wanted rid of it, and, if he bought it, they would deliver it here, right to the doorstep and he could live in it. This strongly appealed to Derek.

"Ah could huvv it in yerr back gairden, an' jist come back intae the hoose furr ma meals, like."

These words, spoken by Hammy, sounded like music to Derek's ears. Being so eloquently put and full of good sense, they brought a big smile to Derek's face, and he immediately offered to assist any way possible.

Sally showed interest but didn't get over-enthusiastic. She had heard many fanciful ideas mooted under this roof when these two males chatted, and she knew of very few taking wings, other than the nonsense they'd been up to when she'd been living with her mum and aunt at Cloverton. A shudder went down her spine at the memory: the four of them becoming involved with drug dealers, the police and the fire service: the absolute stupidity of four adults behaving like naughty schoolboys – and to achieve what? The result of their endeavours was sitting on the window sill – it was Hammy's family treasure – a large 'Ministry of Food – Dried Milk' tin filled with hundreds of long-out-of-date silver three-penny pieces that nobody wanted!

As for being schoolboys, they were anything but! At thirty-one, Derek was the youngest; then add twenty years for her father – a mature and respected bank manager. With them was Derek's grandad and, of course, Hammy too, both over seventy years old! They could have been killed!

Any novel suggestions being put forward by any one of the four, Sally was convinced, must be considered as highly questionable. However, from Derek's point of view, Hammy's idea was being considered from an entirely different perspective, and sounded brilliant. He'd get back to having some you know what, if he was lucky, even if only occasionally.

Toozlethwaite Manor wasn't exactly palatial. This had actually been Hammy's home when he was first married many years ago, long before it was modernised. It was a cottage which used to be part of the local farm property, with two bedrooms, a large living room, a good-sized kitchen, a toilet and bath, and a shower room, and just the right size for two in Derek's opinion – but Hammy was back living here as well under their roof on sufferance for what was now turning out to be a long, short-term solution.

However, it couldn't be said that Hammy was sitting around doing nothing and being a nuisance during the day – only at night. He spent many daylight hours, almost every day, working at his old abode, the farmhouse; residing in Toozlethwaite Manor was very convenient for him, being only five minutes brisk walk along the road.

The farmhouse which, together with the surrounding land, Hammy used to own, was currently being renovated and wasn't yet suitable for habitation. It lay in a mess for a short time after the hurried departure of 'Tipsicorus International', as the cannabis farmers had called themselves. It had made big local headlines and was Derek's big scoop, being the only journalist to appear on the spot at the right time, and therefore the one who manipulated the facts accordingly. For a short time they had the decency to feel acutely embarrassed about the folly of their ways, but dedicated followers of Derek will not be surprised that it did not take long for the feelings of the mad four to become manly pride.

Selling the property quickly was the decision of the shady solicitor in London, the same one who had arranged the original purchase by the gang from Hammy, when poor Hammy's egg business cracked up.

After the fire fiasco – the property was put back on the market by the solicitor, a move prompted by self-preservation. Being regularly involved in dodgy transactions, he required to maintain at least a front of respectability, preferring that the police didn't come knocking on his office door too often. Much to his relief the farm sold rapidly. He was relieved, but someone else was delighted! The big smile on the face of the fortunate purchaser who obtained it at a rock bottom price was the evidence, and the happy man was Alexander...

Now, this largish farmhouse was in the process of taking on a new purpose in life, rising like the phoenix from the ashes, under the new ownership of Sally's father, but this wasn't the first good deal he'd made in the area. A couple of years ago he bought the old cottage, which was nearer the main road, at a bargain price from Hammy and gave it to Sally and Derek as a wedding gift – the cottage proudly called Toozlethwaite Manor by Derek, but mockingly by all others.

This latest opportunistic idea of Alexander's was yet more proof that he'd never been one to miss out on a bargain. In a quick deal, he snatched up the main building and the surrounding land for a song. This time though, Mr Hamish Macintosh would be benefitting, much to his surprise and delight.

Having lived for a large part of his life in the big farmhouse before having to sell, Hammy would have dearly loved access to sufficient finance to have enabled him to purchase it back for himself.

As there was no chance of that, Alexander generously offered him the opportunity to return to the old place as a tenant manager. It gave Alexander a warm glow, deep down, to think that he'd helped his fellow conspirator to climb back up a few steps of life's ladder.

It was not planned for it to remain a farmhouse though. Alexander had big ideas, ideas that he hoped would reap dividends for him in the future, and these were ideas that Hamish was charged with bringing to fruition.

Hammy jumped at the chance.

On what was now a building site, Hammy was the man in charge.

For the last ten months work had been underway, extending the existing structure to create a small country hotel. The main building displayed a distinctive character, so the extension was well thought out and sympathetically designed to complement it. Hopefully, the end result for the new complex would be very attractive.

The weather had been favourable for external work, and everything was progressing satisfactorily. Long gone were the two barns, which sat there during many of Hammy's years in Newingsworth. One structure was easily removed anyway, due to it having been almost destroyed in their recent escapade. At the start of the project, Hammy had made a particular point to the driver of the digger who was levelling the ground and scooping out soil for the additional foundations.

"Mind noo, keep yer eyes skint furr mair treasure..."

The young driver nodded and smiled at Hammy, obviously thinking – he's Scottish, and at his age maybe getting a wee bit wandered – just indulge him.

No more 'treasure' was found.

Hammy was obviously conscientious and carefully monitored and cajoled his team if there seemed to be any danger of slipping from the main plan. In consequence, the work was moving forward very well. Although tending to be a gregarious person with everyone knowing when he was in a room for example, he was different with this project: subdued and modest at any mention of his excellent progress.

For him it was something different he was doing, being giving a second chance to succeed, a chance, he suspected, maybe he didn't deserve. There was no showiness with regard to this task; he settled for a warm glow of self-satisfaction, and the hope of repaying his debt to Alexander in some future way.

Although quietly confident in his abilities to achieve the completion of the current part of the job, it was the next stage, looking beyond the building work, that somewhat unnerved Hammy.

As well as the building alterations, the use of the adjoining fields was also planned to change. In the future, cows would not be wandering around these pastures, nor would the free-range chickens be returning, which was Hammy's business before he sold up. No, Alexander intended the surrounding grassland to become a nine-hole golf course – a feature of this country-style hotel that should pull in the punters, he hoped. He accepted that its creation would not be an overnight job, so the finished golf course would be a more distant objective.

The golf course would be the big challenge. Although applying no pressure regarding the timing of the course preparation, Alexander was leaving it to Hammy to organise the construction, and even to design it, if he chose. His only stipulation: as quickly as possible.

To be honest, Hammy had a few doubts.

It was not the timescale which concerned him; he could work that out somehow; it was the design, hmmm, where should he start with that? He hoped there would be no request by anyone to see his credentials or qualifications, or anything silly like that. Should he buy a book? Would that help? He'd have to do something, he supposed, because until now, the nearest he had been to a golf course was seeing the 'Open' on television – that was always 'braw', and he enjoyed watching it – otherwise, Hammy had not the foggiest idea about the game.

Perhaps, in the not too distant future, he would talk a bit more seriously to Alexander about that...

4

Unfortunately for Derek, the work entailed in the new hotel development was not an overnight job by any means, and Hammy was becoming ever more happily ensconced in Toozlethwaite Manor.

In her dealings with Hammy, Sally appeared to accept the current live-in situation amicably but, every so often when she took it out on Derek and especially at night if he cuddled too close, there was a twinge of guilt telling her she was treating her husband unfairly – it wasn't really his fault.

Of course, Derek eagerly pushing Hammy's proposal for a change in sleeping quarters was to be expected, but for Sally to gradually see it as having benefit too was a pleasant surprise – certainly to Derek. He gave a silent cheer. Yes, a caravan could be a great idea.

Hammy was eager, intending it to sit in the back garden, but how could the lane be negotiated by a car towing a caravan? It was a very narrow lane, with crumbly edges. Shouldn't the car driver be the best judge of the method used, Derek offered? Good idea! Exactly how the caravan should be manoeuvred into a final resting place, can be decided when it is delivered, they both agreed.

The lane accessing the cottage should not be considered lightly; this Derek knew to his cost. It was never meant for heavy traffic and had not been upgraded – ever.

In the days when the cottage was the home of Mr and Mrs Macintosh Senior, other than the farm tractor being driven cautiously by Hammy, it was rare for any vehicle to venture along the lane. When Hammy's parents had been alive and staying there, if they'd wanted to drive, which was less and less as they'd aged, they left their car parked back at the farmhouse. It seemed sensible to them to have a safe place for starting and ending a journey, and to use only the well-surfaced farm road. The lane was really only for the passage of the cows, ponies or bicycles in those days.

There used to be a shortcut, using a rickety foot-bridge to cross the stream, and a gap in the hedge to squeeze through, which permitted access to a path leading to the main farm road. By this means, when they'd given up driving, the elderly pair could be easily picked up by car if they wished a toddle into town with Hammy, or Sybil, his wife. The narrow footpath was well-used by them while they were resident, but both died a long time ago.

The cottage lay empty for many years with no-one using the footpath, and gradually nature worked its wonders; the bridge rotted, the path vanished, and the hedge grew to fill the gap. So, nowadays, half a mile of unpredictable road surface was the only access to the grandly called 'Toozlethwaite Manor' and was the only way home for Sally and Derek, and any visitors who cared to call.

Derek could not forget a major fall-out with Sally because of his involvement with a pretty young lady on that stupid lane... The basic flaw was the lane but it didn't get a mention. He was landed with the total blame – and he had truly suffered, and that little misunderstanding took a long while to live down.

As he stood gazing vacantly along the length of this troublesome access, he did remember some bits of that mishap as being more pleasurable than others. Yes ...very pleasurable indeed ...those buttocks ...but back to reality – mustn't have any silliness with this caravan.

How would they get it into the back garden?

In preparation, he and Hammy already had removed part of the fence, but the difficulty would be the turning circle at the front of the cottage – it would surely be much too tight for a car towing a caravan. Derek certainly didn't fancy the alternative – driving a car backwards all the way along the lane, especially with a caravan attached, but then again, what would Derek know about driving backwards? He couldn't even drive forwards.

As a non-driver, Derek could only marvel at the skills shown by those who successfully navigated this narrow space, especially taxi drivers, but they always drove forwards and could turn easily at the end. At least one person he knew had also been moving forwards – and still managed to go over the edge.

His mobile sounded, and as expected, it was Hammy. He was in the car, with the fellow who was selling him the caravan; they were on the way over and would be arriving shortly.

"Can ye meet us at the end o' the lane, Derek?" Hammy was shouting into the phone. "This big dumplin' beside me, tells me he couldnae possibly drive half a mile backwards up oor lane wi' the caravan. Wid ye believe tha'? He's obviously no' a very guid driver, ah'd say."

What...? The young gentleman driving gave Hammy a less than pleased look. He thought he was doing the old guy a favour, selling him his treasured possession for only fifty quid and, in addition, towing it here from the far side of the town at no extra cost. Having been warned about the lane being very narrow, and having crumbly edges, he'd already concluded it would be more sensible for the van to be manually and carefully pushed by three people. Yes, his intention was to help – until Hammy's words caused a rethink...

Being called a big dumplin' by this old, overweight, Scottish windbag sitting next to him, didn't sound like a compliment, so he was having second thoughts, and... Stuff this for a caper, it was now decided; the van will be disconnected, and ...in quick time I will be offski. Football is on telly in an hour and I can watch it after all – the whole match!

Almost there, he was told, turn right at the sign to 'Tipsicorus International' which he did, and half a mile after leaving the main thoroughfare, they came to the junction of the farm road and the lane. The driver left his vehicle, walked over, and looked along its length. It could now be properly assessed. The cottage looked very far away: the lane, ridiculously narrow.

With a barely perceptible nod of the head, the young man ratified his own earlier decision: yes, confirmed – it will be the football – definitely!

Slipping back into the driving seat, he then expertly swung the car and van into reverse, and slickly moved the van into position at the start of the lane. He would at least help them a bit by reversing it over the railway sleepers, which served as a bridge over the stream, and take it partly along between the thick hedgerow and the crumbly edge of the bank.

Reversing again, over the bumpy bridge, was done expertly, but also with considerable caution – there was no leeway for error, particularly in reverse. He applied the handbrake, and the old fellow opened his door.

"Guid man, noo jist hing aboot, wid ye?" said Hammy, getting out of the car with difficulty, to go to the rear of the caravan.

The car wasn't in brilliant condition he knew but, sitting at the wheel, the driver visualised the many additional scratches which would now be added to the passenger door as Hammy forced it open to squeeze passed the hedgerow. The thorns on the hedgerow were not doing any good to Hammy's clothes either, as he squeezed his way to the rear, but that mattered little – he was focussed on what had to be done.

"Ah'll now hae tae dae the controllin'," was his mumbled decision as he surveyed the scene.

He would walk backwards along the lane, waving his arms at the driver to guide him. This bloke would surely manage if he was shown what to do. Yes, that's what was required. The boy driving – he was young and needed a wee bit of a confidence boost...

So Hammy stood majestically in the middle of the lane and began the procedure.

The big dumplin' in the driving seat, was very wary as he reversed a little farther. Yes, he was being guided, but exactly what was the Scotsman doing? What was that signal meant to tell him? He's scratching his nose? He's taken out his handkerchief... Now, he's blowing...

As any sensible person would do, the driver ignored him, and the caravan was manoeuvred backwards about fifteen yards –

successfully and independently, but that was it! He'd done his bit.

The old caravan took up the full width of the narrow road. With it now sitting squared up and pointing along the lane, and with Hammy at the far end, the young driver got out of the car, glad to be stepping on the little bit of level ground still remaining on his side and, smarting at being called a big dumplin', uncoupled the van. He felt in his shirt pocket to make sure the fifty pounds had not been pinched back by that cheeky Scotsman and, finding it still there, he smiled happily, got back into the driving seat, and restarted the engine.

The big dumplin' opened the window, and looked out. He couldn't see the old duffer and Hammy couldn't see him, but nevertheless, he waved a vigorous v-sign as a fond farewell and zoomed off home to the football...

Derek was already outside when Hammy phoned and started walking the length of the lane to meet them. He was curious to find out what the driver thought was best. He could see Hammy coming towards him, and he could also see the back of a very old caravan filling the lane. It did not look in good condition from where he was and as he got closer, it looked worse.

"Hi Derek, so far so good, eh?" enthused Hammy. "Urr ye feelin' strong then? The three o' us urr goin' tae huv tae push an' pull ma new hame alang ...but jist hing oan a meenit..."

Hammy swung on his heel and returned to the rear of the van.

"Urr ye there, laddie?" he shouted to the big dumplin'.

There was no response. He gave the rear of the van a couple of hits with his hand.

"Urr ye deef? Can ye no' hear me?" he cried again.

Hammy clearly remembered the conversation with the driver on the way over: If ye canny reverse wi' this, ye'll be giein' us a haun' tae shove it up the lane, wulln't ye?

These were his very words, and he also remembered the exact words of the young bloke, the cheery reply: Of course, big man!

"So, wharr is he? Ah canny see 'um?" he muttered.

It was awkward leaning out to look around the end of the caravan, but there was little to see at the front. No driver... No car...

"Aw naw, he's no' awa'? The cheek o' some fowk!"

He sheepishly turned to Derek, "It looks like, uhmm ...we urr own wurr ain. Thurr's jist the two o' us. We're goanie huvv tae hurl this muckle big contraption alang the lane, uhmm ...a' oorsels."

Why was Derek not surprised?

"Right, I'll stay at this end and pull," Derek said, taking command, "...and you go to the other end and push."

Hammy was mumbling away to himself – he still hadn't got over the cheek of the young driver...

"OK? Now we mustn't, for heaven's sake, let it get near the edge," instructed Derek, as Hammy scrambled along the slope, leaning on the side of the van.

Now standing close, and seeing in detail the large object he was about to manhandle, the thought that went through Derek's head was that this surely was as close to a load of scrap as any road vehicle could become. Rust was showing everywhere, bits were hanging that shouldn't hang, and tyres showed shiny patches of metal. Even he could see they were illegal, but at least, this rust bucket wasn't going anywhere from now on. He corrected the thought. It had to be moved for half a mile along a lane with crumbling edges, before it would reach the planned spot in the back garden. There it could be left to die quietly.

Then again, looking on the bright side, Hammy was going to be sleeping in it, which meant 'hanky-panky' might return for yours truly and his lovely wife – if he could remember what it was. Yes, some good could come of it, rusty or not.

Derek looked back along the lane at the distance they were about to travel. Was it really only half a mile? There was certainty that the length would not vary whether you were running, hopping, crawling, or pulling a rusty caravan, but Derek just knew it was going to feel considerably longer.

Back at the cottage, Sally wasn't aware of what was happening. She had been washing the dishes when he slipped out quietly – to avoid having to wet his hands. He should let her know, Derek realised...

Sally's mobile sounded.

"Sally, Hammy and I are going to be late for tea," the phone told her.

"What do you mean?" Sally replied. "Where are you? I thought you were in the garden."

"Hammy's caravan has arrived – we're at the end of the lane," responded Derek, "and if you'd like to come and help us pull it along..."

Sally gave a derisive laugh, "No," and the call was ended.

So they began.

The potholes and ruts on the lane's surface did not help. The pair of them managed to start some movement, and as it was a reasonably level surface, it didn't take too much effort to actually keep it going, however moving it in the correct direction proved difficult.

This awkward beast immediately began to veer left – towards the stream, as if it needed a drink. They stopped heaving and pushing, and investigated. It was either due to the lack of pressure in one of the tyres or else the brake was binding on one side, they concluded. Whatever the cause, it was impossible to keep it moving straight ahead. Could this become a danger...?

Derek took this temporary stoppage as an opportunity to regain his breath – it was hard work. Then a worrying thought occurred to him. If he, a relatively young, and fit, thirty-two year old was already struggling, how was Hammy managing? Should he ask him, bearing in mind that Hammy was nearly forty years older? What if the old fellow collapsed and died?

"Hammy, are you still alive?" he shouted, and as the words came out of his mouth Derek realised it wasn't quite what he'd meant to say.

"Hammy, are you feeling ok?"

Yes, that sounded a little more caring.

"Why, whit's wrang?" a grumpy Hammy replied. "Um ah no' pushin' hard enough furr ye?"

When the rain began, the wheels nearest the stream were sitting very close to the crumbly edge of the slope. For a few minutes only light droplets fell which would have bothered no-one, but then it very quickly got serious. They were about to have another go at moving forward, when the heavens opened. With a rush and a struggle, self-preservation became very important. In a mad scramble, the pair of them slithered along the sloping banking, and with difficulty opened the side door and clambered into the van. They were much happier inside hearing the drops outside play a thunderous rhythm on the roof. At least they were dry.

The floor was at a funny angle, Derek thought. The front wheel was either sitting in a pothole, or possible not doing its job properly, obviously as dodgy as the rest of the van. Sitting inside, dry, looking out at the rain pouring down outside was marginally preferable to being outside, even though it was a disgusting smelly space. Anyway, it wouldn't rain for long.

It was tiny, and claustrophobic.

Derek sat and wondered how someone could design this to be lived in, with so little space and having to serve so many different purposes. Ways had been found to put items to double use; tables to beds, seats becoming secret storage places for cushions and clothes, and a tiny sink able to be hidden away when not needed.

Hammy started looking in the various cupboards and it became obvious that this van had been sitting unused for a long time. The fishy smell did not appeal to Derek's olfactory sense and it became stronger when Hammy opened one of the little doors and found the tin with the remains of cat food.

Hammy was going to sleep in this?

The inside would require a deep clean before he could possibly survive in here. Maybe I could help, thought Derek – by getting Sally to assist. She would like doing this, and she wouldn't have to start this evening. Tomorrow is Saturday – no need to rush.

Hammy was having difficulty pulling open the locker door opposite where Derek was seated, but he was determined. He pushed his foot against the sink, managing to get his whole weight into action and...

As the catch gave, and the little door swung open, Hammy fell back onto Derek's lap, and Derek's back, in turn, slammed onto the side of the van. They didn't see the wheel outside start to slip, nor the road surface begin to crumble, but they could feel the movement – and panicked. Both jumped up and the caravan rocked again, and the sliding hastened – it was starting to slip down the banking, very quickly...

Off balance, both fell back against the sloping wall of the van, helping it on its way. It slid down the six feet of the banking into the stream and stopped abruptly. Luckily the water wasn't deep but water was flowing fast and it was muddy and still raining heavily.

A moment ago they were sitting on the road, now they looked through the front window and saw the world at a funny angle. The corner of the van had settled in the mud. They could see right along the stream. Hammy grabbed the door handle but he was going nowhere. It opened outwards. The door was resting against the far bank.

They looked at each other. This wasn't their first time in a scrape together. Teamwork – that's what was needed, wasn't it? Efficiently working as one was the technique – even if it had not worked last time!

Looking from the front window again, Hammy could see the water level increasing rapidly, due partly to the heavy rain still pouring down, but owing more to the dam now created by the caravan. Worse still, the water level wasn't just increasing outside; in many places this rust bucket was leaking badly and water was flooding in – fast!

"Yerr phone, laddie," said Hammy, trying to appear in control of his faculties. "Ye'd better get us help quick-like, 'cause ah'm no' a very good sweemer!"

Derek's feet, when he looked down, were almost covered. New shoes – ruined. The phone... Where is it? It wasn't in his pocket.

Meanwhile Hammy was trying to open the roof-light, and wishing his figure more sylphlike; he had not a snowball's chance of squeezing through.

Whit a shame! Sweaty's goat nae chance either but at least we will both drown the gether, was Hammy's sad thought. Ah've lived a full life, went through Hammy's mind, but Sweaty here is only a laddie by comparison. It's jist no' right furr him tae huvv tae gang sae young but ...oh thank Goad, he's fund the phone – in his other poaket.

"Ehm ...Sally," Derek spoke gently, in the knowledge that they may never be face to face again. "I am afraid we are going to be a bit late. You see..."

"Oh Derek, it's fish, and it's ready now and I'm going to be very annoyed if the pair of you don't appear at the dinner table right away..."

Derek visualised his dear wife, with disappointment written all over her face and her little foot being stamped petulantly in anger – but he could understand.

"Sally, we are going to drown..."

"Now, don't be silly Derek. The rain wasn't that heavy. You've been out without a coat before and survived."

Hammy snatched the phone from a woebegone Derek.

"Look lassie, we urr stuck in the caravan in the ruddy stream and the bloomin' thing is fillin' up wi' muddy watter, an' we dinna want tae droon! Can ye be gettin' help furr us? Like – righ' noo? Please..."

"Oh right, Hammy, but look after my Derek, will you? He's inclined to get over-excited." Derek wasn't excited but he was getting very wet – up to his knees, so far.

"I'll ring the fire brigade," said Sally, rising to the occasion.

5

Though it seemed like an eternity to Derek and Hammy, help arrived after a very short time, lights flashing and siren sounding, much to Derek and Hammy's relief. It was distinctly uncomfortable standing there in muddy water, now passing their waistbands and, though it was no longer raining, the water level was continuing to rise.

The fire crew banged on the roof to check someone was still there and still alive, and to confirm it was still worth their while to swing into action. Releasing live personnel from dangerous situations always appealed to this particular crew, as against the removal of corpses. For some reason, that procedure invariably proved very unpopular.

Being told that shortly they would be safe, gave immense pleasure to the two wet-ones inside, but when the Fire Chief shouted to them that the intention was simply to open the roof of the caravan with their giant tin-opener, Hammy objected strongly.

"Ye canny dae that tae ma new hame. Dae ye no' ken, ah've tae sleep in here, ya crowd o' muppets. How wid ah dae that, wi' a jaggied big hole ower ma heid?"

This was not the response the fire crew expected. Usually in circumstances like this, they would be showered with gratitude, so, not surprisingly, "Hell mend 'em..." was the collective response from the crew outside. The fire chief was forced to step in and take control to prevent his men going off home in a huff and leaving this grumpy old sod to sort it out for himself.

"Could you not just pull the caravan back onto the road using ropes?" asked an agitated Sally, having run along to give moral support even though her carefully prepared meal was now being ruined.

Now, in the minds of this highly skilled and eager-to-prove-how-clever-we-are team of firemen, that surely was not the way to handle this crisis –much too simple. Anyway, what did she know...? Pull the van out – using ropes? How ridiculous...

"Well, I suppose we could," admitted the fire chief, reluctantly ...and that's what they did but, as the van was dragged and bounced back up the gradient, though they knew it was wrong, these dedicated rescue workers were delighted to hear repeated cries of 'Ouch!' and 'Oh!' echoing from inside the van, as Derek and Hammy were thrown around the tin box until, eventually, the van was on solid horizontal ground, exposed to view in all its glory. Now, being Chief was special on occasions like this: having the honour of releasing the trapped pair. The first person seen by the rescued and grateful sufferers would be him; he could glory in the credit.

However, he should have been less eager. Had he considered where the van was moments ago and what it might contain, before turning the handle of a door that opened outwards, he might not have been soaked by the deluge that poured out, which washed him down the slope and into the stream.

"Oh you poor man!" shouted Sally, sliding down the bank to the aid of a dripping and embarrassed Chief, while the others were content to look on, suppressing grins with difficulty. "Let me help you. You were so brave. Come along to the cottage and have a shower and get cleaned. I'm sure I could rustle up some coffee and cake for you while you change. You others..." and her tone changed as she turned to Derek and Hammy, and the remaining firemen, "Pull the stupid caravan along to the garden, and get it out of the way. If you do it properly you might get some coffee and cake too – but be more careful this time."

Sally was muddied and in a foul mood. The Fire Chief had lost face, was soaked, and glaring fiercely so none of the others, including Derek and Hammy, considered it wise to react in any way other than to comply. They did as instructed, and eventually a sad looking rusty caravan found its final resting place in the back garden.

A little later, when Sally was cleaned up and sufficiently mellowed, she allowed the fire crew to relax in a crowded living room, on soft seats. Derek and Hammy sat on the hard ones.

"I remember you," the fire chief said suddenly, now that he was looking at and seeing Derek properly. "You had something to do with the fire at the farm last year, hadn't you? And you are a journalist too, if I'm correct."

This was said accusingly, and disparagingly, even though he was a guest in Derek's home. Derek shrank down a little in his seat feeling guilty, though there was no reason why he should; he'd spotted a possible crime and he'd phoned for help, so this comment irritated... At the time, Derek suspected Andy Woodstock, the policeman who'd suddenly become his friend, to have relit the fire – to save disposing of the evidence in a more official manner.

"Yes...?" he offered cautiously, but then he decided appearing defensive was not a good idea. Reacting like that made it look as if he had done something criminal, so, he changed to a better form of defence – but it was only a gentle attack... "You were looking for a dead body, weren't you?" he said to the chief. "You told me that at the time. I distinctly remember. You were convinced it had been a gangland cremation, was what you said. You said you didn't want me to quote you on that, but you were certain, weren't you, even though the police were getting annoyed. Were you correct then? Did you find – the body? ...No? Was it embarrassing to be wrong?"

Derek remembered well the circumstances of that night: Alexander, Hammy, Hector, and him: what they'd found: the hole they'd dug: the fire they had started, and the luck they'd had in escaping.

He also knew there was no body. He and Hammy had dug the hole, searching for Hammy's 'family jewels'.

The fire chief was the one with the gut feeling – a corpse. He had been less than popular, haranguing the police into digging for ages almost everywhere in the barn – to find nothing. He'd backed down eventually, feeling a little foolish at having been proved wrong.

Derek's bluff was paying off – the fire chief glared back at him.

"Maybe I could do another story for the paper," Derek continued, "...about the fine work you did, saving us today, and how everyone had a good laugh when you then fell in the..."

"No, I don't think that would be a good idea," the fire chief quickly interrupted, "...and we have important work to be getting on with. Come along men."

So, the fire crew were off, leaving Derek and Hammy to remove the burned meal from the oven and conjure up some sandwiches in an attempt to pacify a short-tempered Sally. The evening meal was ruined and, without doubt, the fault would be identified as his, but, although Derek felt bad, it was at least comforting that this time the blame was to be shared with Hammy.

6

It was now Saturday morning and, wisely, Derek had second thoughts about suggesting Sally should become involved with the cleaning of Hammy's caravan. When she rose this morning, obviously the static was continuing from the previous evening, and this got up his nose. Did she have to continue it? Nor was he the only one suffering. They'd tried apologising, both of them. Last evening, Hammy grovelled to Sally – and to as high a standard as he was able – but to no avail. Ok, so the meal was ruined. Yes, it would have been delicious, but there was surely no need to go on about it; acting as if it was the first time this had happened to anyone. They said sorry last night, didn't they? What else could they do?

He could easily have rhymed off many other occasions where it had all gone pear-shaped and he had suffered; however, it would have been very unwise, he recognised. These unspoken thoughts remained locked in his own head. It was not the right time; there would be another opportunity...

Today therefore, much against his principle of not getting involved with physical effort, Derek was actually helping with the cleaning of the caravan but, though he and Hammy were perspiring, they appeared to have made little progress. Thanks to the muddy water, the van was now in an even worse state than when Hammy bought it. Removing the part-empty cat-food tin that contributed to the aroma made a difference, but, after the episode in the stream, it was also likely that smelly pond life could be surviving in a multitude of places inside this tin box.

Derek often wondered what actually floated down that stream. It was a good job the rust holes were letting some of the water escape.

The cushions were foam rubber. When the caravan filled up yesterday, most of them floated around, and absorbed water through the many holes in the plastic covers. These were lying out to dry on the grass, but they would probably end up unusable.

It wasn't just the tin of cat-food they'd found abandoned.

Other things discovered in the various cubby holes made it look as if it might have been used for dirty weekends, but surely only when the van was in a liveable state in the dim and distant past. They found odd socks and ripped tights, several empty wine bottles, a man's shirt with one button remaining, and an embarrassing amount of assorted underwear, much of the feminine variety. This debris was handled wearing rubber gloves, placed carefully in black polythene bags, and sealed; they were taking no chances...

The van was now sitting in a sunny spot at the back of the cottage in what was presumed to be its final resting place. Bricks were supporting each corner to take the weight off the poor old tyres, tyres which had given all they could give.

"It jist needs a wee lick o' paint an' it'll be righ' as rain," said Hammy, which caused Derek to question the man's sanity.

Earlier, Hammy insisted that the power be connected up because they could put in a heater and dry out the inside much quicker, so they ran an extension from the cottage and connected up.

There was a flash – and a bang!

Of course, water and electricity are not happy companions, as they found when they opened the caravan fuse box. Hammy fixed that – while Derek repaired the fuses for the cottage... Maybe they could do without the heater, they decided – as if there was a choice.

Then Hammy started talking about the flower beds he wanted around the outside of his new temporary home and, having obviously been thinking about it, began rhyming off various shrubs and perennial plants intended to make the caravan look more 'lived in'. It was beginning to sound as if Hammy was planning to camp in the back garden for a very long time...

Derek became slightly anxious.

Sally appeared in the doorway at that precise moment carrying two bottles of chilled beer; forgiveness at long last for last night, thought Derek. Maybe now was the time to talk about how hurt he and Hammy had been by her treatment of them.

Someone was going to have to tell her that behaviour like that didn't impress anyone, and it was his place to do it. She would have to accept that she shouldn't have been stamping her feet in a huffy manner like a spoiled child. It was just a little burned food, was it not? It wasn't as if he and Hammy had planned it. He would also explain that he was only saying this for her benefit, so that it would make her an even nicer person.

However, wisdom continued to prevail today ...he kept his stupid mouth shut!

7

At work it felt a long day for Derek. He wasn't under pressure for copy for the Gazette; his contributions for the next issue were ready and complete and he'd met the deadline with ease this week. It was more the fact that he did not have to push himself that made it seem long and tedious, coupled with the inadequate story-line he was engendering for his own book; more realistically and sadly, it was his almost total lack of story line that was creating frustration for him.

Pedalling home, he hoped that Sally had already started preparing tonight's meal. He was looking forward to something to make him think straight, and food might help; fresh inspiration was desperately needed – maybe even a change of subject should be considered...

Sally had not been in a good temper when she left the office before him. He hoped that in that intervening hour her mood would have improved. With any luck, by the time he arrived home, she would have returned to being her normal smiling and loving self but, if not, look out Hammy, because if you are there before me tonight, you will suffer first.

Not knowing the cause of Sally's bad mood wouldn't help in humouring her when he got home, he realised. Working together every day at the Gazette had its good points for both of them, but on the grumpy days...? So he was a bit apprehensive about the approaching evening. Bad moods tended to return to the cottage with them.

Unfortunately, the moment he opened the front door, he recognised that the time delay had not diminished Sally's grumpiness.

Thankfully Hammy hadn't suffered – but only because he wasn't there. Sally hadn't seen him. Maybe he'd sensed the vibes...

"Hello Sally darling, I'm home..." he called out cheerfully. "How are you doing?"

"Don't start...!" was her less than cheery response. Oh ...right....

A note was sitting on the table.

'Dear Sally an' Derek, Wish me luck wid ye, cos ah'm oot in the caravan the noo – ah'm goan furr it. Dinna mak' oanythin' furr me at teatime, cos ah've hudd some food tha' ah made mahsel'. Ah'm awa oot tae ma new hame an' ma new sleepin' quarters – an early night'll no' dae me oany hairm. Ye'll no' be needin' the hoat watter bottle when ye go tae bed, ah hope, cos ah've goat it, jist in case, ye ken. Ah hope ye dinna miss mah pleasant company in the evenin', an' ah hope tae survive tae see ye again furr breakfast – yerr freendly ludger, Hammy.'

Derek's mood brightened as he read the note – no third person this evening. Yahoo! At long last! No Hammy in the house! Missing you already!

Oh, how Derek had looked forward to reaching this moment, but it wasn't supposed to be like this...

Now it was here and it was just the two of them, unfortunately, the way Sally was behaving – in a foul mood – he sensed it could turn out to be one of their less enjoyable evenings. Joining Hammy outside might be worth considering!

There was a wry smile on his face as he realised that Hammy's timing was perfect – getting out before Sally starts ranting.

Yes, they were alone, but what Derek guessed earlier was proving to be correct now – her mood was not improving – and it did not take long before he put his foot in it. He managed to say something which must have been wrong, because a reaction followed. He wasn't sure what it was but somehow he succeeded in starting her off. Only little rumbles to begin with, but she rapidly warmed up and it became a tirade and all flowing in his direction, and then the discussion became more focussed...

It was because of that tree – that damn giant sycamore, the one that had been standing on the same spot for decades, loved by the rabbits, with masses of burrows in the tangled roots, which Derek guessed must lead to a bunny kingdom underneath. This was not the first time it had been mentioned, which made the situation considerably worse.

The tree causing this controversy grew just beyond the boundary of their cottage garden at the back of the house, and was the one that you couldn't possibly miss when you looked out of the back windows. Tonight it was the fuel for Sally's ever-increasing ranting.

To be honest, Derek told himself, that particular tree seemed a threat from the first day they came to live in the cottage, but more pressing matters in two years of marriage had caused any action needed to cut it down, or even to reduce its size, to have been forgotten – or dodged. Tonight, she was claiming it could be dangerous, and it was his fault, of course.

He knew there would have been another reason to get the argument going if it hadn't been this one, but whatever, it just so happened to be that tree this time. He should have done something.

Yes, he was guilty this time, but Derek considered this guilt to be on a technicality only – it was guilt through doing nothing, which surely must carry a penalty of lesser severity than if he was actually misbehaving, but why would Sally not accept that logic?

Their last major row was all due to him; he freely admitted that. He had been drinking 'a little excessively'. Yes, yes, yes ...he'd also been wearing her clothes (which incidentally Derek claimed was her father's fault for encouraging him). Derek accepted that there had been good reason for blaming him for those things, and he was willing to accept he was at fault – but tonight? Surely not!

Derek's well reasoned explanation did not convince his wife, and he felt hard done by. Surely it was the tree's fault for growing so damn large...

When he reflected afterwards, yes, he had been incredibly condescending, dismissive, and unsympathetic about her fears, and not the caring, loving husband he should have been – but she had refused to be reasonable about it. He would have been willing to accept some of the points she made; he might even have admitted that he was in the wrong again; now ...it was too late.

Those tree roots, Sally believed, were infested by the rabbits to the extent that the stupid tree could fall down in a strong wind. In the process it would damage the house, and more importantly, she could be hurt if she happened to be in the house at the time. Significantly, there was no mention of it mattering if he were the one in the house...

Wrongly and foolishly he had suggested that a stupid tree wasn't something to get upset about at the moment, now was it? Well ...not just before mealtime, on an empty stomach. It was time to eat and he was starving and, anyway, that tree now belonged to her father. He owned the land now, so, if it was anyone's problem, it was her father's – not his.

"I don't want my house flattened by a silly old tree," Sally had said.

"...Whose house?" Derek responded sharply, "Shouldn't you have said ours?"

"It was my father who bought it for us, so it's more mine than yours..."

"Oh, so being married has little to do with it then?"

"Well, you aren't behaving like a caring husband, are you?"

"Look, calm down. You are beginning to talk silly."

"And you couldn't care less if I get flattened by that wobbly great tree out there?"

"Now, you are just being downright stupid!"

"Stupid? Am I? Stupid...? Yes, stupid for having married you!"

"Look, I'm sorry. I didn't mean it like that..."

"I'd say you sounded as if you meant it very seriously, and I'm not willing to remain here – in danger from that tree – or in the same house as you for one moment longer..."

At that, she went into the bedroom, packed her little suitcase which was a perfect size for attaching to her bicycle and, with that dinky, pink case in her hand, made for the front door of the cottage.

"I'm going to Cloverton, and will remain there until you return to your senses and apologise, and do something about that tree. You just don't care," she declared – and was gone, slamming the solid wood door as hard as it had ever been slammed in the one hundred and twenty years of its existence.

He watched through the front window, with increasing discomfort, hoping that it had been a bluff about leaving, but then realising as she fastened the case in position and cycled off along the lane without a backward glance, that she was serious. What was even worse, she hadn't prepared the meal, and he was starving.

8

It wasn't the first time he'd had to make a meal, but it was a while since he made a meal only for himself. When it was just the two of them, before Hammy arrived, the meal making routine had become one of sharing – alternating nights for each to do the cooking; then Hammy arrived.

Hammy's turn came only now and again. His speciality – his one and only dish – was scrambled eggs on toast, and there is a limit to how much of that anyone could enjoy. His turn tended to be limited to once a week, but he surprised them now and again by ordering pizzas; delivered directly to the cottage, ready to eat, and brought by a young fellow on a push bike. Clearly even Mr Hamish Macintosh got fed up with his own scrambled eggs.

As a consequence of his cooking regularly, Derek became reasonably proficient with a variety of ingredients and their preparation, but tonight, even though he tried hard to concentrate on the food-making process, and to follow Jamie's recipe exactly, his Oozy Mushroom Risotto with Spinach Salad tasted less than appetising, and all because of one missing ingredient – his dear wife.

He looked out at the tree and cursed it. It just ignored him.

The caravan sat there. Derek could see the flowery curtains were closed, the ones Sally donated for Hammy's comfort, and which flattered the rust bucket. As Hammy was at this moment still out there, presumably cosily snug in his now moderately hygienic and fresher smelling tin-house in the garden, Derek presumed that he couldn't have heard the shouting and arguing, or he would have appeared at the door to complain about the noise.

It would have been very embarrassing to have to explain that Sally had cycled off into the night and wasn't coming back.

He could visualise his elderly friend lying in the pull-out bed, at peace – snoring away as usual. Tonight, Derek would be far enough away from that sound not to be disturbed, and had to be thankful for small mercies...

For certain there would be no-one to disturb him tonight; sadly, no Sally; happily, no Hammy. It was all quiet in the cottage, silent in fact, and Derek was going to be lonely tonight. Plenty of space for him climbing into the double bed, all by himself; he would rather have had Sally next to him.

A lovely aroma came from the pillow where Sally normally laid her head. Each breath he took reminded him of the person who should be sharing this mattress. He put her silk jimjams under her pillow – he couldn't leave them there – visible – to torture him.

All round the bedroom he could see her clothes – scattered asunder –Sally's style and he wouldn't have it any other way – except when they caused him to trip.

Oh dear ...she has gone without her furry toys. Sleeping without them could be difficult for her. She always has them at night, but here they are: the little cuddly figures on her pillow, her favourites, Mr Squirrel and Wise Old Owl, just sitting there, smugly, mocking Derek and his loneliness.

He didn't deserve to be abandoned, nor should he be suffering with a feeling of guilt like this. It hadn't really been his fault this time, Derek told himself, but that did little to reassure him. He lay on his own pillow and closed his eyes, cleared his mind and thought of blank spaces – like the blank space beside him – where his Sally should be – and he was wide awake again.

His second attempt began more successfully. He started to drift off, into oblivion – until the rear window began to make a noise, a repetitious noise, a persistent rattle, a chattering that couldn't be ignored. It wasn't loud, just enough to prevent sleep. This was something else he should have fixed. It only happened occasionally, and tonight was an occasion. He was wide awake again, lying concentrating, counting the seconds of silence. The silences were very short.

Ah, it's stopped. No, it's started again...

Sleeping was not now an option. He sat up. Maybe reading a book would be a good idea, but the nearest reading material was in the main room. There was nothing on hand to read, so, he did without ...and the noise continued. If he was to get any sleep something would have to be done about that window and there was no one else to do it, so up he got.

A stiff breeze had sprung up as the evening had progressed, though he hadn't noticed anything earlier. It was windier now than when Sally cycled off. The slight breeze behind her at that time would have helped her on her way to her parent's home. It had certainly not hindered her leaving – it would have taken a hurricane in her face to have stopped her...

He found the window catch was a little loose so, some folded paper was jammed into the gap and the chattering stopped. Chattering, oh dear, and Sally was back on his mind...

Why go back to bed? He wouldn't sleep, he just knew it. He flopped into the soft easy chair in front of the television. Anything on telly to put me to sleep, he wondered? He switched on and flicked a few stations, and found The Horror Channel, and why not? Ah, 'The Texas Chainsaw Massacre', again? It had been on so many times, but he'd never watched it because this sort of film was always silly, and childishly done; laughable, really...

He fetched his dressing gown, and wrapped it around himself, forming his own little lonely cocoon as the film began. In no time at all, he was having regrets. He was definitely not laughing, but he couldn't switch off. It seemed worse with no-one else in the cottage. Were the doors locked? It was dark outside...

When it began to get bloody, he hid behind a cushion ...but he kept peeping out. He shut his eyes tightly so that he couldn't see the action ...but the sound permeated his brain ...and again he peeped. And that's the way it was until the end: totally compulsive peeping. At least he survived to the conclusion of the film – most of the poor demented souls he'd been watching, hadn't.

I'll never get to sleep tonight, he told himself dolefully, as he removed his dressing gown, hanging it tidily on the hook on the back of the door (he'd been trained differently from Sally). He climbed into bed, and despite having watched all the gory bits on that disgusting film, he dropped off.

Yes, he fell asleep, but it was to be a troubled sleep. He tossed and turned, his left leg kicked out, causing his duvet cover to slip to the left, then it was dragged back unconsciously up to his chin, exposing his feet. His body tensed as an arm flew upwards, as if swatting an annoying fly, and banged against the other pillow disturbing Sally's cuddly toys. Now his head was under the pillow...

...What's happening? Where am I?

I'm in the garden! I am ...freezing! My pyjamas – I am still wearing my pyjamas – why am I still wearing my pyjamas? I can't still be asleep but nothing is real! The cheese! I shouldn't have had the cheese!

Why can't I sleep like a log? A log? Log? It's that damn tree, isn't it...? Go away sycamore tree ...please... Just leave my conscience alone – now! You are annoying me! It's your fault that Sally left me and ...whatwazzat?

There it is again ...something on the ground ...behind the tree ...hiding... If I go round this way ...slowly ...and quietly ...I'll see what it is ...Gotcha!

What the...! It's Mr Squirrel! Am I glad to see you ...but just a moment, what are you doing here? This is my dream!

'Sally told me to keep an eye on you. She said "Sweaty might do something stupid when I leave him" – which incidentally was stated in confidence, so don't tell her I squealed – and here I am, to stop you – me and Wise Old Owl. There he is, up there, on his favourite branch in his favourite sycamore tree. He knows all about it too. Say, 'Toowit-toowoo,' for Sweaty as you usually do, Owly. You do know that's his party piece, don't you Sweaty? Usually no-one can stop him chattering away...'

'Toowit-toowoo...'
'Attaaboy Owly. You tell 'im...'

What's that supposed to mean, for goodness sake? I hope he's not laughing at me, and don't call me Sweaty! I'm not in a good mood you know.

'Oh yes, we know that, and that is why Wise Old Owl has just asked if you are safe with that chain-saw in your hands; ooooooh ...and with the blood all over it? Have you cut your finger?'

What chain-saw? Oh ...this one... Ahaa... I am going to chop down this tree. Sally says I must do something. I want my Sally back. I hate this tree!

'What about the birds ...and the rabbits...? Don't you care about the world around you? Putting all these dear little people out of their homes? Where will they live? Are you a monster?'

I can't help it and I am not a monster but the tree has to go!

'I think at least you had better discuss that with the rabbits first ...don't you? They were saying that they were most unhappy. They might decide to take some serious action, you know.'
'Toowit-toowoo...'

What is he on about now?

'Oh dear, he says from where he is sitting, he can see an army of angry-looking bunnies, carrying little shovels, coming over the hill from the next field to give assistance to their poor friends in the basement, below this tree – friends that you are wanting to make homeless. Oh dear! Can you feel the ground trembling too, no...? Can't you tell something dreadful is about to happen...? They will go for your foundations, mark my words ...and if Sally's house falls down, you will be in even bigger trouble, and you'll have no home

either, and it will have served you right... They will have got their own back and Sally will be most upset. I will tell her that I tried, but I'm not sticking around to be involved in any carnage. So, you are on your own, buddy – I'm off...!'

Derek awoke in a sweat, fighting with the duvet cover which obviously had taken a considerable dislike to him, and tumbled out of bed.

"Sally, Sally ...I'm so sorry, I won't let them." and then he remembered.

He stretched himself, and rubbed his eyes. He felt awful. Putting on his slippers he went into the living room. What time is it? It was difficult seeing the clock; after eight, but still dark this morning; that was unusual? He could hear the noise of the very strong wind as it found the gaps in the window frame. He went over to the back window to look out but all he could see were leaves – leaves and branches pressing hard against the glass. The light was being completely blocked out – for a very real reason...

He should have listened to Sally – that damn tree has fallen down.

9

It was after eight a.m., it was dark, and he was standing trying to see out the back window but couldn't because of the leaves; and then the horror of the situation became suddenly clear to him – the caravan – the tree had dropped right on top of the caravan. It was his first night out there... Oh no!

Hammy's first night in the van; but also ...his last.

Derek covered his eyes, eyes that were rapidly filling with tears. He closed them, rubbed them, and opened them again, hoping it was all his imagination – that he was still dreaming – but no. He had let this happen. It had been his responsibility to do something; there was no getting away from the truth. He should have taken action before – when Sally complained the first time. If only he could turn back the clock. Oh, why is he always so stupid?

The tree had obviously hit the ground. That enormous ruddy tree had toppled over, in the wind, onto the garden – on top of Hammy's tin home – on ...top ...of ...Hammy, the sweetest of men.

The caravan has been crushed, and so has...

"Hammy..." Derek wailed, and fell to his knees, sobbing, "Hammy, Hammy, Hammy... I'm soooooooo sorry..."

He covered his face and wept.

"Whit's wrang?" said the voice from the spare bedroom.

"It's Hammy!" cried back Derek "I've killed him... Ohhhhh...."

"No ye huvnae, ya stupid gommeral. Ah'm here, am ah no'?"

A vision in blue and white striped pyjamas had appeared at the spare bedroom door, scratching away at the normal places, and rubbing his eyes.

"Ye didnae expect me tae stay oot in thon howlin' gale did ye?" was Hammy's grumpy comment.

Derek's tearful face looked up.

"The tree... The caravan... You ...you are not..." he spluttered out.

"Whit?" said a still half asleep Hammy. "Whit are ye goin' on aboot?"

The relief felt by Derek was incredible. This lovely person had miraculously returned from the dead, which made him want to leap up and throw his arms around the elderly man standing there,

Luckily for both, the temptation was resisted, and Derek simply sat on the floor with his mouth hanging open in a most undignified way. He would have to tell Sally that Hammy was alright – right away. She would want to know. Where was the phone? There was a hesitation though. What would her reaction be, sympathy – or scorn? He could only dial and wait to find out.

"Hello," said Alexander's voice.

"Father ...Dad ...Alexander... I never know what to call you..." spluttered Derek.

"I'd much rather you didn't call me at all," replied a smirking father-in-law. "You are lucky to catch me. I was just about to leave for the bank. Shouldn't you be going to work today?"

"I have a problem – well, it's partly your problem. The big tree ...at the bottom of our garden, outside our fence, on your land – it's fallen down!"

"Oh... And you are you under it?" laughed a caring father-in-law. "Thank goodness Sally is over here with us. It would have been a terrible surprise for her." There was a moment of silence as a thought suddenly occurred to Alexander. "The cottage ...it hasn't damaged the building, has it?" This response may seem a tad heartless but it was not because Alexander felt nothing for Derek – it was the natural reaction of a man who was afraid the cost of substantial damage was about to be dumped on him.

"No, it's only the garden it hit, but..." Derek admitted, and out it all spilled.

Alexander was forced to learn how, last night, Sally had foreseen this. She'd had a premonition. That very sycamore tree was accurately predicted to fall... (It could be said that Derek was being a little generous in attributing the premonition to Sally, considering she had been saying it for many months before. If she was to be given the credit, it would be due only to repetition, rather than good timing.) They'd had an argument, Derek continued, and that's why she'd left to stay at Cloverton.

Of course, Alexander already knew all that. Sally had made her side of the story perfectly clear last night – as soon as she arrived.

The flattened caravan and Hammy's near-death experience also got a mention, in hushed tones; Derek still could feel the effect of seeing what he'd thought was Hammy's demise. To Derek's consternation, Alexander found this hilarious ...so, Derek asked to speak to Sally instead, because his wife would at least understand and be sympathetic to the dreadful shock he'd had – and she would return home to the cottage to comfort him, maybe.

"Oh, you are too late for that, Derek. She left for work before I came down stairs. She was saying some wonderful things about you last night – sorry, that's a lie. You'll have to see her at the office. And Derek – please take her back home again. I can't stand the pressure."

As they hung up, Derek decided that, as far as the office was concerned, today would have to be a 'sickie'. He would catch up tomorrow. Today, he would have to do something about that blessed tree.

"See you, young man, you should be lookin' oan this here as a blessin' from above..." explained a sanctimonious Hammy. "You urr lucky, an' ye should ken that, cos ye've still goat me – an' thon tree. An' ye can thank it for fallin' – ye've goat enough wood noo tae keep a' the fires goin' in a' the hooses in the toon – furr the next ten years."

10

"Do you remember the great job you did last year when Derek had that issue with the silly blonde, and you acted as go-between? I certainly do. I couldn't forget it because, Spider, you were wonderful."

These were Sally's very first words when she arrived at the office.

Spider tensed. He could feel it coming. It was nice to receive the compliment, but he sensed that there could be a downside to follow. Whatever was about to be said next, he also knew, should elicit the simple answer – no.

"Do you feel up to the task again?" asked Sally.

Spider, normally of a pale complexion, blanched visibly. Surely they hadn't fallen out again, he thought, but it was obvious they had. He could remember the effort of doing the go-between thing last time and how it put years on him. How should he answer?

The trouble with having a conscience, and he hated it, was that it usually made him do whatever was right – and what are friends for if they can't do a bit of mediating when pushed, he asked himself, but deep down, he still wanted to say NO!

"Of course..." he smiled.

Derek hadn't arrived yet. He was late.

Rob was on the phone, locked away in his office as usual, but due to the partitions being paper-thin there was no privacy, and all he was saying was being heard clearly by Sally and Spider. Derek would have heard it too, if he'd been there.

"Yes..." said Rob. "No problem ...tomorrow then... Oh my goodness, that is terrible... Yes, I understand... That is very serious... The house...? Your friend...? Squashed flat...? Will have to be taken away? Oh dear ...it's as bad as that? ...Yes, of course... I'll tell her... Good luck."

Hearing only one end of the conversation can be quite frustrating to the listeners. Rob came out of the office and looked seriously at Sally.

"That call..." he said, cautiously, "Now, how can I put this? There's been ...uhmm. There was a little problem at home, a lucky escape, but he said that you would cope, Sally."

Sally's heart skipped a beat. Something has happened to Father, or is it Mum, or was it Aunt Thelma? Are they all right?

"He said you were made of stern stuff, and probably would not be concerned anyway, but if you were, he emphasised you mustn't worry about him – too much... He'll try to handle this dreadful situation on his own. Oh, did I say the call was from Derek?"

From Derek! Thank goodness for that; she hadn't realised it was only her husband at the other end of the phone, but what she heard sounded very serious though. Flattened...? House...? Friend...? What was going on at all? Was it the cottage – her cottage? What has he done this time? Derek was always causing trouble...

"What actually happened?" she asked Rob, beginning to feel just a tad anxious. They may have fallen out but Derek was still her responsibility, wasn't he? The fact that he had phoned was a good sign – him being able to – it meant he wasn't lying unconscious somewhere, so she could relax about that.

"He said not to tell you," Rob said sheepishly.

"He said what?" and her eyes opened wide.

"He said not to go into any detail with you. I think it was because he thought you might get too upset... Oh, and it was very unfortunate about your friend, Hamish? His first night in the caravan and..."

Yes, she knew Hamish went into the caravan last night – for his first time, sleeping there ...so...? "Could he not sleep then?" she queried laughingly, and then a more sombre thought occurred. "Oh no... He died in his sleep? Is that what happened? He was very old..."

but she became more anxious as she remembered the word 'flattened' was overheard earlier, but surely, he wasn't...? Ohhhhhh...!

"No, no, no... At least, I don't think so..." offered Rob, as he backed into his office and closed the door again, hurriedly. He remembered the discomfort suffered by Spider and him during the last fallout, so, it seemed wise not to get too deeply embroiled, yet. That would come soon enough if the normal pattern ran.

On one hand, Sally wanted desperately to phone Derek directly, to find out exactly what had happened, but her pride, and the eagerness to remain aloof, prevented her. Anyway, it can't be that serious, she decided, or he would have rushed immediately to me for help, although if he has had to arrange Hammy's funeral...

No... Derek wouldn't even attempt to cope with that on his own... I'll let him suffer a bit. When he eventually does decide to ask for my assistance, I'll make him crawl.

Although Rob already accepted that a key member of staff, in the form of Derek, would not be appearing today, he considered the absence to have been very bad timing. Imagine, foolishly choosing to have both major home repairs and a marital upset on the same day – and when it was coinciding with the very day Sally was to be needed to do child-minding for his two youngsters.

This extra pressure on Sally, the inevitability of her being upset about Derek, could disrupt the plan. It was possible she would not be willing to child-mind...

Thomas and Raymond, now four and five respectively, were proving to be even more of a handful these days to their parents, so the prospect of Sally refusing was horrifying for Rob – he might have to do it himself!

Normally the boys would be at school but his wife failed to mark this holiday on the calendar. Unfortunately for Rob, having two youngsters on the loose on this particular day clashed with Elizabeth Sheldon's meeting in the town with three of her female buddies. She wasn't going to let these two little blighters spoil her day, even if it was her memory lapse which caused it, so the problem was being passed on to him. This had been decreed before he'd left home this morning.

"You are their father, for goodness sake!" his wife informed him, as he buttered toast at the breakfast table, carefully absolving herself totally of any responsibility.

Rob would have to either take a day off work, or solve the problem in some other way. It was going to be some other way was his decision, and the other way, his solution: land them on Sally. The plan had been to ask her whenever she arrived this morning, but that was before she entered in a foul mood. Of course, today's arrangements were further confused by Derek's absence. Should he tell her just now, get it over with? No ...a bad mood ...doomed to fail. He'd ask her later, when she's in a better frame of mind.

That was his decision at the time, but, as on previous occasions, he forgot... It was now after mid-day and he hadn't asked her yet. Don't panic, he told himself, everything has calmed down now, and she has never objected in the past, so it will all be fine. I'll ask in a moment...

Just after one o'clock there was a noise on the stairs – and Rob's memory was jogged. He hadn't talked to Sally, and she'd gone to lunch.

"Hello darling," he said to his wife, Elizabeth, and did the usual kissy-kissy routine that made him feel foolish in public. In front of Spider, it felt even worse, but his wife always insisted...

"Hello boys," he said to Thomas and Raymond, who just ignored him and made for Derek's empty desk and computer.

Spider was quick. He shot over and diverted them while disconnecting the power supply to Derek's desk. He knew Derek would be a tiny bit upset if he returned to find all his work deleted by two pairs of rogue fingers. So, they just had to be content bashing at a dead keyboard and playing with the office sharpener, destroying as many pencils and biros as they could find.

Returning from lunch, Sally's face fell. She read the situation immediately because this was not the first time she'd been landed with the boys; and there could have been better days to choose. Feigning sudden illness was a thought which occurred to her. The parents would be expecting her to magically become Mary Poppins and whisk away their delightful offspring to another world, and that was not going to be easy the way she felt today, but nevertheless she forced a big smile.

"Hello Sally," said Elizabeth. "You're looking well today and obviously eager to get out and about with the boys, I'll bet. It's much more fun than sitting in a stuffy office all day, eh what?"

"Oh yes..." Sally lied, knowing full well that as usual Rob forgot to warn her. Rob just grinned, shrugged his shoulders and made a 'Sorry, Sally' face, behind his wife's back.

"No family on the way for you yet?" continued Elizabeth.

"No," Sally smiled back.

"You can't be trying hard enough," laughed Elizabeth.

"Obviously, something like that," Sally replied through gritted teeth, while thinking, what business is it of yours, you nosy cow; I'd be scared to have a family in case they turned out like your two little monsters...

"Would you like to go to the cinema with Sally this afternoon, darlings?" Elizabeth asked her little dears, who were throwing the remains of bits of pencil and biro at one another.

"No!" was the clear and immediate response from both, as if they'd rehearsed it.

"Yes, of course you would," continued Mummy, totalling ignoring them. She smiled down and patted their heads in the correct motherly fashion. "So, they're all yours, Sally. Enjoy yourselves, everyone," said Elizabeth, as Sally and Thomas and Raymond were happily ushered out of the door by a mother who had other things to do.

As the door closed, and Sally left the office with her explosive charges, Spider heard the loud sigh of relief exhaled by the parents. Rob and Elizabeth were smiling at each other, though, to Spider's eyes, Rob's smile was somewhat forced.

Poor Sally, thought Spider.

Down the stairs they clattered, with Sally being amazed when she reached the street level; she'd managed to keep pace with two fleet-footed youngsters without any of the three tumbling down the stairs.

"The Pirates of the Caribbean, how about that then?" she asked, and grabbed their hands before they could gallop out into the street.

"Yes, oh yes!" they replied happily.

They liked Sally, and they could behave for her if they chose to – which was quite unlike when they were with either, or both, of their parents. On these occasions for the children it was always anything goes; mob rule by two. (Witnessing your child's mad infuriating behaviour, but being totally incapable of doing anything to prevent it, of course, was one of the dubious joys of being a parent.)

Luckily for Sally, Thomas and Raymond had decided, today was to be a behaving day. Saying the word 'pirates' had been a winner for her, and by the time they reached the cinema she was in a very good mood, mainly because the boys were still behaving.

Being a little older now, communication was possible. The boys appreciated Sally actually talking with them and listening to what they said. They were used to instructions being barked at them by Mummy and Daddy, which they could, and did, ignore. Sally was different.

Anyway, Sally was relaxed. Yes, being away from the office was a good thing occasionally. These two little boys, they actually could be lovable on their good days – like today.

Inside the multiplex cinema foyer it was noisy and busy. They bought the obligatory popcorn, but spilled half of it on the way to their seats in Cinema One. During the film, all the popcorn wasn't consumed, but neither was it totally wasted. As they munched, some of it was saved for later by the sticky stuff being spilled all over their clothing, finding folds and pockets to hold it fast. Sally discovered some stuck to her clothing too, but she didn't mind because it happened when they'd cuddled up close to her at the 'scary bits', which was nice at the time.

They were little angels all the way through the performance.

Sally couldn't help it: she couldn't truly call them adorable, but she did find she really liked them. Now if they were mine, she thought, they'd be treated so differently, loved more, and cuddled more, and we'd be a proper complete family – and that thought made her feel all broody. Maybe now was the time to be having a family. On the screen in front of her, every so often, Derek's face was appearing on the body of Johnny Depp. She was feeling all lovey-dovey. Yes, it felt right, now could be the time...

The film came to an end and the lights went up. All three of them were smiling, having enjoyed the experience of being with each other, and for having watched such a super film. Hand in hand, they sang loudly and happily, as they went back along the road, and when the noisy trio arrived back at the office it was with big grins on their faces after a great day out.

But where were their shoes?

Now there is a thing, thought Sally but not really caring about a little problem like that – she was happily in the clouds. The two boys had removed their shoes in the cinema – and forgotten to put them back on again. They had walked back to join Mummy and Daddy in their stockinged feet – and not one of the three had noticed.

Rob and Elizabeth were mightily impressed by Sally's technique, whatever it was. They were so proud of their little angels. They were behaving the way good little boys behaved. They were doing everything Sally asked of them, and without question.

Of course, with their parents, the boys immediately reverted to type, but that was to be expected anyway. So, everyone continued smiling, even though there would have to be a return trip to the cinema on the way home to uplift two pairs of shoes. As this footwear was purchased for both as recently as two weeks ago, Rob hoped they had not yet been dumped by the cleaners in the refuse bin.

When they left, the office went quiet again, and Sally sat back at her desk with a dreamy smile on her face. She was still pleasantly broody.

11

What had she done?

Four days ago, there she was working away feeling perfectly at home in Detroit, Michigan. Having lived there almost twenty-five years very contentedly, she looked on it as her city – but she'd foolishly given in to him. No desire to move had ever been considered previously, and anyway, if Detroit had been good enough for her folks for most of their life, why should she have any reason to complain – or to up-sticks and leave? However, that is exactly what she'd done...

It was the middle of the night, which always makes life appear much worse, and she lay unable to sleep; her eyes were open but she was seeing very little of this small dark bedroom other than where the beam of light from the street lamp outside squeezed through the gap in the curtains; the dingy wallpaper thus exposed did little for her morale.

"Why in Heaven's name did I agree?"

The words were mouthed soundlessly. She needed to talk but there was no one to listen. It was frustrating that he could be lying next to her like this and sleeping soundly when she felt so upset. After all the happy times spent in a city she knew and loved, here she was in a godforsaken little town that she didn't know, and a town which was nowhere near anywhere either.

London – now that is big – the capital of this miserable country, but it is so far away. If only she were staying there. It for sure would have been more like back home, all hustle and bustle; yes, things would be happening there – exciting things to do all hours of the day and night – but here she was in Newingsworth, in the middle of nowhere – Deadsville.

The journey from her home to here was dreadful – a nightmare she was trying hard to forget. Going from one airport to another, waiting around in noisy and busy terminals, grabbing indigestible food and eating it hurriedly, then finding out, of course, that eating it hurriedly had been totally unnecessary because she was to be going nowhere for many hours. As she'd sat there, she couldn't believe the length of delay they were announcing could be possible – but it was, thanks to a stupid volcano called something unpronounceable.

Time dragged. Visits to the airport shops were tried but after the second and third viewings, although it helped with the time wasting, her interest in each shop palled. She bought a paperback and tried reading, attempting to absorb herself in a tale of passion, but couldn't retain concentration. Sleeping was an option that many people around her were taking but, as an announcement for her onward connection could be missed, dozing was the best she could manage – and afterwards she felt worse.

The 'people watching' just happened: something she drifted into. Sitting bored, gazing into space, her attention progressively was taken up by anyone who moved. Their behaviour disturbed her, not that they were doing any wrong. Sometimes it was to stretch stiffening legs, other times to fetch a vending machine drink. Couldn't they sit still, for a little time at least; look, another toilet-break for that woman, she's just been...

The most annoying movement seen was of those who gathered their belongings and walked out of the area brandishing boarding passes for flights to still-accessible destinations. These persons were showing off that their life still held a purpose, but worse still, it was the manner in which they did it – blatantly – with a smug smile. It was not fair. This behaviour caused her considerable displeasure.

Everyone was suffering delays, of course, but who cared about the others. She realised later, that compared to what it was to become in a few days, she got off lightly, but that didn't make it any easier at the time.

Not being a good traveller didn't help either. Everything associated with being transported around the country or the world had the ability to irritate her. There was no simple reason for her discomfort. Travel pills didn't help the agitation and claustrophobic effect of being in crowded places, and though the airport was bad enough, it was heaven compared to how she felt on the planes. It was just the way she was and she couldn't help herself.

Choosing, whether to use the direct flight to London from home, or the more economical one via New York, had been difficult. Foolishly and regrettably, economics won – hence the delays and discomfort – but at least the final coach trip from London had been acceptable, and on time.

Now having arrived, she was lying in a strange bed, using someone else's old mattress, in a rented house, in this blessed town, so how could she possibly sleep? And the street name? Buttercup Avenue – yughhh...

She turned and looked at the prone partner beside her.

Obviously, and to her great annoyance, the discomfort in her unsettled mind was having no effect on Sam whatsoever. He was dead to the world. He could sleep through a tornado – and at this moment was making just as much noise. She used her elbow judiciously, and though Sam grunted in agony, the pain didn't waken him. He just turned over, but at least the snoring stopped.

How would Mom be coping without her? With the time difference, she guessed, it would be near closing time in the restaurant after, as always, a very busy evening.

Did her friend meet Mom's expectations? Had she risen to the occasion? Maggie Thorne was her replacement. She and Angie worked together for four weeks in preparation for the departure. Someone had to take Angie's place and Maggie was it – the chosen one, and specially chosen – by Angie.

Everything required for the job was explained carefully to her; the opportunity to perform the duties over and over, under Angie's watchful and critical eyes, was given. It was hard work. Towards the leaving date, it did seem that she understood the job, and was remembering everything. However it became clear that though the skills were there – the confidence was not.

Angie continued to do all she could with Maggie until her time came to leave. The intensive training given was the best possible, in Angie's opinion, but the end result disappointed. Would another couple of weeks have helped? Apologising to her mother for failing her only brought a wry smile to that woman's face. She was not in the least perturbed.

"Maggie may not be perfect; and Angelina, honey, you'll be missed; but..." was the motherly reaction.

Surprisingly, Mom seemed unconcerned by the changeover of manager. In fact, she also appeared oblivious to the trauma being experienced by her one and only daughter, leaving home for the first time in twenty-five years and finding it difficult to abandon a mother who would struggle without her.

"...I'm a big girl now, and you are too, Honey, so I think we'll both cope," were Mom's comforting words, "And the world out there will still keep revolvin'..."

It may have been crocodile tears from Mom at the parting, but even so, it was sufficient for Angie to feel that she would be missed a little...

She shifted her position in the bed, roughly, half-hoping that Sam would be wakened and then he'd comfort her but no; Sam slept on...

It was wrong, Angie admitted to herself as she lay there, to grudge Sam the enjoyment he seemed to be getting from his new job – just because she wasn't happy.

His old teaching post back in Detroit had been driving him bananas. The same post since leaving college, and every evening the same grumbles – kids who weren't interested in learning anything, especially the subjects he was trying to cram down their throats, Mathematics and Physics.

To compete with the toys that they couldn't do without was impossible. He continually failed in class to prevent them playing with their expensive cell-phones and iPods. They were all experts with those. It was second nature and the same all over school, and it was getting to him. What was the attraction of these electronic gadgets? These kids couldn't live without them – they all had them –

it was an addiction.

He needed out – a change – anywhere!

Sam was possibly the only person in the school, and that included the school's head teacher, who didn't regularly upgrade each time a new gizmo appeared on the market. Sam's own cell phone, the most basic model, sufficed. His hard-earned dollars wouldn't be wasted on those sorts of things.

To save enough to marry Angie; his cash was destined for that simple task. They'd lived together for a long while already, sharing the large home that Angie's mom owned, so as well as getting married, Sam was desperate to have his own place. That home would be for him and Angie only, and of course, for any little ones who might happen along.

When they'd both been back in Detroit, they'd found conversation about Sam's day at work to be almost impossible. Getting the frustrations out of his head couldn't be done in the short time between him arriving back and Angie leaving for work. In the one waking hour where their lives overlapped, his grumbles had to spill out rapidly or not at all. Anything said was at a fast rate.

Anyway, in her rush to get out, it was unlikely that Angie ever really heard very much of it.

The chance for a change came about, thanks to Google. With the restaurant taking up all of Angie and her mom's time, Sam being on his own each evening had free reign of the computer. He stumbled on the possibility of an exchange visit with a teacher in Britain, a job at a High School in a place called Newingsworth. A twelve month temporary exchange was on offer, but becoming permanent was also shown as a possibility.

This was it – a dream chance – an entirely different environment. He'd be teaching kids who would want to learn, he told himself – that's what British kids were like. Well, he hoped that's what they would be like. It would be a long way to go to fail...

The name of this town was familiar. Pop was originally British, and Newingsworth was where he'd said he was born and brought up. Could this be the same place? In the days when Pop was on the road doing the gigs, Sam as a youngster tagged along with him and recalled this town being talked of with affection. Occasionally, particularly after a few beers, Sam remembered Pop rambling on about regretting having left.

Travelling about the States had all been a bit too much for his father at times but, as a musician, that's what he had to do. Sam was with him most of those early days and at low moments his father would start reminiscing about the good old days back in the UK. It always sounded magical and peaceful to Sam's young ears, compared to the busy city hotels they usually frequented. From what Sam could remember though, his pop gave little detail about that earlier life, although the boy who'd sat contentedly on his pop's knee back then had been very young and inattentive...

He would apply for this post even though he had no chance; hundreds of teachers already lived over there. He would be in competition with them; still, it would do no harm to send it off, and so, sending the application was done with little hope of even getting a reply: receiving an actual offer came as a shock!

Suddenly the pressure was on. He began to have doubts about his sanity in applying in the first place. This opportunity was quite unexpected, and suddenly a whim was becoming a reality. Greater doubts developed when Angie proved unwilling to move.

"But don't let me stop you," she'd stated with questionable sincerity.

When she'd then called into question his premise of children being different in Britain, he began to have more doubts. They are the same all over, she'd said, only good when it suits them. That was somewhat deflating.

Not having Angie enthusiastically urging him on was disappointing, but only one chance was likely to come his way. It was daring; it was stupid; but now was his time. This was it. So, the offer was accepted, he committed himself, and Newingsworth was to become his new challenge...

Five months later with his boyish enthusiasm helping him become established in the post, his dream of succeeding was becoming a reality and so far he'd been lucky. He had been warned on arrival by his new headmaster that the American accent would be a hit with the pupils initially, and that the effect would probably wear thin after a while but so far, so good...

After three months, he'd plucked up the courage to invite Angie to join him. He could now support them both. She would love it over here, even if it turned out to be only a long holiday. His phone calls, his texts, his emails, all sent from the new school, extolled the virtues of this fine town he was in, and slowly he was winning her over. Back in Detroit, as the months progressed, Angie's determination not to leave her own home town was gradually wavering – and then she gave in and agreed.

Now here she was, lying on someone else's mattress, wide awake, beside her partner in his own cosy dreamland, in this scruffy house, in a street with a stupid name – in Deadsville. Worse still, her dream partner had started snoring again.

She was already having serious regrets.

12

Stuck in Newingsworth; three weeks in this god-awful place, no friends, no-one to talk to, and Sam at home only in the evenings and at weekends. During the day – bored...

Where are the jobs I was supposed to walk into? The few restaurants that are here don't want managers, they already have them. There were possibly opportunities for waitresses or dishwashers, but only by joining the queue, and anyway, that is not what I want. I am a skilled and capable manager and I can earn good money.

The visit to Slatterfoot Job Centre proved remarkably unsuccessful. She left there totally disheartened, convinced that calling it a Job Centre was a doggone lie.

Only one organisation in the area seemed to be advertising for staff, but not through the Job Centre. Their advert she found in the local paper, but it proved to be only of a slight interest, mainly because the money was derisory. She could be working like a slave in a Call Centre. It offered odd shifts which could vary with all sort of patterns, day and night – and yes, it was a job, but...

She believed sincerely that Call Centres were designed to allow disgruntled members of the public to use a phone system to do nothing less than give dog's abuse to some poor fool at the end of a telephone line; someone who'd have to sit and take it because it was their job; someone who was just grateful to have a job of some sort and it wasn't fair! At least that was the reputation these jobs had back home. She had little doubt the UK version would be the same, and

...no, no, and no again, I do not want to prove it is the same in this country. I am not desperate for money so I'm not interested, thank you very much!

The house was clean – from top to bottom. Her time was not being totally wasted. The paint surfaces were washed down, however that meant the chipped paintwork was now well and truly exposed, and though the carpets were clean, it was more obvious they were worn. Even the bed was squeaking more than when she arrived at first – but at least there was good reason for the squeaks. She had missed Sam, a great deal, she hadn't realised how much. There had been a lot of catching up to do...

Right now though, she was on her way to the supermarket.

She'd been there a few times already. It was a large building, and not too unlike those back home. Bisko's it was called. This organisation hadn't reached the States yet, but it was the biggest in this area and had a monopoly, as far as she could tell. For what she had seen of the shops in the town, it was very likely that this supermarket's presence killed off the smaller local businesses. Many shops were lying disused.

Bisko's car park always seemed to be full, but there would be no worry about parking spaces for her – she had no car. Spaces for bicycles and motor bikes were specially marked, though she had none of these either. As she was passing these parking spots, she noticed an old fellow arriving on a motor scooter and manoeuvring into place. The noise of the small motor was distinctive. She hadn't seen many of these back home. In the States it was more usual to have a big car, or a motor bike, or nothing.

Suddenly she felt uncomfortable.

That old guy was giving her funny looks. Was there something odd about her today? Why was he staring at her like that? He nearly knocked his scooter over. Close your mouth old fella, she thought – it's not a flattering look. Is he just a dirty old man who can't help himself? He looks like a guy who always has to be undressing females in his mind? Every country has them obviously! That's all she needed... Should she give him a V-sign, or just the finger? Which do they do here? Though that's probably considered very rude in a dump like this – could cause a bigger problem, she thought – she might get arrested.

Deciding to ignore him, hoping he would go away, she went to collect a trolley. In the storage area she found them chained together. Some place this, she thought, having to lock up the trolleys in case they are stolen? For heaven's sake, who'd want to steal a goddam trolley – and huh! A pound coin was needed!

At least the money system was understandable, but she was having difficulty accepting the prices. Petrol here costs a fortune compared to back home: couldn't yet tell with the food...

She was halfway up the first aisle when she realised she'd managed to select the trolley with the dodgy wheel, probably the only one. Her lucky day and she'd found it. Live with it she decided, but had to concentrate to avoid hitting other shoppers. It felt better when she realised how most of the other trolleys in use gave the person pushing exactly the same trouble.

Some fruit first – healthy food and good for you. That she knew, because her mother pounded it into her head when she was a kid. Now she couldn't understand how anyone could resist eating fruit if it was available, and here there was plenty on display. She knew Sam was not a big fan, but she would be changing some of his habits – starting with fruit.

As she glanced up to avoid hitting someone with her wayward trolley, something caught her eye. It was the old guy – the scooter guy. He was watching her again – the cheek of him. He looked startled when she looked straight back at him. Pick on someone else, old boy, or I'll trample you under my heel, she muttered under her breath. Brave talk, but it was unsettling her. She carried on. Ah, a fresh pineapple, now that must be bought, that is something Sam will hate...

Probably beforehand she should have made a list of all the things required, but she did have all the time in the world, and could stroll leisurely round the store making random choices. She could even double back, if necessary, to collect anything missed. Look at all these aisles to choose from. She could wander along in any direction, and take all day if she wished.

It was more fun going the opposite way to everyone else. She took perverse pleasure in that. More eye contact that way, even if it was hostile because she was crossing people's paths. In here with all the customers around she didn't feel quite so lonely, even though they were all concentrating on their own shopping – except for that old guy again...

He dodged back round the corner of a unit when he realised she was looking back at him. She stopped and stood her ground, and continued looking at that same spot until his head appeared again, and was then retracted rapidly. That's fine, she whispered to herself, injure your neck, you silly old fool...

Could this be a stalker? Could it be – really? This sort of thing happened in the States, but it usually was for film or TV stars, not normal ordinary babes like her. Now this was something. She had her very own stalker... Sam will be jealous, won't he? She could already imagine his complaint later – why is it your day was much more exciting than my silly darn school lessons?

Not true though was it? This wasn't really exciting. In fact, it wasn't nice at all; amusing at first, but now it felt uncomfortable, and it was starting to irritate. Should she complain to the store staff? Would they believe her? Would they just laugh and tell her not to be silly? She decided it best if she just let him be, he would get fed up in a little while, surely...

But he didn't.

She didn't have to look to check for the old guy again – while she selected the fresh bread and chose some cakes as a reward for Sam if he ate the fruit, she could feel his eyes on her. Down the tinned foods corridor she went, passed the frozen food units, up the electrical goods lane, pushing a trolley that didn't know how it should be behaving even though she kicked it every so often to get it back to the proper direction. There he was, every time she looked.

So, she went on the offensive. Angie hurried towards him, but somehow he had vanished by the time she reached that spot, and when she turned around he'd made it to the opposite end again. He was maybe not as old as he looked, or else he was fitter than her.

By the time she arrived at the check-outs, she was relieved to see that he was no longer there, but, as she stood in the short queue, it was a very odd feeling she experienced. With him not watching her any longer – it was almost as though she had lost a friend...

13

For six days a week she was an ordinary granny, an ordinary granny doing the ordinary things that ordinary granny's do – but on the seventh day, she was different. She became 'Granny Wisdom, the local radio Superstar Agony Gran' – that no-one recognised in the street. Her seventh day was a Monday. She was *special* on a Monday...

Having lived there for a very long time, almost all the residents of Blytheton Road were known to her. The few she didn't know could be considered to be fly-by-nights and not worth knowing. They all knew her too, of course, but to them she was simply Granny Smith, sometimes Mrs Smith, wife of Hector. She had a Sunday name – Daisy, but that was known and used by only a select few.

It was certain that none of the locals were aware of her alter ego, Granny Wisdom, even though they had probably listened every Monday for months. Her identity was a well kept secret. Anyway, the full local radio show wasn't being done by her now – much too exhausting. Arthur and Charlie, Derek's pals from the park, took over as the hosts, but Daisy was still required. In their Monday two-hour show Daisy contributed a live weekly twenty minutes, as part of the programme, and supplied answers to pseudo-anxious lovelorn telephone callers. 'Have a Heart' was her spot. She made it fun and the MOGGIES were still out there rooting for her...

Her current task at home though, was re-training her husband; making him use the name he'd called her before she became 'Gran'.

Since Derek departed Blytheton Road to get married, leaving

them on their own, she had been trying to get Hector to call her Daisy again, like the old days, but he was finding it difficult changing his established habit. She had been his wife for nearly fifty years but, having called her Gran for thirty of those years when Derek was with them, 'Gran' was deeply embedded in his brain. It would take time...

Routine was important to Daisy. The brasses were polished every day, except on Monday's: she left early to go to **"LITTLE RADIO fm'** for the broadcast on that day. Her house always looked spick and span, and she was proud of it; windows clean, washing on the line if the forecast was for a dry day, curtains pulled back to the correct position, and the little garden kept neat and tidy, with thanks to occasional visits by Derek to cut the grass and the hedge. Routine always had been important to this bustling-about older lady particularly in the bringing-up of a grandson – and, of course, in the fussing after his grandad. Another thing was certain too – it had been a happy home for the three of them.

Now she worried... Where is Hector? He should have been back by now. What could possibly be keeping him today? My goodness, look at the time, nearly eleven o'clock, time for our cup of tea. I'll put the kettle on – that'll encourage him... He'd better not be doing this to annoy me... Where is he?

For a long while, Hector had felt guilty about resigning from his morning newspaper deliveries, mainly because he still considered himself to be fit and capable. It niggled also, having done the same paper round for so long using the squeaky old bike of his, that he could no longer claim to be the oldest paper boy in Newingsworth – maybe even in Britain – or be recognised as having the oldest bike ever used on a paper round. It may all be history now, but it had made a good story in Newingsworth Old Folk's Club...

His early morning round ended nearly a year ago and thankfully any guilt was long gone, as far as Daisy could tell. Anyway she was the one working now. The job on Mondays at **'LITTLE RADIO fm'** meant extra money, giving them both the chance of additional goodies, and though Daisy harboured no wild desires to buy anything special, she had encouraged Hector to splash out on something.

For years he'd dreamed of one day having another motorbike.

Learning and using one during National Service led to him having his own bike for several years after leaving the army. When he and Daisy married, his treasured possession went up for sale and the money helped buy their first furniture. Forty odd years ago a motorbike would have been the perfect choice to buy, but not nowadays, and mainly because of Daisy. She couldn't be his pillion passenger on a motorcycle – she'd be ill.

So, the next best thing, they decided, was to 'make do' with a motor scooter: a little less powerful and less hair-raising for the pillion passenger. Daisy was in agreement with that, so the Vespa was purchased.

However, saying 'make do' sounds like a disappointment – a poor second best. No way – the Vespa scooter was his adult toy, his for almost a year now, and the novelty still hadn't worn off. He used it almost every time he went for the shopping, happily roaring off like a boy racer.

Still, it was unusual for Hector to be five minutes late. She hoped nothing had happened to him. The roads were so busy around here, and as for that car park at Bisko's, it was a nightmare. She was glad she couldn't drive.

She reluctantly goes on his scooter pillion, but usually keeps her eyes tightly closed at the busy bits, and when he is overtaking, and going round corners – and almost all of the rest of the time too...

Phut, phut, phut, phut, phut, phut...

Ah, thank goodness, she thought, there he is now, and opened the door for him. He stood with a bag of shopping in each hand but with an odd look on his face. Daisy's immediate thoughts were of an accident – he'd hit something – someone had run into him...

"Oh ...D-D-D-D-D-Daisy..." He staggered in with the bags, and dumped them quickly on the floor. He didn't look well.

"What's wrong, Hector? Have you hurt yourself? Did you hit someone? Spit it out..."

"L-l-l-let me sit d-d-down... I've had a sh-sh-sh-sh-shock." His face was ashen, and he was trembling. "D-d-d-do you believe in g-g-g-ghosts?"

"No, of course, I don't," she replied dismissively.

"Because I've j-j-just s-s-s-seen one – a g-ghost ...in B-B-B-Bisko's."

"Don't be ridiculous, and you've always said you don't believe in ghosts either."

"A b-b-blast from the p-p-past it was. Our M-M-Millicent... I s-s-saw her ...this m-m-m-morning," he was getting quite agitated, "in B-B-Bisko's, b-b-believe me. Our M-M-Millie ...in the b-b-bread q-q-queue."

"You need a strong cup of tea – with two sugars," she declared. "Maybe even something stronger. You haven't been drinking with Hammy again, have you? You haven't been to the Club?"

"N-n-n-no..." He flopped back in the chair.

When she came back in, he was a little calmer, and some of the colour was back in his face. "Now, let's start again," said a very practical Daisy. "You saw someone who looked liked our Millicent in the supermarket, so now you believe in ghosts. Is that right? Is that what you said?"

He looked up at her, now feeling foolish.

"She l-l-l-looked just l-l-l-like I r-r-remember her."

"Hector, your memory is of a young girl. Our daughter was an eighteen-year old when she went, and it was over thirty years ago she left home. Are you forgetting that Derek is now a grown man?"

Daisy looked sadly down at her dear old husband, remembering her daughter's departure. Her thoughts were much clearer than his. Her memories were *very* clear, and painful. It had hurt her more than him at the time, but the past couldn't be changed. She had tried to put it behind her.

"Anyway, did she remember you?"

"G-g-gran, d-d-d-don't..." he started back.

"Daisy, please..." was quickly slipped it in to remind him, and to fill the natural gap... "What did she say to you?" pursued Daisy.

"Now, d-d-d-don't be silly. I d-d-didn't speak to her..." He gave his wife a pitying look – but he wasn't finished... "Everyone knows that g-g-g-ghosts c-c-can't t-t-talk..."

14

The disaster – it really had been foreseen by her. The tree fell down exactly as she predicted.

It was a special power; she could feel it – even though the argument on that night was simply down to her being in a foul mood, and any old subject would probably have gone the same way, but it wasn't just the tree. There was the caravan...

A full week had gone by since she'd last been at the cottage – and the same length of time avoiding communication with Derek about anything other than work; however, he spoke to Spider, and Spider was speaking to Sally; so the destruction of Hammy's caravan was now known to her, and this was so obviously another example of her premonitions.

The single word 'wreck' was the first thing to come into her head the moment Hammy appeared with that van, she was able to claim. To have 'recognised' that must have been due to her special power too.

There was no dissuading her on that. It had nothing to do with her seeing what any other person with eyes could have seen – that it was a rust-bucket from the start. Oh no, no... It was another premonition, and it felt spooky...

Anyway, premonitions or not, she was refusing to return to the cottage until the mess was cleared up, and of course there was no question in her mind, Derek had to be made to suffer. She could guess that he would be missing their intimate cuddles, just like all men. Then again, so did she, but she could be strong. She didn't need that sort of thing, well, not until Hammy found another home...

It wasn't as if Sally didn't see Derek during the week. He was there; he was near her at work every day at the office. When he came close, she wanted to hug him and say sorry but no, that wasn't possible – he had to suffer. He was getting more like her father every day. Last year he was wearing her clothes, but her father at least had an excuse for dressing as a female; he was an amateur actor. Now, very much like her father, Derek was daring to argue back. Therefore, any dealings she had with her husband had to be at arm's length, though in truth the arms didn't play a part.

It was poor Spider who was under pressure. At Sally's request he was reluctantly performing as the go-between again. Spider liked them both, but he would have appreciated each of them so much more, if only they'd left him out of it. Their arguments often meant that he couldn't sleep at nights. He wasn't able to concentrate properly during the day and feed Rob with winners like he used to, and he was a tiny bit scared that if the winners didn't appear, Rob would look for an excuse to be rid of him. He needn't have feared. Rob's betting compulsion meant he appreciated any help or support he could get from Spider. He would settle for just the occasional winners.

Anyway, being in debt to the bookie was a way of life for Rob. The odd times that he'd won substantial amounts never failed to make him nervous. He couldn't cope with winning. He always had to return to his normal state as quickly as possible, to ease his mind and not surprisingly, returning to owing his bookie was easy.

Hammy was doing a great job in the garden at Toozlethwaite Manor. Not on his own mark you, he had plenty help. His building team from the hotel construction site, who were commandeered into assisting, had worked hard and the debris was almost now clear of the crushed flat caravan. The removal of a few remaining loose branches, and the rust bucket would be totally exposed. The curtains Sally donated to brighten Hammy's new quarters could now be seen sadly fluttering about at ground level, where the windows were. The caravan had been a good idea but....

Each night, after the storm, Derek had come back home to the cottage, pleased to see Hammy had managed to organise the clearing of yet another part of the tree. The work of rebuilding the farmhouse and hotel had been temporarily curtailed to allow the team to cut and remove the wood, and was being done without seeking the permission of the man who was paying their wages.

It was Alexander's land and probably, in a court of law, he would have been judged to foot the bill, so Hammy felt justified in doing this wee job for Derek; he was saving lawyer's fees and arguments and Derek had agreed not to mention it to Alexander. Derek, however, was secretly convinced that his father-in-law would be well aware of what they were up to and craftily turning a blind eye to it.

For all the work being done in the clearance of the tree, Derek felt deeply obliged to Hammy. As a surprise, and a grateful thank-you, he'd successfully located another well-used caravan, this one being in a much better state than the first, and he purchased it secretly for Hammy. This time, it would not be brought near the cottage. He'd organised for it to be delivered to the farmhouse – a great deal more sensible – the road to the farmhouse being wider and safer than the cottage access. There would also be a suitable parking place clear of the building work, and it would still be only a five minute walk for Hammy to come back to the cottage for his evening meal. In fact, it was planned to perfection...

Hammy was delighted when he was told. As it also meant that Hammy would not be in the cottage overnight – Derek was delighted too.

The cottage could become their own again and he'd have Sally to himself and, unless something else went wrong, it would happen soon because he had been forgiven. The coolness was still there though. He was informed of this, in the time honoured way, at the office on Friday by the go-between so, when Derek received the news with delight, it wasn't Sally who was given the hug of delight – it was Spider!

Sally was returning – on Monday evening, and although the heavy stuff was all now gone, there was no chance of clearing the back garden of all the smaller bits of debris still remaining. It was still an eyesore. So, Derek and Hammy blew up balloons, and added streamers, around the cottage, and placed a large banner saying 'Welcome back' at the front door.

The plan was to divert her attention, and with any luck, she would not then notice the mess. And that idea worked – a treat. Well ...yes ...it seemed to have worked a treat, but that was from Derek and Hammy's viewpoint.

In reality, for Sally, the pleasure was diminished somewhat because of the other surprise awaiting. As she came in the door, they reminded her it was Monday – it was her turn to make the meal...

15

Hammy was now sleeping in the caravan beside his workplace nearly a mile away, and Derek's conjugal rights were being enjoyed again: two very big reasons for Derek to feel good. However, there was an even bigger reason – a great idea for the book subject emerged earlier today thanks to Anton; one that would be far better than any of the failures he'd been toying with up to now.

A whiff of optimism was in the air this evening and Derek was feeling enthusiastic and upbeat. The little tremor of excitement that he hadn't felt for ages was back because this idea was almost certainly going to be a winner. He could feel it in his bones, he just knew. This was it!

Derek liked Anton. Sometimes his coffee wasn't perfect, but it was always drinkable, however, Anton was someone who never called him anything other than Derek. That meant a great deal to a person who, for nearly thirty years, unfortunately owned a much disliked nickname.

'Sweaty' was not a word he'd even understood when young, but having been known by that for so long, it was proving next to impossible to encourage everyone to change. He still couldn't avoid being Sweaty when he went into the park. He'd given up on Charlie and Arthur. He'd no chance of success with them. They just didn't want to change, and enjoyed making him squirm, but in fun; he liked them as well, so he lived with it...

Thankfully for Derek's blood pressure, fewer and fewer of his friends were using it these days, but the fact that Anton had never called him that made him special in Derek's mind. Yes, he did like Anton – a lot, and even more so because today had been 'inspiration day', thanks to the cafe owner.

Earlier in the day, Derek visited the Old Astoria Café – a fairly regular occurrence – and was chatting to Anton when the idea occurred; something just clicked.

These days, Anton visited his own cafe less and less, so it was lucky for Derek that he'd been there at all. The cafe was owned by Anton and he'd worked in it for most of his life, in fact it had been his life, but do I have to work so hard, he'd asked himself three months ago? The answer, he decided, was no ...the time has come.

So now, his son looked after the place, with some extra staff, and, Anton being at a certain age, was able to step back, relax, and look on himself as the well-matured 'bigga cheese,' the boss in the background. His presence was not required for the daily routines any more. Popping-in now and again would be all that was needed.

Although he claimed to have to pop-in regularly to check that all his customers were being properly cared for, it was not necessary; his son was very capable of running the place. No; the real reason was to do with living on his own. He needed to maintain contact with the outside world; he needed to continue to meet people and this was how he did it. An appreciative audience in his own cafe was always assured – and it kept his extensive knowledge of local gossip up to date.

Having lived in Newingsworth all his life, owning and running the cafe for a large part of it, he would be hearing the tales of the neighbourhood circulating freely every day, and each of these days, facts were being slipped into the filing system of his ample brain. Anton became the equivalent of the local historian, but with nothing written down. It was all locked in his memory. That, unfortunately, was the historical weakness – his memory wasn't as good as it used to be.

Nowadays, his tales tended to be serialised. The missing parts of a particular story could be added, sometimes many days later when eventually remembered. Of course, they would only be relevant if the original person was there to listen – and still wanted to know.

It always interested and amused Derek how these days Anton's memories were bits of a story, bits that would lead to other bits, and these bits, coming together forming another totally unrelated subject – probably of more bits. Again today, Anton had been reminiscing while Derek was having a cup of coffee. The radio played in the background as the old fellow spouted-out random tales from his past.

Some customers only pretended to listen. They would smile every so often while Anton talked to them but, as their eyes glazed over, Derek could tell that their smiles were occurring at the wrong moments in the story.

Those less tolerant made it obvious, after being served, that they wanted to be left alone. These were the ones who made a big job of opening up the newspaper blatantly after placing an order. Often though, Derek watched them pretending to be reading or doing the Crossword, or the Sudoku, but they would actually be straining to hear Anton's 'tale of the day' being told at another table.

Derek wanted to hear Anton chatter. He was always listening for amusing stories with a local flavour in the hope of writing them down and using them as articles for the Gazette. Being a weekly paper, he considered serialised themes could run for weeks. It maintained readership interest but, more importantly, kept local readers habitually buying the paper; essential for keeping him in the job.

Anton was sitting opposite Derek when it happened. The trigger was the voice coming from the radio, that of a Rapper. It was some new young kid called 'Dig-me-fast-man', or something like that – Derek wasn't sure he'd heard it correctly. Anyway, rapping was not Derek's favourite type of music and obviously wasn't Anton's either but, as it was being given air play, none the less, someone somewhere must like it.

Tricky phrases and rhymes were being rattled out by a guy that these two coffee-drinking critics cynically considered was being paid wrongly for his offering. To their ears, there was only rhythm to be heard. A melody was sadly lacking... That type of noise meant nothing to anyone over twelve, complained Anton.

"Now backa, when I was the mucha youngerra man..." he began. Anton's reminiscing tended to start this way, or with something very similar. "Moosic... It was realla moosicca backa then. You could hearra the toona they play – inna thees Cafe. Yea, these guys, backa then, they playda toons, the realla toons. And eacha day, they woulda be inna here, inna thees Cafe I tella you, talking about realla rocka moosic..."

"What guys?" asked Derek, as the second coffee was placed in front of him. That simple little question was all it took for Anton to launch into today's topic.

Anton knew of a band, a local group, from about thirty years ago. It was before they made it big. They'd used the cafe as their base and sat and chatted about how successful they planned to become. Like most youngsters, they had daydreams, but the unusual thing was that these kids made their dreams come true. Anton remembered them as school-kids – reasonably mature school-kids mark you – many years ago working away at normal classes in their final year at the High School in town.

They were very much appreciated by the town's young folk. During their final school year, as a class-act rock band their reputation steadily grew, with a large local fan club following them loyally to wherever the gig happened to be in the area.

'Fort Knights and a Damsel' they were called back in those early days, four boys and a girl.

After playing together for almost a year, they were 'discovered' by several agents, and offered contracts but, to succeed, not surprisingly they were informed they would have to leave home. They were given the chance of living and recording in London, or Detroit. The youngsters chose the American studios, where to them the big time beckoned.

Anton remembered there was a bit of a scandal about them, something to do with one of the boys and the girl getting up to some mischief. After that, only three boys and the girl chose to leave Newingsworth. They apparently picked up another musician in the States, who then stayed with them and became a permanent member of the group. That is when they became 'Rabid Revenge' – a change of name and a change of style coming out of the new guy joining, and that was it...

There was no more to be contributed, certainly not names. These were not details Anton was capable of recalling. He said he could picture them in his mind and could give vague descriptions of them as youngsters, which was not very helpful, but it was a start.

To Derek they sounded a presentable group of individuals, and presumably made a great noise, though Anton hadn't been as addicted to their music as the genuine fans were. Being much older than the band members and their followers, no doubt, contributed. It wasn't his scene and anyway, he had a cafe to run.

The change of style when they went to America did not impress him either, he continued, but a lot of people over there must have liked them. As far as he knew they had been very successful in the USA, a big country. Strange, they had made very little impression on the UK music-scene, or if they had, he was not aware of it.

Derek left the Old Astoria Cafe feeling as if he'd had six espressos on the trot – he'd had two. Well fired up with enthusiasm, he desperately tried to avoid forgetting any of the detail mentioned by Anton. From now on, every single word could become valuable...

He rushed home to tell Sally and his words spilled out fast and furious; this was something he could work on; this was a big moment...

"Oh..." she said, in an airy-fairy way, "...that's nice..."

16

Derek was out of the office all afternoon again – at the cafe, at least that was Sally's suspicion. These visits were becoming a habit and not correct behaviour to her mind. She hoped her husband was doing the work he was being paid for and not getting carried away with whatever he was chattering on about last night. She knew that Rob would not be happy if he found out Derek was skiving. One thing was very obvious – the office was quieter when he wasn't in it.

Spider was on internet searching for unusual stories for the next issue and also phoning to check that the regular advertisers still wanted space. Every so often, the print machine at the back of the room would chatter for a short time, and then the room would return to a peaceful silence.

Rob was supposedly busy in his own office doing the work of an editor but, being the boss, he was allowing himself to keep an eye on how this afternoon's choice of winners was progressing. So far, it had been a pleasant experience for a change, so he was anticipating an unusually successful end to his day but, he reminded himself, the day hadn't yet ended. He'd had days like this before...

Sally was sitting day-dreaming with happy thoughts bouncing merrily around in her head. Weren't children wonderful? The day-out she'd had recently with Rob's two youngsters, they enjoyed themselves, didn't they? She certainly had. It was lovely when they'd cuddled close and she'd put her arms around them, one either side. It was only a film, but at times they were terrified of Cap'n Jack Sparrow and his merry band of pirates. When some parts of the noisy mayhem up on the big screen made them jump – and startled her too – she'd been the one they'd clung to for comfort. Yes, it was becoming so obvious... She liked children and children liked her. What if they were her kids? Would she feel the same, she wondered – probably even better...

Maybe now is the time...

Her working day was over. Sitting on the settee sipping a glass of white wine at this time in the early evening was unlike her. She sat dreamily waiting while her dear Derek prepared the meal. He was head chef tonight, currently in the kitchen, about to surprise and delight her with whatever he was concocting from Jamie's Cookbook.

It was Friday and no work tomorrow. She hoped Hammy wouldn't appear – she was in the mood... Normally it would take a lot of gentle persistent persuasion to warm her up – but, oh no, not tonight. Sweaty, slaving away in the kitchen for her, totally forgiven now that the mess outside was all cleared away; her second glass of wine was in her hand; yes, this evening the atmosphere was perfect. For her, it will be tonight and all night, if she gets her way. She was eagerly looking forward to having (to put it delicately) a lot of rumpy-pumpy...

He was making the meal, it was his turn, but he was behaving a little strangely tonight muttering unusual phrases to himself; had been ever since he came home. Had he been drinking before coming home? Seems to be very pleased, repeating the same words over and over, to do with work maybe? Was it in case he forgot them? ...Now he was moving around the kitchen using sort of dance movements and saying the words rhythmically and looking as if he was trying to keep his movements in time, but with difficulty.

His behaviour in the kitchen tonight was a tiny bit disturbing. She could see the strange cavorting – the worrying thought that he is going to spill something, or burn himself, for sure – and spoil the mood! This was not like Derek at all, and now he was into a little song. The tune was barely recognisable – Frere Jacques, maybe? Derek was not a singer...

"Vapid Vengeance, Vapid Vengeance
I'll get you, I'll get you,
Hot Knights with a Damsel, Hot Knights with a Damsel.
I'm hot too. Woo, hoo, hoo."

And then he was back at the beginning, and on it went, again, and again...

'Vapid Vengeance,' as a phrase, didn't make much sense in Sally's ears, but the other sounded more promising – hot nights with a damsel. It matched her mood, and well ...as long as the damsel was her, she could personally guarantee that tonight will be one of the hot nights...

How silly of me not to notice, she thought, but how fortunate – and it's so obvious, now. Derek is in the mood too...

Little did she know – Derek was on a different planet.

Now normally, as far as relations with his wife were concerned, Derek would have picked up all the 'be-prepared' signals. In all the time they'd been married, he had certainly not been known to ever miss a chance of sensing and being ready when the moment arrived – for a little bit of that – but it wasn't happening tonight.

However, it was mealtime...

His food was a success, and his preparations, even with the strange song and dance, well worth the effort. His woman loved it. More loving looks were directed at him when he topped it by carrying through a delicious dessert. For Sally, the grand finale was a relaxing coffee in the easy chair – and then he was on his feet, clearing away the dishes.

"Just leave those..." she said in a sexy whisper. "Take it easy, Derek. That can be done later."

"No problem," he replied airily, "It'll just take a moment."

He cleared all the dishes into the kitchen and left them there with a clatter, then came straight out – and over to the computer. He sat down and switched on.

"Are you going to be long at that, darling?" she enquired gently, but suddenly with a little uncertainty being felt by her. "I'm going off to bed – early. Shouldn't you have an early night too?" she purred. "We don't have to go to sleep right away. We could ...uhm ...you know..."

"Serious stuff this," he said without looking up. "I've a lot of searching to do. This is it. It is going to be a great idea – enormous potential. I can tell tonight's going to be the night..."

Obviously, two great minds were going in different directions and it didn't take a bucket of water to cool her down. These wrong words at the wrong time did it very effectively, causing her hot switch immediately to turn to 'off'. With a glower in his direction, she rose – and went to bed in a huff, to read a book, and to remember. Derek would pay for this...

Still the penny hadn't dropped. He'd no idea of his missed opportunity, nor did he appreciate how many other misses his dear wife would be promising because of this.

His mind was internet.

There is bound to be something on the web about this rock group, he told himself, there always is; something with which he could begin to construct a story. Some geek, who wants to show how smart he is will have created a web page somewhere, he was sure, no matter how obscure the subject someone will have had the compulsion to put it on the World Wide Web.

He was almost certain that when he looked, he would be finding there was more than one geek out there, and all wanting to share their knowledge with him.

'Vapid Vengeance,' was all he'd need to enter and, abracadoodliflip, an enormous list of web sites would sit up and beg for his attention.

Doing this was so rewarding... He couldn't ask for a better task. Any moment now, in this household, someone would achieve satisfaction, and then could happily go to sleep.

One thing was certain – it would not be Sally.

17

Derek was so wrong. After the confidence only moments before of anticipating information leaping out at him – it didn't. WWW was letting him down, not performing to expectations at all, and that for him was truly mystifying.

He had carefully input 'Vapid Vengeance,' and got nothing, absolutely nothing, well, certainly nothing musical. The spelling was checked – no stupid errors – but still nothing. His search for 'Hot Knights with a Damsel' was just as unsuccessful. Nothing appeared at all, well, nothing related to what he was looking for?

Why? Why, why, why...?

Had he remembered the wrong names? No... Of course he hadn't. That thought was dismissed with scorn. Him, doubting his own memory... Never... Who was it had been saying the names over and over from the instant he left Anton, even made up a little tune to help, and, obviously couldn't possibly have forgotten them? Me! ...They were continually repeated all the way along the road. In fact, to be absolutely certain, the names were even written in the little notebook.

The notebook was fetched from his jacket hanging in the small hallway – and there it was, written clear as you like... and he read the words aloud, to prove how correct he'd been: "Rabid Revenge"...?

Ah... not Vapid Ven..."

Now a lapse like this was disconcerting to someone who recognised the extent of Anton's memory problems. He wondered to himself if Anton had been as young as him when his malfunctions began...

It started to pull together a little more effectively when he googled the two bands, with the correct name this time, having managed to remember both wrongly... That was humbling. 'Hot Knights with' indeed – it should have been 'Fort Knights and...'

When re-input, the very first site he selected put him right. This is what happens when you become too cocky, he told himself. In fact, the names they used as a band were confirmed, just as Anton said, 'Fort Knights and a Damsel,' and who later became 'Rabid Revenge'.

He liked the names. The original one, used when they were young and just beginning, was cute. The second signalled their move into the big time and a change of style, the sort of name to get them noticed. It had more of an edge to it for heavy rockers.

Wikipedia had a page about them. There were many others, as expected, but none of the websites could help him discover how to make contact. It would have been great if he could have found that; the personal touch was what he was looking for. A phone number to enable him to speak to the band members directly – that was what he was wanting. Maybe he could get in touch via the internet.

Of course, he reminded himself, this will be possible only if they are still alive. What if they are all...? Think positive!

He guessed they would have settled with homes in the USA, because that is where the band made its name. There could be no certainty in that though.

Could they still be doing the circuit? If they were, surely a web site would be advertising their concerts and selling tickets for them: but there was nothing like that to be found, so it seemed unlikely. Many old bands these days were back on the road, split-up long ago, but no doubt reformed in the hope that the public remembered them well enough to replenish vastly depleted bank accounts. If they were out there, and alive, why would they miss the chance, he wondered?

In his mind he was clear in his aims. If he could contact each one individually, he would encourage them to comment about each other. Being stars he would expect heads to be swollen, otherwise they'd be very unusual performers. Each would be the most important person in the universe. What he was hoping for, in addition to the inevitable anecdotes making themselves the sole hero, was that they would spill the dirt on each other. Derek reckoned that could pay big dividends. A bit of 'divide and conquer' usually led to spicier stories. 'Squealing' it was called at school – though your mates rarely loved you afterwards, he remembered....

Derek looked at the details given in the Wikipedia entry, but oh-oh, there may be some doubt in this information. 'This article needs additional citations for verification, etc.,' it stated at the top of the page...

Anyway, no harm in reading it ...nothing to lose...

'...This band was formed originally in 1981 in the United Kingdom, while its members were still attending college. They had some success as a new wave rock band but only at local hops and dances in their home town area. On graduating from college the band remained together in its original format of four males and one female, continuing to play locally. The group was recognised as being raw talent by two commercial organisations who then vied for their attention. Contracts were offered by a US recording company based in Detroit, and a London based British one. The American contract demanded that they transfer and work in the USA, whereas the UK contract required that they perform only in the UK and European circuit. The money, and the far greater scope of opportunity offered by the Americans, won them over and they signed a contract with 'The FIZZINGLE Music Corp.' in 1982. The four boys and the girl bravely left Britain and established their new base in Detroit but a major upset occurred when a change of personnel almost destroyed the band. One person became homesick, and had to be replaced by a local musician. Luckily the gap was well filled and a new sound emerged, a sound which helped them make their mark almost immediately. Under their new name 'Rabid Revenge', they were introduced to an American audience which immediately took them to their hearts. Their fame and fan base and incredible popularity rapidly grew from that moment. 'FIZZINGLE' their record company, had been a small organisation and only modestly successful until they signed 'Rabid Revenge' and they went big with the band. The effective coupling of the band, and the studio, generated a string of *smash hits. 'Rabid Revenge' became and remained favourites for their hard and distinctive rock, and their popularity gave them pulling power capable of filling the biggest stadiums in the USA for more than twenty years, as a result. American citizenship was taken out in 1985 by all four British band members. As they grew older, they reduced their stadium performances but continued to get together to perform and record hit albums, but on fewer occasions, and in 2002 the group split up. For all their years of success in the States, surprisingly, they remained relatively unknown in the United Kingdom, and Europe. The FIZZINGLE Music Corp. closed-up their shutters on the same day that their money-making group, 'Rabid Revenge', gave up.'*

Back when this group started into the business proper, Derek had been only one year old, a little young to be aware of the goings-on of a rock band. Living with grandparents, who were the least likely people to be interested in what was happening in the world of rock and roll especially abroad and in the States, obviously ensured a large gap in Derek's knowledge. He saw this ignorance as an advantage.

For him to write a book, all he needed were some hard facts, stuff that he could embellish, with the band members' approval of course, and already he could sense that there was something to go at. The really interesting stuff would require some digging, no doubt. Now, provided no-one else had beaten him to it, this was a story waiting to be told – and sold.

Derek looked down the list of their hit albums on the screen; this was the material which brought them fame and he was surprised to see that they had refused to move forward to the CD format. All their albums were issued, at the group's insistence, as 12 inch vinyl, with sleeve covers of their own designs.

1982: 'Dark nights get darker'
1983: 'Pressure under decompression'
1983: 'Nail the lid down tight, baby'
1985: 'She hadn't cut her nails'
1986: 'Cross eyes don't please me'
1990: 'The marks came out at the laundry'

1991: 'Finger scratching bitch"

1998: 'You're nothing, believe me'

2000: 'Love has rusted'

2002: 'Where can I park my branding iron?'

This wasn't just any old rock band. They had been locals at one time, youngsters who were born and brought up in Newingsworth but, more importantly, locals who made the big-time, and any books about locals sold like hot-cakes. His would definitely sell well, especially if he got agreement from Rob for publicity in the Gazette.

He was on to a winner. He could see himself being in demand on all the talk shows, though maybe not all. The morning ones meant very early starts. He would avoid those...

According to Anton, the five original members had definitely lived in Newingsworth, this town, Derek's town. Back then in the 1980's five local youngsters forming a band would not have been unusual, but being spotted as talented would certainly have been. They had all attended Newingsworth High School and when they left, stayed together, targeting fame in the music industry as a young enthusiastic rock group.

To think ...they'd hung around Anton's cafe all those years ago and the way Anton told it, it sounded as if the cafe had been the next best thing to a gang hut. Individual names weren't able to be recalled by Anton, but no matter... There they were, on the website, no photographs though.

Two girl's names were shown. It looked like the first dropped out. She was only identified by a single name, Millie, copying Madonna maybe, Derek guessed. A useful and practical thought occurred to him: if all of them were born here, there must be relatives left in the town. Tracing them shouldn't be difficult, and they, themselves, would probably be eager to be given a moment of fame, wouldn't they?

Wouldn't lots of people in the town know of them, too? Derek thought about Alexander, his father-in-law, would he be about the same age group as the band members? He's not exactly the most likely person to have followed a rock band, though. Derek surmised he should be considered to be on a par with Gran and Grandad Smith.

He would ask him anyway.

Derek ran a print of the individual names, and dates.

Millie – vocals, keyboards – 1981 to 1986.
Sadie Truman – vocals, keyboards – 1986 to 2002.
Growler / Jonathan T Jones – percussion – 1981 to 2002.
Twister / James Hoist – bass guitar – 1981 to 2002.
Sailor / Theobald Walters – lead guitar – 1981 to 2002.
Steven Thwaite – vocals, rhythm guitar – 1981.
Bonzo / Frank Wolfeson – vocals, rhythm guitar – 1982 to 2002.

For all the original band members not to have stayed together for the duration of their success was surprising, though maybe not so unusual. Having known each other at school or college, and having lived in the same community would have seemed to be a reason for sticking together to support each other, and in turn be supported but, for them, like most bands, circumstances probably changed along the way. Derek's guess was for clashes of personalities to have been a cause and living out of a suitcase wouldn't be much fun if you had gone off each other. Obviously, they will have had their differences and gone their separate ways.

It was now two o'clock in the morning and sensibly he should give up for the moment. It had been a great evening, and look at what had been achieved... He felt good, very good, in fact. He would have to tell Sally because obviously she would want to share his delight at the success he'd had. Where is she?

"Sally?" he shouted.

There was no sound.

She hasn't gone to bed, has she? If she has, she might have said... Hmmm, I hope she's in the mood for some hot loving, because I feel ready.

This has been a fantastically great day...

"Sally, I'm coming to get you, Honey..." he murmured.

Poor Derek, we know that his hoped-for 'hot loving' is destined not to be, but he will find that out for himself, in a moment, won't he?

At times, into every life, there comes a little disappointment.

18

A fact already clearly established was that Daisy did not believe in ghosts. She knew it was silly to even imagine that there could be such a thing as a ghost, but, and it was a very important but, she could understand now why Hector was shocked. The likeness was amazing.

Daisy had been wandering around the store, looking to replace the electric kettle they'd used since Derek was a young lad.

Nearly twenty-five years beyond its guarantee period the kettle lasted – until today, and it went 'bang!' and Hector immediately came out with, "That is ab-b-b-solutely ridiculous. We've only just b-b-b-bought it!"

Hector makes a habit of grumbling about the stuff they sell nowadays, but he really should not have been complaining about this one, having had it for twenty-six long years: a grand old piece of quality British workmanship. This kettle certainly gave good service, and now, this kettle had given its all.

"Well, g-g-g-get the s-s-same a-g-g-g-g-gain," had been Hector's words as she left the house – after she'd pointed out its age...

The trouble this morning was that she couldn't find a replacement of the same make, in fact, what annoyed her was that though the shelves were well stocked, there wasn't a single one of British manufacture. She looked at all the shiny kettles sitting there. On every box stocked by this British superstore, Bisko's – and she checked every single one – it was clearly stated and, apparently from the size of the printing being proudly proclaimed by them in large letters: 'Of foreign manufacture'. She felt quite sad not to be able to buy one that was British, but a kettle was needed, and Bisko's had the best stock in the area, so it was no use trying elsewhere.

The choice was pot luck from then on. How can you tell the good from the bad? The price seemed the only indication, and what a price too. Hector had better not find out what the replacement was costing.

When it came to decision making, there was a well-tried method she always applied for a choice of this nature. Closing her eyes, she turned left, walked two paces, reversed, and then went four paces in the new direction, stopped, and turned towards the display, still with her eyes closed, and deciding it would be the one on the second shelf from the top, she opened her eyes.

Simple: there it was; the one in front of her nose – made in China, of course. She lifted the carefully selected item from the shelf, and turned to go to the check-out – and that is when she saw her.

Very like Millicent indeed ...a little slimmer than she was at that age, as Daisy remembered her, but looking every bit as lovely as Millie had been. Everyone has a doppelganger somewhere in the world, she had heard said, and this had to be the proof. It was incredible. Here this girl was – in Newingsworth, and one thing was clear – she was no ghost.

Just out of curiosity, Daisy wondered where the girl lived. A strange feeling suddenly came over her, almost as if she knew this young female ...a slightly dizziness... Stopping for a moment ...taking slow deep breaths ...Daisy began to feel better. Should she go over and tap her on the shoulder, tell her how alike she is to her Millie, she wondered? No... That would probably upset the poor girl. She would just follow her...

Daisy was better at shadowing than her husband – at least she thought she was. It wouldn't do having the girl getting worried about an old woman following her around the superstore. Keeping at a good distance and looking at the products on the shelves while moving along the aisles avoiding actually looking at the girl – that was the trick. She would keep watching her out of the corner of her eye. This girl could not possibly notice her, she convinced herself.

The girl stopped.

Look at what she is choosing, going for the cheapest soap powder

– not a good idea... She would have to be stopped and told how unwise that could be, because it wasn't as economical as the slightly dearer one – better to go for the other...

Daisy almost stepped forward to assist but suddenly realised it would be a foolish move, the wrong thing to do. She stopped immediately. The sudden change caused another shopper coming behind to bump into her in the process, and it was apologies all round.

Moving farther away seemed sensible because drawing attention was not what Daisy wanted, but the store was getting busier and it was becoming more difficult to keep visual contact. She noticed the girl's trolley was well stocked so her shopping must be nearly completed. Feeding an army of children it looks like, thought Daisy and yes, she was right! The checkout is her aim now...

Hector would be wondering what was keeping her, but she would have a good story to tell him when she got back home this morning. She could say she'd seen a ghost too...

There were long queues as usual. It was a very busy store. Sensibly, she chose a different checkout lane from the girl, but found it so slow. It is incredible, she thought, that no matter how many tills were in use there are never enough ...the girl is being served now, but what's happening on this lane?

The checkout girl on Daisy's lane went to change an item and the queue stopped moving. Come on, come on ...Daisy mentally urged – the other queue hasn't been delayed, but what's the girl up to? She's abandoned the full trolley, and only removed some of the things. That's strange; she's just buying some of the items... Why isn't there someone operating this check-out? Can't someone else take over? Look – the girl has paid now – and she is leaving...

"Excuse me," Daisy said to the two people in front of her as she squeezed passed, because she did not want to lose sight of the girl; it would spoil the story she was going to tell Hector.

The beeping noise was loud but not enough to disturb her concentration.

The girl was walking across the car park now, a full bag in either hand. There was still visual contact. Daisy hoped she wasn't going for a car because if that was the case she would never learn where she lived.

"Excuse me, Madam," said the voice behind her as a hand grasped her shoulder, holding on firmly.

"What?" she responded, rather rudely which was most unlike her, but she hadn't time to stop and chat with someone just now. That girl was...

"You are coming with me to the Manager's office," the harsh voice spat out. "We always prosecute shoplifters."

Daisy looked at the kettle ...in the box ...in her hands. Unfortunately, Hector's cup of tea was going to be greatly delayed this morning...

19

When Sam arrived home Angie was furiously stomping about the house throwing cushions at the wall trying to get it out of her system. With only a few cushions in the house, the same ones were lifted and thrown over and over, and still it didn't calm her down. It had happened again – a little old female this time. The first time had been once too often, but now...

"What is it about this damn country? Weren't the British supposed to be reserved, keeping themselves to themselves? Now, two damn stalkers, and both ancient! Is there a local society to encourage this sort of behaviour?"

Sam could only stand and listen...

"It might even be the way they keep fit? Probably in this country, they send out government leaflets, 'Dear Senior Citizen, stay active longer – chase an American.' I shouldn't have come here..."

Sam could tell there was more to come...

"...And she thought I didn't see her following me all around the store. Godammit, at one point, I thought she was going to tell me I had gotten the wrong damn soap powder!"

"Calm down, Honey. Are you sure she was following you?"

Now, that was the wrong question to ask, he found to his cost. She looked destined to go on about it all evening, which could be in conflict with the class homework he was hoping to check. Concentration would be difficult in these circumstances, so it would be a late night for him.

"Have you contacted your mom?" he asked hoping to break the

angry mood and move her on to a different subject.

"Yes."

Success – but he would have to keep working on it.

"And...?" he pushed a little.

"I've been texting her all afternoon. She says to contact the police..."

Maybe he hadn't succeeded after all, the subject hadn't been changed.

"Look, how about I go with you next time to this supermarket, Angie Baby?"

"Don't call me that..."

"Sorry, Sweetie..."

The mere mention of the 'baby' word from him was unacceptable. Angelina couldn't handle that. The timing of getting wed and having a family was fraught with danger for Sam. He wanted to make a move soon, she didn't. Being partners for almost five years seemed long enough for Sam to feel comfortable with the idea, but there was something in Angie's past that made her distrust men, even him at times, and especially regarding marriage and kids.

Angie was greatly influenced by her mom, Sam had found.

"Wonder how the restaurant's doing without you?" he ventured.

"They're managing..." she replied grudgingly, then, "Why are they following me? What have I done to them? Should I go to the cops as Mom suggests, Sam?"

It was a chance to state an opinion, he should be grateful for that, but he had to be cautious in everything he was saying. She was wound up tight tonight. If she exploded, he was the only one in the vicinity – he would suffer...

"Tomorrow, I've no school, so we'll go together to the superstore. We don't have to buy anything. You just point them out to me and I'll deal with the situation."

The two causing the bother were both elderly, according to Angie, which sounded the sort of people he could take on. He was never one for fighting at school, or anywhere else for that matter, so anyone less strong or less fit than he was could be considered fair game. He would be well able to handle an old couple, with hands tied behind his back, and blindfolded.

"Fancy a drink?" he asked.

"Only if it's a large strong one," she replied in a calmer voice.

She had been curious about whiskies on the shelves this morning. One had a name and a price that appealed to her, so, a giant bottle of 'Glenfaroogie – Very Highland Special' had been purchased – only seven pounds. It was a bargain, especially for one imported from somewhere exotic – and such a large bottle too.

Drinking whisky was not a habit of theirs – in fact, neither had ever tasted it. Sam poured two very generous helpings.

"Cheers, my little Pumpkin," he whispered in her ear.

She liked when he whispered in her ear, and gave him a peck on the cheek in return. They raised the well filled glasses – and downed the contents in a single gulp, the way it was done in the films.

Both choked and went a bright shade of red.

Obviously, they watched the wrong sort of film...

20

Both were feeling decidedly unwell, and not in the mood for visiting a supermarket simply to get nasty with a couple of silly old people.

To prove Sam's point on the presumption of whisky being an acquired taste, last night, they forced themselves to have another glass each. To their regret, the only thing proved was that in the early hours of the morning Angie was up at the toilet, pouring the contents of a painful stomach into the water closet. Sam hurried her along, caring not a jot for her suffering because there was only one water closet in the house – and he needed it desperately too.

This morning, the heads didn't want to be associated with the bodies – breakfast was not even mentioned but, no matter, Angie's problem at the supermarket would still require sorting out. Although he did promise to help, today he now wished he hadn't, and then it occurred to him: it could turn out a total waste of time if the old couple didn't appear. No matter, he would have to go through with it – for Angie's sake.

"I'm not well..." she moaned. "You go yourself."

She just wanted to suffer in her bed, alone, so it took a lot of gentle persuasion to win her over. She had to be convinced by Sam that she might still be able to rise, get dressed, and be capable of going with him and that, truly, she was still alive.

He felt more sympathy for her today than he did in the middle of the night and would have done what she asked of him and gone alone, but, how would he recognise this troublesome pair of stalkers?

She was made to rise.

Speaking to the manager at the store would be the best bet, he reckoned. They would have CCTV cameras, every store had them these days, and the evidence would either be there already waiting to be found, or the company could organise to watch out for the next time, if it happened again.

It was a struggle but, eventually, and reluctantly, Angelina and Sam set off – to bag a brace of stalkers.

Coming from the other direction, Daisy and Hector strolled along arm in arm. For many, Saturday was the main shopping day of the week; for Daisy and Hector, every day could be a visit to the shops, if they wanted – retirement allowed almost total freedom. It was a sunny day and the weather forecast was good, so from choice they were walking together rather than using the scooter. The scooter was for when Hector went alone, and anyway, stretching the legs was beneficial at their age. There was no rush, all the time in the world, although Hector wanted back before the rugby match started on telly in the early afternoon – but that was hours away.

After yesterday's kettle episode, Daisy felt a little uncertain about going back to Bisko's and hoped it would be a different security man on the door. The embarrassing incident was still very clear in her mind. Yes, well and truly caught she was, and when marched to the offices, she was convinced she would be in jail within the hour. The security man gleefully had been thinking the same – his first successful capture of the week; a mention of this incident would appear for certain in the next company newsletter with him receiving the credit.

As for the timing – wasn't it fortunate for Daisy that Friday was a working day for Muriel?

She'd been coming out of the cash office just as Mr Colin Barton (Cocky Colin as he was known to the rest of the staff) was passing. Muriel was obliged to step back out of the way, but was disturbed to see an elderly female being manhandled by this obnoxious big oaf – an elderly female who turned out to be someone she knew – and that the lady, unfortunate enough to be held firmly in Cocky's grasp, was Daisy.

"What's wrong? What's happened, Daisy?" she asked.

"You can just keep your big nose out of it, thank you very much!" was the friendly reply from Cocky Colin.

This was the normal sort of reaction people could expect from the sour-faced burly security man but, his response, rather than brushing-off the interfering cashier was the red rag to ensure Muriel would become involved. This nosey cow is about to spoil my moment of triumph, Cocky realised right away, as she insisted in joining them for the visit to Mr Tomkins.

With the security man at the front, and Cocky and Muriel throwing snide comments at each other, the group barged into the manager's office, interrupting the telephone call to Head Office. This did not please Mr Tomkins at all...

His call was abruptly ended, and he had barely turned round to acknowledge their presence when Colin Barton launched into his version of the story. Mr Tomkins was well aware of this man's nickname and the reason for it, and anticipated a fanciful tale; Cocky didn't disappoint...

"The job I do has its dangers, but it is my job and I have to be brave..." was the dramatic beginning, and he went on to explain how he'd had to be especially alert because of the recent spate of thefts, but today, by being highly efficient he had foiled a big one this time.

"Don't be taken in by appearances," he told his boss, with a knowing look, and continued about how this deceptively mild-looking old woman was trying to creep off the premises without paying for a valuable company product, and how she'd been stopped by him after a serious struggle.

Mr Tomkins saw before him a respectable looking elderly lady, half the size of the security man, standing patiently holding the packaging containing a kettle. Although obviously not impressed nor intimidated by the security man, she was embarrassed by what had happened.

Mr Colin Barton continued by expanding on how she'd attempted to fight him off, viciously, and that because of his injuries, he would probably require time off for a doctor's visit – but only after handing her over to the police.

Daisy stood open-mouthed. She thought she had come quietly...

"I know this lady," Muriel interrupted "...and there must be a mistake, because she would never deliberately have been shop-lifting."

She told Mr Tomkins how well she knew her, that there was a family relationship, and went on to explain what a delightful and helpful person this lady really was, and all of Muriel's words rang true with the boss.

"...Although it looks as if she could be getting a little forgetful," she ended, feeling awkward saying that in front of Daisy.

Not surprisingly, the manager trusted Muriel more than Cocky Colin, but the security man wasn't giving up easily.

"This woman is the leader of the gang of shoplifters that I've been trying to catch for months," Cocky claimed. No, he couldn't prove it he had to admit when Muriel laughingly scoffed at his story, but to which Cocky Colin immediately retorted that she wasn't one to criticise him! What about her security problem in the Wages Office not so long ago, the robbery and the kidnapping? What did she know?

There was obviously no love lost between the two of them.

"So, just you keep out of it!" was probably not the best comment for Cocky to make towards the cashier in the manager's office.

"Put a sock in it, you!" from Mr Tomkins brought Cocky's story to a rapid conclusion... He regretted not having fired this man long ago. He totally disbelieved every word said, and not for the first time, and on top of that he couldn't stand the fellow, but he held his temper. He listened sympathetically to an explanation of forgetfulness from a very shaky Daisy, which concluded with an apology for causing all this bother. Thankfully, Mr Tomkins believed her, in fact, to the extent that she was given, in return, an apology for the failure of the store to stock British-Made electric kettles...

When agitated, Mr Tomkins was inclined to grind his teeth. It was a bad habit; he knew he did it, and wished he didn't. Muriel had seen this happen many times and she'd learned it was a warning sign. This was always a signal to leave.

"A little more care in the future?" Mr Tomkins offered to Daisy as he opened the door, and the three moved to leave, "...but not you!"

The door was closed, leaving Mr Colin Barton behind.

Smiling to Daisy, Muriel stopped for a moment. They stood in the corridor and listened... Silence ...and then, inside the office, the shouting began...

Daisy was extremely grateful to Muriel, who'd been delighted to have helped anyway. To relax and recover from the shock of it all, the two of them sat for ages in the canteen afterwards having a chin-wag. Then as a precaution, Muriel went with Daisy as she left the store, and made sure she paid for the kettle.

Not surprisingly as a consequence, yesterday, Hector's morning tea, and lunch were much later than normal.

They were nearly there now. It was a nice day and therefore a good reason to go to the supermarket. As a matter of fact, almost every day there was some reason for Hector, or Daisy, to visit Bisko's. Today, other than to buy a newspaper, nothing was actually needed. They had almost reached the store, successfully having navigated the busy main road, when they saw Thelma approaching from the opposite direction.

It was almost a daily occurrence for Thelma too, but for her it was also a social occasion – the opportunity to pick up gossip whenever she bumped into anyone she knew. To make a small contribution towards her keep, not wishing to be totally beholden to her brother so to speak, Sally's aunt looked after the house at Cloverton, and visiting Bisko's was part of her contribution. Nowadays Muriel was finding working full-time as the cashier at Bisko's to be tiring. She very much appreciated her sister-in-law doing the shopping for the three of them and, even though Muriel wasn't overly hard-pressed at work, having the household chores done by Thelma was guaranteed to earn her continual gratitude; Alexander never even noticed.

By co-incidence the three of them arrived outside the store at the same time – Thelma, Daisy, and Hector – and stopped to have the inevitable chat, well; the two women stopped. Hector wasn't one for standing blathering like that. He preferred his chat to be with Hammy, his mate, and with a pint of beer in front of them while sitting at a table in the club. It conserved energy that way.

Hector left the two women at the front door, rabbitting on about how Muriel helped Daisy yesterday. He went to collect a newspaper. Ensuring he missed none of the daily news in the other papers – without purchasing them, of course – was part of the routine. He preferred the presentation in his own paper, the one he actually bought, but he was of the opinion that by reading the others he was taking a balanced and unbiased approach to the news. Many of the local males did that, and it really infuriated staff responsible for that section of the store ...but Hector's intentions abruptly changed. She was here again – the ghost – and he was immediately drawn into the chase.

She was wandering around with an empty trolley. Hector couldn't stop himself, and followed at a distance so that she wouldn't notice him. Up one lane, down another, and still not a thing selected. She was obviously having difficulty finding whatever she was looking for.

He knew this store better than the majority of the store's employees, and had experienced the frustration at not being able to find the item wanted. He felt sorry for her. Should he offer to help? He couldn't very well go up to her and ask what she was looking for, could he? Of course not, he didn't know the girl, and that sort of behaviour could get her worried ...but he could stand at the end of the aisle, and smile at her on passing, and she might ask him where she should look. Yes? Good idea!

Back along the lane she came a few moments later – but she walked on without even seeing him. She did give a funny wave of the hand, he noticed, but it wasn't to him. He was ignored, oh well ...and he was still convinced that she looked like his Millicent...

Hector went to pay for his newspaper, and left her to it. She would find what she was looking for, eventually, without his help. He weaved his way towards the large entrance, through the incoming crowd that was acting as if it was the Special Sales Day. He'd make his way out now to join his wife and Thelma, presumably where he'd left them and presumably still yapping – and they were, still at it. He turned towards them as he unfolded his morning paper.

"Just a goddam minute, buddy," said the threatening voice.

Hector turned as hands grabbed his lapels and a face pushed close to his.

"I saw you and I'm warning you..."

That was as much as Sam could communicate before he was attacked by two females wielding handbags extremely effectively who rushed to protect Hector from a mugger.

"Hit him harder, Thelma!" yelled Daisy.

"I'm hitting him as hard as I can, Daisy!" yelled back Thelma.

All Sam could do was to let go of Hector and put his arms up to protect his head. His arms took the battering instead, and only for a few moments he stood his ground. These Brits were going to win, even though they were older than him. His heart wasn't in it – so he ran.

Afterwards, the thing that annoyed Hector was the tearing of his newspaper. It was in tatters! He had just paid good money for it. There was no need for that sort of behaviour... Look ...it couldn't be read.

He heaved a big sigh of relief. Thank goodness the girls were here; and ...wasn't it sensible to have read all the news in the others?

21

And the news travelled fast...

Thelma, having rushed back, conveyed the information to Muriel who was at home in Cloverton because it was Saturday. You can't keep excitement like that to yourself, was the motto, and that's why Muriel immediately phoned Sally at the cottage. She was horrified to be told by her mother of the mugging.

However it was Muriel who felt pressured to do more.

A member of her extended family – it was Sally's husband's grandad, to be precise – had been mugged, but also, and importantly, it had happened at Bisko's Newingsworth, and even more importantly, as Cashier she had to think of the Company's reputation, particularly after yesterday's embarrassing situation at the store for Daisy.

Something would have to be done...

Mr Steve Tomkins, the senior manager at Bisko's, was lasting well in his role. Continually his duties challenged him, but he could take pride in his achievements because, year on year during his tenure this store was successfully improving sales. His reputation at Head Office was well established.

Being recognised as conscientious and hard working in a fairly pressurised job gave him satisfaction and was financially rewarding but, for him personally, it was a gruelling task. Consequently, recharging of his batteries was becoming an urgent natural need before exhaustion set in. This was the first Saturday in three months he would be taking off. For weeks, he had eagerly looked forward to this undisturbed long weekend with his wife and his three children – but the phone was ringing.

In his home, answering came automatically to his wife, mainly because her husband was rarely there, so, she was the one who lifted it to her ear, fearing the worst.

"It is Muriel, your cashier," she frowningly told him, "Wants to speak to you...."

"No, it can't be Muriel Davidson, tell her I'm..." he whispered, and hoped his wife could think of a better excuse than his tired brain could conjure up.

"Look Muriel, I'm very sorry but he's not able to..." Mrs Tomkins tried to say, but the caller was persistent, and so, eventually his wife was forced to submit, and hand the device over.

With considerable reluctance, because he did not want it, he took the phone and listened. Hearing Muriel insist that he had to be involved personally, back at Bisko's this morning, because it was serious, was not what he wanted to hear today. His wife certainly didn't want him to go. Mrs Tomkins, who saw little enough of the father of their children, was standing in front of him furiously waving her arms and making annoyed faces telling him he mustn't give in!

Muriel won...

From different directions the pair made their way to the Store, then straight to the control room, Muriel, full of enthusiastic, righteous indignation about the incident, and Mr Tomkins ...anything but!

In the special secure room, the CCTV footage was run, and checked, and there it was. It was a relieved manager who was able to confirm the incident at least as having been recorded as it should have. (It was before his time, but an undetected system failure had been the downfall of the previous boss. As the one who had suffered the consequences, Muriel knew all about those events with great clarity).

All cameras were working correctly this time with the recording clearly showing two persons to be struggling – an older person, male, and a younger person, male also. Another two could be seen to join the fray. These two were obviously females, and using handbags as weapons. The poor mugger in the end seemed to get the worst of it with the handbags obviously beating the living daylights out of him; leaving him little alternative other than to scarper.

Without sound, the antics they were viewing could have competed with a Keystone Cops silent film, and almost made it seem worthwhile for Mr Tomkins to have come in. He started laughing.

"This would look quite comical if it was played faster," he said out loud, "...and then could we try playing it backwards?"

It was a playful question, to lighten the mood; he might as well enjoy it now he was here, but Muriel just gave him a look.

"Oh – sorry," he said.

He hadn't been serious and now felt slightly embarrassed, but also niggled. He had been dragged out on a Saturday morning, a holiday that he'd been looking forward to, to look at some silly slapstick on video, and then made to feel guilty for smiling; criticised by one of his staff, one who was smirking – but not at the video – just enjoying his discomfort.

This spoiled holiday was her fault. It was no longer amusing. He began to grind his teeth and feel annoyed...

Zooming-in was attempted, focusing on the heads of those concerned, but facial recognition of any of the four was impossible. Camera positioning had been fairly arbitrary at installation, many years ago. The camera above the front entrance was the one which successfully recorded what had happened, but the position of it meant tops of heads and shoulders were all that could be seen.

This was becoming irritating. He wanted done with it.

Muriel was easily able to recognise Hector's bald pate, which was clearly distinguishable from the short haircut of the mugger but, as the mugger was the person they were attempting to identify, recognising Hector was of little help so it would not be practical to pinpoint the individual properly for the police. Mr Tomkins could therefore see no justification in having the local constabulary involved. Had his morning been spoiled for no reason then? No, someone will have to suffer, Mr Tomkins decided...

"The Security Person failed to do his duty!" spouted out Muriel.

It was galling to the manager having Muriel pointing that out to him. He was going off her rapidly... "...And the protection of the customers in the vicinity of the store was Bisko's responsibility," she continued, a fact that he well knew and, of course, which he had to accept – to the disadvantage of his blood pressure.

Grinding teeth...

"Who was on duty then?" he threw back at her, and, as usual, she knew everything including staff names.

"That would be Colin Barton," she was able to tell him. Normally, Mr Tomkins would have been delighted by Muriel's intimate knowledge of the store's goings-on, but somehow today, it was getting on his nerves... "You'll remember, it was him you were talking to yesterday," Muriel was happy to point out, but decided to say no more when she noticed his jaw movements...

It was unfortunate for Cocky Colin to have been on duty yesterday and then again today. Yesterday, it was a shoplifter 'getting off with it' as far as he was concerned, and he was the one who finished up getting the rollicking. Life's not fair. Today...? What's up this time?

Here he was in Mr Tomkins' office again, and being asked why hadn't he done something about it?

"I wasn't there..!" was the confident reply.

"Ah..." and his boss's eyes narrowed, "So, where were you?"

"Coffee," was the rapid response.

There was a smug grin on Colin Barton's face as he claimed a legitimate excuse – a ten minute rest break, his legal right; and that part was emphasised. His boss was grinding his teeth, so it seemed wiser for Colin to stop grinning. This time though there was little he could be criticised for.

Mr Colin Barton left the office after only a few minutes – blameless, although feeling somewhat less cocky.

Cocky Colin was seriously bothered though, not by the questioning, but because this interrogation by the boss was done in front of that interfering cashier, Davidson. This was the second time that the female from wages office had seen him put under unjustified pressure. He would remember that...

Back at home, it took all the remainder of Saturday for Mr Tomkins to calm down. Thankfully, by Sunday he was relaxed and enjoyed a pleasant and undisturbed day with his family, so much so that when he went to sleep on Sunday night, he was actually looking forward to getting back into action ...at work ...on Monday morning.

Though Sally was at home when called about the mugging – Derek was not. When he left he'd said he would be somewhere in town.

He was: drinking coffee at the Old Astoria Cafe, and having another chat with Anton about his book. The cafe location had not been mentioned earlier to Sally, in case of criticism. She was reacting strangely this morning, after rising in a real growling mood. When he tried to relate the success he'd had on the web last night and his new ideas about the book, for some obscure reason, she didn't want to know.

He couldn't mention Anton's, so, a more plausible reason for going out had been necessary: going to do an interview, one he should have done on Friday, with two old ladies who were claiming to have a cat who could open a tin of sardines on its own.

Sitting in the cafe, his mobile sounded – and it was Sally.

He panicked – she was checking up on him. He'd been rumbled. If he answered while he sat here at the table, she would hear the noise in the Cafe over the phone. He jumped up, spilling his coffee as he did so, and rushed out, then found he'd panicked for nothing. She wasn't checking on him at all and he hadn't needed to spill the coffee, but it was serious.

Poor Grandad, imagine, him being attacked outside the supermarket. How could this have happened to his dear old defenceless grandad? Why would some thug do such a thing – mug a harmless old man – Grandad was never allowed out with much money anyway?

Derek returned to his seat, perturbed by Sally's message, feeling sort of foolish for the rapid exit. Anton nonchalantly replaced the coffee, passed the sugar – and the 'Rabid Revenge' story continued from exactly where it stopped.

This was most unusual: Anton actually remembering where he'd reached and seamlessly continuing, but Derek couldn't stay to listen. Reluctantly, he asked for another stoppage. He had to meet Sally.

What chance was there of Anton restarting this story at the right place next time? Probably very little, Derek decided as he left...

His grandparents would be in a state of shock; he and Sally were in agreement on that fact, so they were meeting in town and then going over to Blytheton Road to comfort them. Derek conveniently remembered that Gran usually bought a large steak pie for a Saturday night. While they were there, if they got the timing right, they could maybe get a share of the meal.

Hammy would be back at the cottage, but he could fend for himself for once.

When they arrived at 12 Blytheton Road there was no state of shock; both grandparents were coping admirably after the incident, Gran perhaps better than Grandad. In fact, Gran seemed quite exhilarated. She had been beating the living daylights out of a mugger, and thoroughly enjoying herself at the same time, she happily told them.

"I presume you are here for the pie..." she added, looking at Derek.

At Buttercup Avenue, Sam was being told off.

"You were going to protect me, you said, and then an old man and an old girl said 'boo' to you and you ran off," Angie was grumbling, "...And you didn't even come back for me!"

He didn't need to be told of his inadequacies, he knew them only too well. Anyway, it wasn't just one female who'd attacked, there were two, and they'd been fierce. He was glad to have escaped ...and his arms hurt. Damn pensioners – too bloody fit, nowadays. He'd only wanted to warn the guy off. Maybe he should have said 'please'. Was it his bad manners annoyed these Brits so much?

Sam felt lousy and now he was asking himself why he was here in this country. Worse still, he'd been the one who'd encouraged Angie to leave her mother, her job, and her home, to be with him. He had let her down – badly.

Maybe her mother was right in what she was suggesting – go to the police. That is what they should have done in the first place, rather than try to sort it out personally, but what would the police say? Would they want evidence? There was none. Anyway, what kind of evidence could possibly be obtained?

And then, Sam suddenly had an inspiration. All was not lost.

It is amazing what you can come up with when you sit down and really concentrate. Yes, a plan... He could use his cell phone; it could take a good picture. In fact, he and Angie both had cell phones. Get a photograph of one, or maybe even each of the stalkers. The phone could be used to video too. If they recorded what was happening on video that would be even better – indisputable proof, surely?

Why not do it tomorrow? Yes, they could go back again on Sunday morning. That troublesome pair would almost certainly be there again. They were probably the type to buy milk and bread and a newspaper, every day.

Putting it to her, he found Angie to be less than enthusiastic; Sunday will be a different routine, she said. Yes, but only because it is a thicker newspaper on that day, Sam responded; they'll be there ...but this humbled, bruised, ex-mugger had great difficulty convincing his girl-friend that this latest idea was a good one.

It took perseverance and eventually, with reluctance, she gave in to him, but she definitely refused to accept the idea as being 'good'.

"...But, I suppose it's gotta be an improvement on your last one, Honey-bunch," was Angie's sarcastic conclusion.

22

Sam was cautious, returning to the supermarket the following morning. He was following at a short distance behind Angie, his head continuously darting from side to side and his eyes sweeping the way ahead and behind. Prudence prevailed to prevent him being taken by surprise again by two ferocious women; his arms still ached.

Angie stopped at the jewellery counter. What a fine assortment of wrist watches; the less expensive ones were on display on the counter top within easy reach, with the more valuable ones safely behind well-lit glass at the rear of the unit and under the glass-topped counter. She looked at the watch on her wrist; the same one she'd had for years. When bought, it had been a bargain from the market stall at home. It still worked, but... Hmm, that one looks nice, she thought, leaning over the glass to look at the more expensive display. She wouldn't want a gaudy one, but there were several that she would have if she did buy. Should I? The temptation to spend was strong, well, until Sam caught up and overtook her to hiss something as he passed that she heard, but pretended she hadn't.

"No!" was all he said out of the side of his mouth so that anyone watching would not realise they knew each other, but sufficiently loud and meaningful for Angie to get the message. Disturbingly, to Sam's eyes she'd remained defiantly where she was, gazing spellbound at the expensive items, so of course he had to pass once more and whisper a little more fiercely this time. She smiled and moved away. He was obviously panicking and thinking of the remains of this month's salary – but she wouldn't have spent it – he should know she was not stupid!

It was an attempt to appear casual but they were both keyed up and eager for action with two cell-phones ready to grab; already set to record live action rapidly, for evidence when the moment came.

For three quarters of an hour they wandered around, and nothing...

Was Sam's idea about to fail?

There was no sign of the old man or the old woman. What a waste of time? It was monotonous, moving about without purpose. Angie wanted to talk to Sam to relieve the boredom, but he kept his distance. He wasn't willing to give in yet.

For Angie it was now an aimless walk. Very few people were in the aisles. Eventually she was missing seeing those who were. She was into robotic mode, going through the motions, becoming oblivious to all around her.

Oblivious – until realisation struck, that someone she recognised had hurriedly passed her – the old guy – but he didn't appear to have seen her this time. He was moving briskly and concentrating like mad on something other than her for a change. It was a relief, until she noticed he had something in his hand. She gasped – he was making straight for Sam – and Sam was looking the other way. What should she do? The old guy was nearly beside him. He's not going to hit Sam, is he?

She couldn't stop herself...

"Look out!" she called in panic.

As Sam turned round, he was blinded by the flash of the camera in the old guy's hand.

Angie suddenly realised that by shouting she'd set Sam up for the perfect full face shot, and the only thing that could possibly have spoiled that photo would be that Sam wasn't smiling – he'd presented a face frozen in surprise.

She grabbed for her cell-phone, but too late, the old guy had vanished.

When Sam's eyes cleared sufficiently for him to see again, standing in front of him was Angie. There was a wry smile on her face.

"Looks like you've goofed again, big boy," she said. "Do you always pose for a camera?"

Sam didn't laugh...

23

Sunday afternoons are for relaxing, a time for a husband and his wife to be doing very little, that is unless the wife decides that the husband should not be relaxing. Derek was being informed accordingly...

If he wished, permission was being given to play around on the computer for the remainder of the morning, but not in the afternoon. The afternoon was being designated by Sally as 'in the garden time' and clear ideas existed in her mind of what she would be requiring, but what they were was not yet being disclosed to Derek.

There could be no denying that the garden had been a mess since the sycamore tree fell over so, today, it wouldn't just be tidying up – it was time for improvement. Though the indentations still showed on the lawn where the tree had fallen, the wood had since been reduced to logs for use on the fire. These were stacked neatly outside the far corner of the house, but a multitude of branches and leaves remained, spread around and requiring attention.

Incidentally some of the logs were gone, kindly donated by Derek to the Newingsworth and Slatterfoot Communities Welfare Committee, who arranged uplift; the material was to be distributed to the elderly to reduce their fuel bills. Unfortunately, on investigation, they found the homes of most of the district's elderly were heated by gas or electricity so, at the moment, the backyard of the Community building was rather chock-a-block with logs, but at least Derek was rid of the stuff.

Anyway, a garden should be a colourful picture, or at least moderately tidy, and to that end things were about to change. Sally had a plan. This year there would be flowers. To have flowers, there would need to be flower beds. To have flower beds, Sally's dear husband would be required to roll up his sleeves, and, as they say, get on with it.

Sally was preparing to inspire; Derek would just do...

Unusually, he had very few excuses ready today – the type of reasons needed to avoid physical effort. There was always his need to continue research for the new book, but he knew instinctively, that would not go down well with a determined wife and her plans.

So, here he was, reluctantly, lifting the garden fork and plunging it into the ground – or rather, trying to. His arm jarred. It didn't bode well for the rest of his day.

He looked to the heavens, but no help seemed likely from above. Only a few fluffy clouds and no chance therefore of rain stopping play. Making the attempt for half an hour, then feigning a back injury would be the best bet, he thought; and then he heard the scooter. Sally heard it too and beat him to the front door to welcome the surprise visitors.

The noise of the scooter was a dead giveaway to Derek. There were very few scooters in the district, other than Granny and Grandad Smith's, but, he'd seen them last night, so why were they returning the visit today?

Derek couldn't help arriving at the front door with a scowl on his face and, though due to annoyance at having to do the gardening work, the look was not welcoming. Sally frowned at him, and mouthed, 'Smile', and he did.

"What's happened?" he asked them, forcing a smile per instruction as they dismounted, but, in receiving no answer, he had the disturbing impression they were arriving with bad news – then they took off their helmets.

"How nice to see you, this is a surprise," Sally beamed, and being smart, knew they would hear now.

"We won't stay long," said Granny Smith.

"Wh-Wh-Wh-What's for t-t-t-t-tea?" asked Grandad, hanging the helmets on the handlebars.

Since purchasing the scooter, there was no stopping Derek's

grand-parents buzzing around on it. It replaced the hankering Hector had had for years for a motorbike, and it was great for nipping back and forwards to Bisko's. Right little gadabouts they had become, now that Daisy was getting braver about riding pillion. Holding on tightly, most times with eyes shut, off they'd go – anywhere – just for the hell of it.

Today though there was a purpose to the visit and into the cottage they came. Grandad started talking excitedly as Derek took the coats.

"I g-g-g-g-got him," he said.

"You got whom, Grandad?" asked Derek.

"You *know*... The one who a-t-t-t-t-tacked me yesterday."

He brought out his camera, the new digital one that Daisy bought him for his Christmas. It was far too complex for him to use effectively, but at least he'd worked out that he could press a certain button and get a result – immediately. He pressed the controls and successfully brought up a photograph that was important to him – of a face.

"C-c-c-could you p-p-p-print it for m-m-me?"

"Of course," Derek replied.

He switched on the equipment, connected the camera, and, in no time at all the print appeared displaying the face of a startled youngish man. He looked rather frightening, Sally thought.

Hector explained how he'd gone to buy a Sunday paper as usual, and was inspired to take his camera in case he saw the man who went for him yesterday, and he did see him, there he was. Hector had taken the shot of him and left the store very quickly.

Thankfully Daisy and Thelma weren't with him today. Yesterday, as 'minders' they did a great job, but they weren't up to running away at speed. Today had been a man's work...

"And s-s-s-something else I r-r-r-remembered afterwards, he s-s-s-spoke like J-J-John Wayne ...or J-J-Jimmy C-C-C-C-Cagney ...or G-G-G-Gary C-C-C-Cooper ...when he swore at me."

"You mean he was an American?" added Derek.

"Ah, y-y-y-yes."

"Can I have a print too?" asked Derek, becoming intrigued. "I'll watch out for him. If he was in the store yesterday, and then back again today, he's probably local. We could go to the police, you know."

"N-n-n-n-no. He w-w-w-w-won't try again. He's s-s-s-scared of me."

Hector was certainly proud of how he got one over on the mugger and was quite happy to have that story to tell on future occasions at the Old Folk's Club. What was not mentioned to Sally and Derek was his tale about the 'ghost'. That was for talk between his wife and himself only, their little secret; and of course Daisy wasn't overly proud of having been accused of shoplifting and, although that wasn't secret because others were involved, it would be played low key.

"Would you like a drink," they were asked by Sally, "...whisky, sherry, a glass of wine?

"I c-c-c-can't – I'm d-d-driving," said Hector, "Any l-l-l-l-lemonade?"

"I'm not," Daisy chipped in, "a double whisky please, Sally."

For someone who rarely touches the stuff, Sally thought, this little old lady was letting her hair down, but riding pillion could be the reason.

"Where's H-H-Hammy, D-D-D-D-Derek?" Hector asked. "He's still s-s-s-s-staying here, isn't he? I haven't s-s-s-s-seen him in ages."

Since moving to the caravan, Sally explained, he comes in only for meals, but he'd started behaving naughtily and wasn't coming in for food at regular times. Sometimes he didn't appear at all. This she attempted to say jocularly, but her irritation showed through a little.

"But you knew about the other caravan, didn't you?" Sally continued. Blank looks were on Daisy and Hector's faces. "He sleeps here only occasionally, nowadays," she explained.

"In case a tree falls on him," added Derek.

They hadn't know about that either. Daisy was horrified to think about what could have happened to the poor man if he'd stayed out there on that windy night. Hector was less affected. "He's a j-j-j-j-j-jammy b-b-b-bugger," but he was pleased his pal hadn't been hurt.

"We could go out for a walk and see how the work is progressing up at the farm," Sally suggested. "It's a lovely afternoon, if you fancy some fresh air. His new caravan is up there now. We should bump into him."

Derek was reluctant to go. "I'll just stay here" he suggested.

It wasn't because he wanted to dig the flower beds, though he made that the reason – he wanted back on the internet – he had a book to write! He was over-ruled by both his wife and his grandmother.

"The fresh air and the walk will be good for you," said Daisy, in the same way she always had since he'd been small. How many times in his life had that been thrown at him? As usual, he nodded wisely as if in agreement, and they all left the cottage.

The four of them went at a gentle pace along the lane. There was no need to hurry. Overhead the sun shone brightly in a clear blue sky, the birds chattered away, and the stream burbled pleasantly alongside. Part way along the lane, they passed the scene of the caravan incident.

"Workmen..." Derek told his grandparents, shaking his head. "Dear, oh dear, I've no idea what they could have been up to." A little untruth didn't do anyone any harm, Derek thought to himself as they strolled on, seeing marks that were still very visible on the verge where the caravan had taken control and slipped into the mud. Sally just gave him a questioning look. Derek coloured slightly.

They reached the end of the lane and slowly meandered along the wider road back towards the farm, but no Hammy was to be found when they got there. Being a non-working day, and with no-one around to prevent them wandering about, they were just plain nosy. The conclusion of Sally and Daisy and Derek was that Hammy was doing a wonderful job.

Hector was a little less complimentary of his friend.

"He's n-n-not d-d-doing it – he's just the b-b-boss. B-b-b-bosses d-d-d-d-d-don't w-w-w-work..."

In place of the two barns, which had been totally removed, single level buildings were arranged to surround the old yard and now formed a quadrangle. The insides of these outhouses were still being completed. These would become ten self-contained en-suite rooms, with a small kitchen in each, the idea being that each room could be booked as self-catering, or used as part of the hotel accommodation. Public rooms would be added in the main building when the farmhouse was altered.

Had her father regularly been to see the progress of this work, Sally wondered – if so, he hadn't said? He didn't talk about it too much. It seemed he was leaving it entirely to Hammy.

She had some admiration for her father in the way he handled this purchase. It had been Hammy's home before he was forced to sell up, and being the new owner, her father was giving him the chance to stay in it again. From the chat at their evening meals it was clear that Hammy appreciated Alexander's generosity, and was looking forward to returning to the old place.

Sally liked to think her father was doing it all out of the kindness of his heart, but that was unlikely. It was not her dad's way. She suspected it would not be an altruistic motive. Financial gain was almost certain, in his case.

In the middle of the quadrangle sat Hammy's temporary home, the second-hand caravan that Derek acquired for him – although it may have been third, or even fourth-hand, the state of it – but it was still ten times better than the first one for sure. The picture, stuck outside on the door, was 'Highland Cattle in a misty Scottish glen', and had words that Hammy had added which tugged at the heartstrings: 'Och aye the noo – a Coo'.

They shouted, but no Hammy was to be found on the site. So, they meandered slowly back towards the cottage. Daisy and Hector were invited by Sally to stay for the meal, and they readily accepted, although Derek thought that his grandad had invited himself earlier anyway.

There was the chance that Hammy might even appear tonight ...and he did. In fact, he was already there. He was back in the spare room, which was still considered to be his. It was agreed that if his clothes were to remain wearable, storage would be more successful in the spare room of the cottage than in the caravan.

Hammy was back for a meal, but he was not alone. There was giggling, which wasn't Hammy's – it was a female...

"Hammy..." Derek diplomatically shouted to save any embarrassment as the four of them filed in the front door. Derek knew all about being rudely interrupted...

"Och, ye're back urr ye," Hammy shouted from the room, and the giggling stopped. "Ah didnae know whar ye'd gone," he said as he came smilingly into the living room.

"Hullo Sinbad ...an' its ma bonny wee Daisy too. Ah huvnae seen you twa furr ages. We got back here a wee whilie ago. Urr ye cummin through here, Hen?" he shouted back into the room. "Could ye manage an extra place furr tea, Lass?" he asked Sally. "Ye'll, uhm, ken ma freen..."

It was Thelma who came out of the bedroom, with eyes sparkling, a big glowing grin on her face, and her hair rather tousled.

"Of course," Sally said, "how nice to see you, Aunt Thelma. This is a surprise."

As Thelma came in to join them, knowing looks were shared by the others. Sally's immediately thought – what have you been up to Aunt Thelma? However, she wasn't so sure that she really wanted to know...

24

Convincing Rob to proceed with the idea took time but in the end he was won over. It would be subject to sufficient facts being obtained before total commitment though, so, for a start, a visit to Newingsworth High School seemed appropriate. There, it would be simply a case of Derek asking the correct questions...

To do a Gazette feature about this band, his band, would be a good idea, he'd explained to his editor, and although it was true that they were currently unknown in Britain, they'd made it big in the States – a very important factor. Couple this with the other fact that the group initially comprised four fifths of local talent so, when the band's stories were run, surely higher sales of the paper would be guaranteed?

Out in Newingsworth, and Slatterfoot, and surrounding districts, there must be readers who would have known them as youngsters. They would buy the paper, and others would wonder 'how come they knew them but we didn't?', and they'd buy it too – out of curiosity.

It must be a winner – and could run for weeks. At least, that's what he promised Rob; he hoped he was right.

Now, he'd be able to work on two things at once and with a clearer conscience, and they could be complementary. Working for the Gazette would be official but, at the same time, he would be working for himself on the unofficial part: collecting material for his best seller.

It felt odd, thinking about going back to his old school. After fourteen years away, would any of his teachers still be there? The headmaster was still the same person, he knew that much, it was still Mr Brummage, or Beakie, as he was known to the pupils, but he'd ring first, he decided, approach it diplomatically.

A very friendly female voice answered.

"Good Morning, this is Brenda, can I be of assistance?"

"Yes please. I'm doing some research about some former pupils."

"Oh... I don't think we can supply any information like that, certainly not on the phone."

"That's ok. I didn't want to talk about it on the phone. I was hoping I could have a meeting with someone at the school, someone who would have some knowledge about pupils who left about thirty years ago, or would know where to dredge up the info."

"I see... I think I'd better make you an appointment with the headmaster, Mr Brummage."

"That's fine. It will be nice to meet old Beakie again."

"Pardon...?"

"Sorry ...I, eh ...I didn't... Can you tell me when?"

"Certainly ...would tomorrow at ten o'clock be suitable?"

"Yes indeed."

"And can I take your name, sir?"

"Of course – it's Derek Toozlethwaite."

"Sweaty... Is it really you? It is you, isn't it? I thought so, but I wasn't certain."

"Who is...??? Brenda... Big Brenda... It's been years... I should have recognised your voice."

"See you tomorrow then, Big Boy. I can't wait..."

The call ended.

Wow... Big Brenda... That's a blast from the past. Wonder if she is still willing to...?

25

The old place hadn't changed much but it did feel very odd, walking along these corridors once more. Any moment he expected one of the teachers to jump out and confront him, and bark out the challenging question he was always being asked... *"Toozlethwaite, why aren't you in your class? Walking about as if you owned the place... You are here to learn, boy. How many times...? Oh, I despair for you..."*

It was usually about here it happened, the second floor corridor, just before reaching the science labs. It felt a bit spooky to this former pupil, the one who was almost always caught in this very corridor.

Such memories...

As he was about to pass his old Registration Teacher's room, Derek suddenly became conscious of being on his tip-toes, attempting to walk silently. He relaxed again feeling silly. Old habits...

Vampy Simpson was the one who used to suddenly spring out and frighten the living daylights out of him – a holy terror he was, and always appeared to have it in for 'Toozlethwaite'.

What wazzat? Oh no...! The figure ...coming out of the door... Good grief! It's him, it's Simpson. He is still here...

"Good morning, fine weather isn't it. Oh hello, it's ...Toozlethwaite! Never could forget your face, or name. It's so nice to see you again, and you are looking well. Reliving the old times, eh? Great days they were weren't they? Must get on... Have a nice day..." and the gowned figure swept off along the corridor in the opposite direction, going at double the pace of Derek and to Derek's eyes, still looking like a vampire swooping into action.

'Administration Office' it said on the door, and again, old habits took over... Hair was pushed off his face, glasses polished with his handkerchief, and followed by the same hankie being used to check for a drip at his nose, shoes wiped on the back of trouser legs, and finally the straightening of a tie he wasn't wearing today. He checked his watch...

Only then was the door knocked, cautiously.

"Come in, Sweaty," shouted Brenda's voice.

He entered, and there she was galloping towards him. Big Brenda, bosoms bouncing the way they always did. He remembered them, the suffocating feeling. She grabbed him the way she used to, in a gigantic hug, and the kiss, open mouth and straight on the lips, and her tongue was...

"Brenda, I'm a married man now..." he squeaked and struggled to free himself as the adjoining door opened.

Derek looked over Brenda's shoulder. The headmaster was standing, arms folded, staring at him and shaking his head.

"Still up to no good, I see, Toozlethwaite. You can let go of Brenda, now..."

Beakie hadn't changed, and his memory was as good as ever.

"If you'd like to come into my office and tell me why you are causing havoc in my school again after so many years."

Derek noticed, as the Head spoke, at least he was smiling.

"Take a seat," and Derek did, but he was most uncomfortable.

It didn't seem right sitting in front of the Head. His memory was of always standing before him, waiting to be told what outlandish penalty would be prescribed this time, and, because physical punishment was no longer part of this school's routine, usually being given masses of lines. Derek remembered very often longing for the speedy pain of a cane, rather than the alternative humiliation of lines.

"So, you were after some information, Mister Toozlethwaite?"

Beakie's question brought Derek back to the present. He took a deep breath, and explained his objective. He required some facts because he was going to create a biography of 'Rabid Revenge'.

"Who...?" Beakie responded, not unsurprisingly.

Derek expanded his explanation. Mr Brummage was informed

that about thirty years ago, five of his school's former pupils formed a local band, and played at school dances, and then went on to make the big-time as rock musicians in America. The band when at school was called 'Fort Knights and a Damsel'.

"This is all a bit before my time," the Head said, "but it sounds to me that if we give you the information, in return, you could help us with an article for the school magazine."

That seemed reasonable enough to Derek.

Any factual information he was permitted to have, would be appreciated, Derek continued, but what would be even better would be hearing the memories of any teacher who happened to still be here, who knew them personally thirty years ago. Although Derek went through the process of stating the wish, in his own mind there was little hope of success...

"That would have to be Duckett," said Mr Brummage.

"Yahoo..." Derek yelled out in delight, causing the Head to raise his eyebrows and pause a moment, before continuing... "Mr Duckett is due to retire this year. He would probably remember them."

That name rang a bell for Derek... Mr Duckett, but that teacher was considered to be ancient way back when he was at school and that was almost fourteen years ago. No matter, this was an excellent link, and worth coming for.

The Head shouted through to Brenda.

"Brenda, I need a free teacher. Who is not taking a class just now, please?"

"That would be the new man – Sam Walters," Brenda shouted back.

"Would you like to fetch Mr Walters then, please, Brenda?"

"Certainly will, Headmaster."

Derek thought back to all the lectures he'd had from this man sitting opposite – about shouting in the school!

Brenda went out. Derek heard the door slam, and sat waiting. In the ensuing silence the uncomfortable feeling returned. The silence continued with Beakie just staring blankly at Derek. Derek's confidence was diminishing, second by second, under his old headmaster's gaze. He slid lower in the chair.

And then – all change – it looked as if Beakie forgot his existence. He lifted a red pen and some papers from his desk. He started checking them, with a "Tut-tut-tut," at each error found, which he then slashed at viciously with the red pen.

"Oh no..." was groaned at each mistake – then suddenly he looked up at Derek.

"What's the capital of Uzbekistan?" he fired at him.

"Tashkent," was fired back equally quickly.

"Very good, Toozlethwaite," said the Head with a beaming smile. "Very good indeed, so, your time here with me wasn't totally wasted. I am surprised."

Now Derek felt much better. Impressing his headmaster helped renew his confidence, and he sat up straight again.

A few moments later Brenda returned, followed by Mr Walters. An introduction to begin with, and then Mr Walters was instructed by the Head to find Old Duckett, who could be anywhere.

If Duckett was taking a class, Walters was told to stand in for him and give Derek the chance to have some time to chat in peace and quiet, away from the classroom. This teacher had an American accent, Derek noticed; must be a novelty for his classes.

They were in the corridor when it occurred to Derek – Mr Walter's face – it seemed familiar? The photograph Grandad gave him on Sunday, after the incident at the supermarket, flashed into his mind. The photo... Wasn't this the face on that photo? No... It couldn't be ...surely. This man is a teacher. A teacher wouldn't...

As he walked behind him, Derek fished in his pocket and found it. "Excuse me a moment," Derek said.

The two of them stopped. As Mr Walters turned around, Derek looked again at the photo and held it up to let Mr Walters see it too, and the teacher's mouth fell open.

"What...? How did you...?" he gulped.

"Ah-ha, so you are the one – and attacking old men," said Derek.

"How come you know that maniac?" demanded the new teacher.

"That maniac happens to be my grandfather... No..." Not quite the right way to put it, he realised.

"That old guy – he was stalking my partner..." claimed Walters.

"What? Come off it! You attacked him outside the supermarket," retorted Derek.

"I didn't attack him, I only told him to back off. Angie had never seen him before. I'd never seen him before either. So, why'd he pick on us, for goodness sake?" demanded Mr Walters, "...And he nearly blinded me with that damn camera of his ...and as for these two crazy females, his heavies, I think they were called Daisy and Thelma – please tell them to back off if you know them as well!"

Derek was confused. Not a new experience, but this was not making sense. This man was a teacher and he had a partner – a partner who was being stalked – by Grandad?

"Are you saying you weren't trying to mug him?"

"Mug him? Are you crazy? Why'd I want to do that for heaven's sake? I don't need his money. I have a very unhappy girlfriend at home you know, because of this. You guys sure know how to put a visitor off your country, and my dear girlfriend is giving me all the blame."

"Blame...? Join the club, mate," was all Derek could offer, apologising for the confusion, and saying how they'd nearly gone to the police about him.

"Snap!" was Sam's retort.

They agreed that there was something odd about the whole affair and it seemed to revolve around Derek's grandad, or maybe both grandparents.

To their credit, these two young males decided that talking was better than coming to blows. Both realised it might come to that anyway but, having a coffee first, they decided, seemed wise and that is what they did. Sitting together in the school canteen, each with a cup of the product described as coffee on the vending machine list, they did a lot more talking and slowly eased the tension, and by the time their cups were empty, they were considerably friendlier.

Derek suggested that maybe they could get together some time. Perhaps their partners could meet each other too, and show that the Brits could actually be pleasant to strangers. Sam accepted that cautiously, with a proviso – Derek's gran and grandad must not be involved.

Eventually, they made their way to Mr Duckett's classroom, and Mr Walters took over, as instructed. At least their little contretemps ended peacefully both were glad to admit. They shook hands and exchanged numbers for their mobiles – or was it cell-phones? And Derek was left in the shaky hands of Mr Duckett.

"What's your name again? Toodlepip, did you say? Should I know you?" Derek was asked.

"Maybe... I was in one of your classes many years ago," he replied, "...and please ...just call me Derek," he added.

From what he was now remembering of old Mr Duckett, Derek decided what he had to say would have to be kept simple, and so he took a deep breath and started to explain his current quest in life.

After a very few moments, Derek sensed that Mr Duckett was only taking in half of what he was saying to him, maybe even less, but he struggled on. He recounted what he now knew of the band's beginnings, and then asked what he, as one of their teachers, thought of them as individuals when in his class. For example, were they good pupils? Could they concentrate properly on their school work? Did they leave their musical ambitions outside the classroom door and do what he demanded of them each day?

"What did you say your name was again?" asked Old Duckett.

"Derek... Now what can you remember about them?" he tried once more.

"They were very nice boys..."

"Yes...?" said Derek hopefully. "Anything else you remember about them?"

"No," was the confident reply.

"Oh..." said a disappointed Derek, "...and there was a girl too?"

"She was a very nice girl..."

There was a long silence... "Have you anything else?" asked Derek in one final push, feeling his little bit of hope fade away quickly.

"Yes, all very nice... They had a band, you say... Yes ...very ...uhmm ...nice."

They hadn't spoken for long, but Derek just knew that that was it: his time was up: there would be no more. Very obviously he was going absolutely nowhere with Mr Duckett, so, a figurative towel was thrown into the ring. A warm blanket might have been more apt because Derek guessed if they sat facing each other much longer, dear old Duckett would doze off.

He felt sorry for the current pupils of this teacher, but then again maybe that was unnecessary. Every time they sat in Duckett's class, they probably looked on it as a free period.

So, that was it, a blank wall.

Ah well... Who else could he try? Was there anyone?

He didn't realise it, but he missed an excellent chance. If only he had thought at the time, Sam Walters was an American, and he might have known something about a band that made it big on the other side of the Atlantic, in the country of his birth.

In fact, Mr Walters might have helped a lot...

26

When Gran and Grandad came to the cottage to have Sam Walter's photo printed last Sunday, they didn't say anything about stalking the man's girlfriend, did they? Then again why would they have admitted to that, it wasn't something to boast about, was it?

Was there a reason? Surely they didn't realise they were frightening the girl because that sort of behaviour is not like them at all? Anyway, last Sunday, wasn't there a distraction? On return to the cottage the four of them were given something new to think about and were certainly thrown off kilter – finding Thelma and Hammy ...oh ...yes!

For the six friends sitting round the table in the cottage that evening, many subjects were discussed openly, including the usual ones – weather, holidays, television, news, and politicians and bankers, and that's when it became heated. For these two categories, most of the solutions proposed were either illegal or physical impossibilities.

There was agreement that bankers were all tarred with the same brush, except for Alexander. Alexander was offered up as one of the better ones – a point put forward by Hammy – partly because it was Sally's dad and he was in her house but, more so, because her father was being good to him.

There were other questions buzzing inside the heads of four at the table, questions regarding the two suspected 'lovebirds', questions four of them wanted to discuss – but not just then. Like: when did Hammy and Thelma arrive at the cottage? Were they an item? What had they been up to?

It may not have been the right time or the right place, sitting together at the dining table at that juncture, but a great deal of talk about this new pairing would have to happen at some point. It couldn't be bottled up, that's for sure... but naturally, no discussion would be in front of, or involve, the couple concerned. It may be unfair but the people being gossiped about are rarely allowed the knowledge of what's being said.

Anyway, who would want to know the correct facts when supposition is so much more enjoyable? No questions would be asked of them, but it had been plain to see, Hamish Macintosh and Thelma Donaldson were alone, together, under this one roof, and in the bedroom...

Difficult to believe... Hammy and Thelma...?

However, all six shared the meal, concocted at short notice by Sally, with the enlisted help of Derek, and the food presented was very enjoyable and appreciated by all. Derek helped, but only by doing exactly as instructed, and what he actually did was done reluctantly, him having more important things that he had wanted to do. Blooming relatives...

Though this grudging behaviour may have not been apparent to the others, to Sally it was obvious, but she would save the lecture until later. However, later, she forgot all about it, because it was nearly eleven o'clock when they all left the cottage. Hamish and Thelma went by taxi, and Daisy and Hector left as they'd come, by scooter.

It is an obvious fact: a taboo subject must remain private.

Sally forgot about Derek's telling-off, because she had a lot on her mind; she had news to be passed on. It may be late, but it wasn't too late, she decided. A phone call was essential. Her mother would want to be told... "Hello," said the male voice, sounding rather sleepy.

Falling asleep in the chair after a couple of glasses of whisky was not out of character for her father, and Sally was well aware of that.

"Oh, it's you," was his friendly response.

What was it about her and her father? It was always there. No matter how little she said, there was the feeling that a battle was looming, and that the action could start at any moment.

"Sorry if I disturbed you, Dad," she said trying to be diplomatic and calm, and not cause any annoyance. "It was actually Mum that I'd hoped to speak to."

"Ah, you know she's in bed? Is it really important? I'll have to wake her, probably."

"Oh, yes, Dad, very important," she said.

There was a long period of silence, before Muriel's voice came on the line. She was not in her bed, but in the middle of an exercise which was even more inconvenient. She was having a facial mud-pack. Speaking was not the best thing to do during mud-packing, however, Muriel took the phone from her husband – Sally obviously wouldn't have called at this time of night if it hadn't been serious...

"Mum – is Aunt Thelma home yet?"

"No dear, but she'll probably be back shortly."

The moment she opened her mouth, the mud pack cracked, and would have to be repeated at a later date – for Muriel, they were becoming essential.

"Does she ever stay out late or does she stay out all night?"

"Yes, sometimes, both. Recently, she's been staying with a girlfriend she met a while ago."

"Are you sure it's a girl, Mummy?"

"No, I'm not certain... I'm just going on what Thelma said. Why? Oh ...do you think ...could it be ...is she?"

"Hmmm, I'm not sure ...but I think that she may be ...sleeping with Hammy."

"What? Don't be ridiculous darling. Hamish Macintosh is an old man. There's nearly twenty years difference in their ages. Anyway, Thelma gave up all that sort of thing ages ago ...I think..."

"Well, I wouldn't be too sure. Look, Mummy, I'm sorry to have disturbed you at this time of night anyway, just to tell you this."

"No problem darling. It was important, but, probably we'd better leave it until she tells us."

"I'll let you get to sleep then, Mummy."

"No chance of that now. Good night darling."

Communication, while riding on a scooter, has never been easy, unless the driver and the passenger are equipped with microphone and headphone sets. Shouting to each other while wearing the helmets usually means that pedestrians become more aware of what's being talked about than those conversing, and, as it was very late, there was no chance of discussing this evening's goings-on until they were back at Blytheton Road, and had closed their own front door.

"So, what do you think, Hector?" Daisy asked the moment she took the helmet off.

"She d-d-d-d-did a g-g-great job in an em-m-m-m-mergency."

"What...?" responded Daisy.

"S-S-Sally ...she c-c-conjured up a g-g-great m-m-meal, d-d-didn't she?"

"Oh, Hector, I'm talking about your friend and Sally's Aunt..."

"H-H-H-Hammy? Wha-wha-what about 'im?"

"Well ...you know... They came out of that bedroom looking mighty guilty, I'd say."

"What d-do you m-m-mean. H-H-Hammy and Th-Th-Thelma?"

"Yes..."

"Having a b-bit of ...h-h-h-how's your f-f-f-f-father?"

"Yes..."

"No chance – it'd k-k-k-kill 'im!"

Back at the cottage, Derek's mind was concerned with where he was to go next with his book investigations, but he was multi-tasking; trying to decide whether, or not, the pie dish could be left soaking in the soapy water. He had completed all the other washing up, and by doing the dishes he felt that at least he'd helped a little more.

It was a lovely meal Sally presented, but it meant that the fridge and the freezer were now totally devoid of pre-packaged. A major visit to Bisko's would be required if they were to avoid starvation next week, he was thinking...

"Well...?" Sally asked.

"Yes, all right thanks. I'm nearly finished. Just this pie dish..."

"Are they?" and she gave a knowing wink.

"Of course not ...and there's probably an innocent explanation and anyway, Hammy's much too old for your Aunt Thelma."

"Hmmm... We'll see... Are you coming ...to bed...?" she asked smiling, seductively.

That decided it.

He was functioning normally tonight and couldn't miss the signal, so, under these circumstances – Derek abandoned the pie dish!

27

She was paying more attention to Derek's latest idea for the book. It sounded so much more mature than his previous efforts and probably should be encouraged. To her mind, this time, there was the potential for success. Investigating the antics of a group of musicians, who probably back then were deep into drugs, and sex, and all sorts of other mischief, could turn out to be very exciting. A lot of slimy stones would be waiting to be turned over, with plenty of scope for development of a story.

Could Derek do it this time, she asked herself, without causing any more fall-outs? He could become disheartened and lose confidence so easily – especially when she criticised him. Maybe it would be better if she helped with this one.

"Derek, has it occurred to you that my daddy and mummy would have been at the school about the same time as this band was on the go? You could ask them."

Yes it had occurred to him, but he didn't say so. Derek was pleased at her showing interest – this was a first. He didn't want to put her off.

"What a great idea, Sal. Maybe I could meet your dad and discuss it with him. His memory might be a bit better than old Duckett's. I'll phone him and we could perhaps go out together for a meal again."

"Derek..." and her instructional voice took control. "No dressing up..."

He didn't ever argue these days with that voice, something to do with the distinct threat in the tone. She didn't actually say it, didn't have to, but if he didn't comply...

A special 'boy's day out' with her father last year, had led to a lengthy unsettled period between Sally and Derek, and it was Derek who had behaved stupidly and been caught. "Of course not – no silly stuff this time," he promised.

To tell the truth, doing 'silly stuff' again hadn't even occurred to him, but now that she had put the idea into his head...

"No, definitely not," he repeated to himself a few times.

They were meeting in town today, Dad and Derek, and, for certain, there would be no recurrence of the stupid dressing-up nonsense – Derek wouldn't dare; of that Sally was very confident, but...! She contacted her mum anyway and asked her to check her father's choice of clothing before he left the house. Meanwhile, she ensured that Derek followed instructions.

On Saturday afternoon, the pair of them sat having some grub in the Duck Down Pub, dressed in casual clothing, male version, this time.

"So, what do you think about my sister's behaviour?" asked Alexander. "I presume that's what you wanted to talk to me about. Using your house to ...you know." With a mouth full of Spaghetti Bolognese, Derek didn't consider it mannerly to speak just at that moment, but he gave Alexander a puzzled look – and swallowed.

"No, no. It wasn't Thelma I wanted to talk to you about."

"You mean you don't mind if she and Hammy get up to ...nonsense, in your house. I mean to say – if they are at it..."

"What makes you think that they are ...at it?" replied Derek.

This was an embarrassing subject that he'd rather not be talking to his father in-law about. This was how gossip gets about.

"I know my sister. Remember, we are twins. Anyway, Muriel says so, and she got it from the horse's mouth so to speak – Sally."

"There could be a perfectly sensible explanation to the whole affair," Derek replied, trying to guide Alexander away from that subject, "...I wanted to talk to you about 'Rabid Revenge'."

"I'd mind what I was saying, if I were you. You'll get us thrown out. They don't stand for bad language in here," said Alexander.

"Ha, ha, ha... It's a band. You've never heard of them, obviously, but how about 'Fort Knights and a Damsel'?"

"Oh yes, that rings a bell," Alexander replied, "...but that was a long time ago. Why are you interested?"

Derek went over what Anton told him, and how it now seemed to be a good subject for his book – but only if he could dig up information of interest. So far the results had been pretty dismal, but Alexander remembered something.

"It's a bit vague. There were five of them – yes? And they went to America, I remember that much. They were at school in the year above Muriel and me, but they weren't very nice people as I remember. They behaved like a secret society and were always together. One was a real pain, can't remember which – but their music was good."

"Any idea how I could contact any of them?" asked Derek.

"Some of the parents could still be alive and living in the area, I would guess," Alexander offered. "They'd be the ones to give the clues. The girl had some trouble ...was it here, or in America? Sorry, can't remember. Some sort of scandal, I think. Anyway, I wasn't too interested at the time. I was busy studying and then I went to Birmingham for a few years, so I lost touch with local gossip. Anyway, as I asked earlier, what about Hammy getting off with my sister?"

"I haven't thought about it. I like them both."

"If you get the chance, do me a favour. See if you can foster the romance. Thelma's been living with us now for almost two years, and she's becoming like Sally – constantly arguing with me. It's getting to me, in my own house. So, if Hammy were to run off with her...?"

"My only worry would be if they had children," Derek answered sanctimoniously.

"Could they? Oh my God... I never thought of that..."

28

Derek didn't say anything to his grandparents about having met Sam Walters, or what he said about them. He was still waiting to see if they would raise the subject with him, however, if it was anything like the way they'd hidden all information regarding his mother, they'd say nothing.

It was mentioned by him to Sally though, but explained in a different way. He told her that he'd met a nice American teacher who had an unhappy girlfriend. Wouldn't it be a nice gesture to invite them over to the cottage at some future date and show them that people in this country can be friendly? Sally started to ask why the girl was unhappy, was it a bad experience?

Then he went off at a tangent ...about the book. He was getting nowhere and it was genuinely unsettling for him. He admitted to her about his lack of progress, and was appreciative of what appeared to be her sympathy.

Thinking about anything else for him these days was difficult, and for that he apologised. Because a serious question about the band occurred to him, unfortunately, the nice 'hands across the Atlantic' gesture and the arranging of a get-together with the friendless American couple were both rapidly forgotten. What if the names on the web sites are pseudonyms? If that were to be the case, he realised, there would be no chance of tracing the parents.

Think positive, Sally had told him, so he was about to find out about the names – maybe? Sitting on his knees was the local phone book, not necessarily the perfect answer, but he was at least trying something. All he had to do was to find the telephone number of one of the parents, he only needed one, and any one would do for starters; the rest would just click into place. This phone book was about to solve all his problems. He crossed his fingers. Which name first?

Looking for an uncommon name seemed the best bet. That would be Thwaite, Steven Thwaite, even though he'd only been part of the group before America. In that case, he might still be here himself, in Newingsworth. He could turn out to be the local contact, which would make it all so easy.

"Thomas ...Thomson ...Thorpe ...Thow ...Thursby..."

Turn over page...

"Thyne ...Tibbet... Hmmmm..."

It would appear not. He could find no-one called Thwaite currently inhabiting Newingsworth and Slatterfoot and surrounding districts.

"Though it could be ex-directory, I suppose."

"Pity..." said Sally from the other side of the room.

Is it worth continuing, he reflected? Am I just wasting my time? He was already lacking confidence in his own ability to succeed in this but, he had to ask himself, as it was the first attempt to find a surviving parent and he'd only just started the search, why should this little failure seem like a catastrophe? He was going to have to accept it could be a long slog – and get on with it! Sally was sitting across the room watching him so he put on a brave face.

"Nothing at all?" she asked sympathetically, while silently urging him to go faster than his current snail's pace.

He couldn't give up so easily, could he, not now that she was getting involved and being supportive. She would be really disappointed if he threw in the towel so soon, but... "Not to worry," he replied "I'll try another name... Hoist ..." and though it was a little awkward trying to turn flimsy pages of a phone directory with both fingers crossed, he found the page.

"Hoggins ...Hogshaw ...Hogwood ...Hoist. Ah, this is more like it ...and, there are five Hoists listed." Sally smiled to him in support. "Now which one is the Hoist I'm looking for? I feel lucky on this one. Oh yes, success is close," and he smiled back at Sally, suddenly feeling cocky again. "I'll have to phone them one by one, I suppose."

Investigative journalism meant having to do that, and he'd experienced it before, a real drag. These calls were always just in hope. The high optimism he'd had moments before diminished a little. The first try was to Andrew Hoist.

"Hello..." the male voice answered.

"Hello, are you the father of James Hoist, who played with 'Rabid Revenge'?"

"Pardon? You'll have to speak up a bit. I'm deaf, y'know."

So, Derek repeated what he'd said at an increased volume.

"No," was the short and sweet answer.

Another try, this time it was T Hoist.

"Mr Hoist?"

"Yes, Tom Hoist here," and the same question was asked. "No... I haven't heard of that team. Wee Jamie played for Rosebank Rovers 'under-twelve' team last year, but twisted his ankle. Are you a talent scout? He's a great wee player, but I don't want him signed-up until he's older. I want him to pass his school exams first."

"Thank you, Mr Hoist, but I think I've got a wrong number," said Derek, and hung up.

A female voice answered the next call.

"No thank you, I'm not listening to whatever you are selling, I am on the list, so please go away right now, or I'll call the police. I've had enough of your nonsense."

And all Derek had said was "Hello, I'm..."

The next one sounded as if she didn't get out much, and he had difficulty ending the conversation with her. He'd been invited round to her place for a cup of coffee, or something extra special if he was willing to bring a bottle of something strong. She was definitely not who he was looking for.

A final try with the last name, William Hoist, but Derek didn't get a chance...

"Hello?" said a male. "I was expecting you to ring... You'll have to talk quickly, Petal. The wife's in the kitchen just now, and she could come out any minute, so if I put the phone down suddenly, you'll know why. So how are you doing, Petal? Will I see you as usual tonight?"

Derek hadn't said a word, but Petal, he obviously was not! No, that fellow hadn't sounded like the person he was looking for either.

"Maybe a good time for a coffee?" suggested Sally.

It was a positive nod and a smile, now slightly strained, that he gave to Sally as she left the room. Any confidence possessed by Derek moments ago was gently sliding back down the slope.

"Jones... There won't be many 'Jones's in the... Oh my goodness..."

His smile was no longer visible; it seemed defeat could be on the doorstep, but it had to be done. Get it over with – so the first on the list was dialled... If this was unsuccessful, there will another eighteen calls to 'Jones'. He would not cope....

"Yes, you'd be welcome to come round. Tomorrow afternoon? Of course, that will be fine. We'll both be in," she said.

He found it hard to believe – the very first number he called – and it was the right one...! He'd hit the jackpot! It was nothing less than incredible!

What a pleasant voice she had too, an elderly lady, and presumably Growler's mother. She was the contact he was hoping for. This lovely lady had brightened his life and, thanks to her, writing the book suddenly was possible once more. What a change of fortune...

Sally sensed the difference the moment she came back into the room. There was a confident smile on his face as he took the mug of coffee from her, giving her a grateful 'thank you' – and a peck on the cheek.

A surge of pride surged through her as she looked at the figure that was before her: her Sweaty, standing tall and straight, and full of confidence. It was so obvious; it was all going to work out fine. The only thing to make her feel a little unsettled moments later, was hearing him mutter to himself...

"Thank goodness – I won't have to slit my wrists after all..."

29

"How could I possibly move in with you, Hamish? As it is, you are hardly surviving in this tin box on your own and, anyway, what would people say?" asked Thelma.

"Och, ye dinnae need tae worry aboot whit people wid say, Hen. If they did talk, it wid jist be tae say tha' ah wis an awfy lucky man," he replied.

"It won't be long until the main building is finished. If you want to make an honest woman of me and you are still thinking like this, we could reconsider it then."

Hamish felt a tiny twinge of guilt in his old Scottish heart. Getting married again... What would his dear departed Sybil have said about this situation?

The world stopped turning for a moment as Hammy had a think... Och – why am ah bein' so stupid? If she hudd been here, she would huvv been delighted tae tell me – if ah got married again, ah'd be a bigamist... Sybil had been that sort of a woman – and she could take a joke.

Such an innocent start it had been, his bumping into Thelma one day while in the supermarket. He was staying with Sally and Derek at the time, and taking his turn at doing some shopping for them.

It was during the afternoon and he'd abandoned his work on the buildings for a short while. The job wouldn't stop if he wasn't there, he knew that for certain – these blokes knew what they were doing, and every one of them was as conscientious as anyone could be; more so than he was, he realised.

He had a great team, going about their work without needing any pushing; Hammy suspected they managed just as well without his supervision. In fact, when Alexander generously offered him this job, he had been convinced that he wasn't really needed at all, but someone was, and it might as well be him.

The supermarket visit was intended to be a quick call for milk, butter and bread. He hadn't planned to stay away too long but, when he bumped into Thelma, his absence from the job turned out to be lengthy.

She was doing a similar thing, shopping for Muriel, Alexander, and herself. The other two in that household were at work each day – she wasn't. It was the least she could do. The day they met led to a coffee, then a bite to eat, and then a promise to do it all again, because they'd both enjoyed each other's company.

Since then, they had been together in public but never met anyone they knew, even though the affair started four months ago; that was until the Sunday afternoon – at the cottage when he went for some clothes.

His fresh clothes were kept in the spare bedroom in the cottage, mainly because, if stored in the caravan, they would finish up anything but fresh. Anyway, they were expecting to say hello to Sally and Derek in the passing. Thelma was with him and their intention had been to inform the younger couple that they were now a couple too; they were going to let the rest of the world know gradually...

A pleasant walk from the caravan, in the sunshine, through the fields, and entering by the back gate; that was the way they approached the cottage. Walking hand in hand in the fields felt less embarrassing to Hammy than walking on the road – they might have met somebody.

Finding no-one in the cottage surprised them. There was some evidence provided by the fork stuck in the middle of the grass at the back, abandoned apparently, but no sign of Sally or Derek. Entering by the back door meant they failed to notice the other clue: the Vespa scooter parked at the front.

They were disappointed not to see Sally and Derek, but decided that they could be told another day. Thelma and Hammy, had then intended to have some food together back at the caravan, in privacy, but it didn't happen like that, did it? They both found it hilarious afterwards because Sally, Derek, Daisy, and Hector, all pretended to accept that it was normal for them being together in the bedroom. Probably the worst was suspected, but everyone was too polite to comment.

Hector and Daisy having appeared with Sally and Derek made Hammy feel awkward and, as a consequence, he chickened out of making the announcement. Informing the two youngsters would have been pressure enough – he could never cope with the four folk, but as no questions were asked, no explanations were offered.

So, who knows what was being imagined?

Around the dinner table, that Sunday, every other subject under the sun was discussed, except that they were discovered together. It was as if the bedroom incident had been erased from all of their minds... It didn't happen... It didn't happen ...but it did, and it pleased Hammy immensely.

It wasn't just love though... Meeting Thelma brought practical benefits to Hammy and the work he was doing, and, as well as becoming very good friends, she had been giving advice and suggestions to him on the internal planning of the future hotel.

Take for example, furniture and fittings...

Never having done anything resembling that sort of thing before, how could Hammy ever have selected these items from either a showroom, or a catalogue? When he was young, his mother did it; when he was married to Sybil, she did it; so what could be more natural for Hammy than to get down on his knees and thank the Good Lord for bringing him Thelma.

As for selecting soft furnishings and general decoration for the many rooms, he gave himself no chance of coming up with any satisfactory conclusion there either. He needed help and his 'very good friend' was the one who offered it.

As each week passed, thoughts of themes for the internal colour schemes were gradually developed by Thelma, and shown to her 'very good friend'. Samples of fabrics and makes of furniture that she selected were offered to Hammy for consideration, and always with the proviso... "Perhaps you have better ideas?"

Oh no ...not a chance; hers were perfect...

Every single suggestion she made was seized on by Hammy. He had been desperate, now he was extremely grateful for her help. He couldn't believe it: here she was inviting him to criticise her choices? This man would never be so stupid. The woman was wonderful, and even Sybil would have liked her.

He was delighted – how could anyone have these abilities?

Alexander hadn't wanted to be involved at all in any of the detail associated with the preparation of the new place.

To be truthful, he had even less of a clue than Hammy. He was recognised as a good bank manager, and he could claim to be a passable actor, (maybe a rubbish father?) but that was the sum total, and he was quite happy that way.

Before he was married, he chose furniture and colour schemes himself for his own flat, but when he met Muriel and invited her to live in the flat with him, she refused. It was the atrocious decor. Major changes to suit her discerning eye were demanded, with which he willingly complied, and then she consented to join him. What a relief for him when she took over. Being useless with colour, his own choices were making him ill.

Muriel knew about the planned hotel – from the distance, and only what she'd been told. She had not interfered at any stage in proceedings for the rebuilding work. It wasn't her place to do so. The idea had been his and he had the money, so it was Alexander who chose to purchase the farm and the buildings for development, and she accepted the financial decisions he made as being astute. Well, wasn't he the expert? There was no wish to be involved on her part. Naively, she also accepted that for a new building, things just happened, and anyway, she had her own work.

They were both in agreement – Hammy would be doing a good job. When they did show interest, neither Muriel nor Alexander had any notion that it was mostly Thelma's ideas they were admiring.

How could Hammy enjoy sleeping in this caravan; no space to turn and extremely awkward to keep clean? A shiver ran down her spine when she thought of what Hammy had told her of the first one, and the tree, and what could have happened to him. Completion of the redesigned farmhouse couldn't come quickly enough, for both of them.

At Cloverton, which was still her home, Thelma was getting the distinct feeling that relationships with her brother were slowly going downhill. Familiarity was changing things.

In particular, she knew she was starting to irritate Alexander, though not deliberately. A relationship of that nature between Alexander and his daughter was already obvious to her, and it was happening with her now too. She and Alexander, being twins, were too close in behavioural patterns, argumentative and determined, and yes, she was beginning to overstay her welcome.

Thelma was surprised that there had been no comment, or criticism, from Muriel or Alexander, about her and Hamish. They must be aware, she told herself, though the relationship had not been flaunted or mentioned by her, but Sally had seen them together at the cottage. She would have passed some comment back to her mother, surely. If she had, Muriel had said nothing. At some point, it would have to come out into the open.

She wondered about their reaction. What they will say, when she tells them that she will be leaving Cloverton? Her guess – Muriel will say she would miss her company, whether true or not, but for certain – Alexander will be delighted.

Oh dear... No matter what Hammy says, she certainly couldn't move into this caravan... She'd tried to clean it up more, but there was a limit to what could be achieved. The space was cleverly designed, but the vehicle had been well used, and time had taken its toll. It was well worn too, somewhat like Hamish and me, she reflected. The big difference is, and she smiled ruefully at the thought that, unlike Hamish and me, this caravan has no future.

However, who can really tell what the future holds...?

30

It would be a busy day, but one he was looking forward to. Derek's meeting with his newly discovered 'Jones' contacts was to be at their home early this afternoon, and if their information turned out as detailed as he hoped, the visit could last a while, so, an extremely busy morning in the office was ahead. All the work he was supplying for the next edition would require completion and be passed on by lunchtime at the latest, because he would not be available after then. His afternoon would be spent out of the office – on personal things, and without the others knowing...

The office atmosphere was back to normal. Sally and Derek were at peace, much to the relief of Spider, and this morning there was no tension in the air whatsoever. It was so much easier for the four of them to work together – pleasantly.

Having worked for many years at Saddanbroke's, 'the bookmaker you can trust', Spider knew all about the important things in life: horses, jockeys, calculating odds, and bets which were said to be certainties but which turn out not to be, and how easy it is to become infected by betting fever. Some punters used to give him the impression that they were addicted to losing; they could do it with such regularity and certainty. He also knew how easy it would be for his boss, Rob, to graduate into that category.

Yes, he knew a lot about those things...

Unfortunately, he lacked training and in-depth knowledge of mediation, marriage counselling, and conflict resolution but, each time when called upon, he, Spider Webb, coped. Was it a natural ability for these matters, he asked himself modestly? Though unqualified he had risen to each occasion so, could he now consider himself to be an expert in these fields?

Training or not, with the fall-outs between Sally and Derek occurring regularly, he could claim to be never out of practice but after each spat he felt he deserved a holiday in a darkened room.

Today, Sally was in Rob's office having a personal chat about a proposal of her own for a new feature. It would concern the lack of fashion in Newingsworth and Slatterfoot and surrounding districts. Rob was resisting strongly and as diplomatically as he felt he should. He suspected that a subject of this sort, in an area which cared less about fashion than his cat did, could create the wrong reaction from the public. Sally was pushing the premise that weekly sales would soar. Rob was convinced of the opposite.

Derek and Spider were carrying on with work at their desks but, because of the lack of sound insulation in these office walls, it was difficult not to feel involved. They had to pretend not to be able to hear.

The result was a whispered debate going on between these two, unable to resist commenting to each other on Sally's current subject, while knowing they were not supposed to be part of the discussion. In reality, the pros and cons being debated and the conclusions reached outside Rob's office, were more relevant than Rob's and Sally's.

However, the work Derek had on his desk required decisions this morning, and that is why he was gazing intently at the photos entered for the 'Junior Mr Muscle Competition' spread out over the entire surface. A choice was about to be made to permit one small boy to have a moment of fame.

Of course, for this little fellow, excruciating embarrassment will be guaranteed at some time in the distant future. The photo, not seen for years, will be brought out of a hidey-hole by his doting mother to inform his favourite girlfriend, "It was in the newspaper, you know."

So, who is it to be? Make the decision, Derek!

Eeny-meeny-miney-moe...

"There we are... Master Maximillian Pickles of 71 Pinkerton

Street, Slatterfoot, aged seven years old – you lucky little man. I declare you, Little Mr Muscle," Derek announced, and Spider dutifully applauded.

The next issue's centre pages were designated to carry a montage of the submitted photographs – everyone a winner; which would be followed a week later by, 'Little Miss Pink'; and the next, 'My Dreadful Wedding Photos'.

No doubt, later in the year, he would be regurgitating 'My Potato looks like a...' Now, that one was popular *every* autumn...

The rain came on gently after he left the office, and became heavier when he was well on his way – without an overcoat, or an umbrella. He was on foot and kept telling himself he was doing the correct thing: walking is good for you. Of course, it is slower than mechanised transport in reaching the destination, and if it rains, you get wet, and if it rains very heavily, you get really wet – like now.

It seemed ages before he reached the address for Mr and Mrs A Jones, but at last he'd arrived, here he was – Custard Crescent – terraced housing with number 42 at the end on a corner, with a large garden on three sides of the building for all to see and admire. The garden was well used. Here was a combination of shrubs and perennials, with spaces for annuals, cleverly positioned and making a pretty picture, although slightly bedraggled today. Regimented vegetable plots too, some with little shoots showing, some with quite advanced growth, others simply with name tags at the end of apparently empty rows; all indicating the home of a dedicated gardener, obviously. It must be a lot of back breaking work.

Derek rang the doorbell.

"Hello, I phoned yesterday..."

"You must be Mr..." she said. It was Mrs Jones who had opened the door. "Come in, Pet. You are soaking wet."

He was led into the front room.

"Let me take your jacket," she insisted, and Derek did not resist. "Oh, you will get your death of cold, walking about like this. I'll get a towel."

Back she came with a large bath towel, and he tried drying his hair.

Removing the towel, he stood feeling foolish, with his glasses knocked squint on his face and unable to see properly until he wiped the lenses, as Mr Jones joined them in the room. He was standing in front of Derek and reached out automatically and received a damp handshake.

Here was a man about his own grandad's age, looking fit and healthy. This was the one who was the gardener, Derek guessed. By comparison, the wife did not look as fit as Gran, although they were probably of similar ages; then Mrs Jones helped her husband sit down, so, Derek realised, this man may not be as healthy as he looked.

"And what can we do for you?" she asked Derek.

Mr Jones sat and looked at him. The strong silent type, Derek guessed. I wish he would smile. He doesn't appear to like me...

"But before we talk, would you prefer tea, or coffee?" Mrs Jones asked.

"That's very kind. I'll have black coffee please."

Mrs Jones left the room leaving Derek and Mr Jones seated, facing one another. Derek could think of nothing to say. The eyes of Mr Jones looked straight at him. Derek wondered why he was staring like that – and wished his wife would come back quickly. He remembered the film – The Texas Chain Saw Massacre. The gent opposite looked remarkably like one of the... Derek gave an involuntary shudder.

Oh, thank goodness, she was back. She wasn't out of the room for long, but to Derek it seemed an eternity, just sitting ...waiting...

"Forgive my husband not talking. He has a very sore throat. Being blind is very difficult for him, but he struggles along, and not being able to speak has made it more difficult for him these last few days. Hasn't it father?"

Her question was acknowledged by his silent nod, as she continued, "...Now how can we help you?"

Derek felt awful, having had bad thoughts about this poor man, but the vision of the Chain Saw Murderer was taking a little time to recede from his brain.

He took a sip of his coffee and began. His ambition to be an author was explained first, and then, that his chosen subject for a book was to be a local band, 'Rabid Revenge'. At the mention of the band's name, the expression on the face of the wife changed. His didn't – it was still like the Chain Saw Murderer's just before the attack. Her face flushed slightly, and she looked sadder, and older.

"Oh, do you take sugar?" she asked, as if to change the subject, and when he nodded she left the room again. Derek thought he saw her dab her eyes as she went out.

He took time to look around the room while waiting for the coffee, with difficulty avoiding the staring eyes. There didn't seem much purpose in trying to talk to Mr Jones, if he could only nod. The photos displayed were all of the same young male, he noticed, sometimes standing beside parents, sometimes on his own. They were from early toddler onwards, but though there were many in school outfits, blazers and pullovers, there appeared to be none beyond that stage.

That was a bad sign. Had he died young?

No, of course he hadn't. If this was the right house, then their son was Growler, Jonathan T Jones, and he had been a member of the band until they'd finally split – unless Wikipedia was leading him up a dark alley?

There was another fact. When she left the room the second time for the sugar, he noticed a stack of LPs sitting at the side of his chair. Knowing, this time, that he wasn't actually being observed by Mr Jones, he had a good look at the cover on the top of the pile; then she was back again...

"I am very sorry, Derek ...we may not be able to help ...about the members of the group," and she looked genuinely sad.

Oh, oh, he thought. I have wasted my time ...and then he thought of the title on the cover of the vinyl he'd just looked at. 'Where Can I Park My Branding Iron?' Wasn't that was one of theirs, one of their later ones? Could even be the last album they recorded – if he remembered correctly. He glanced at it again, while Mrs J went for biscuits. There's a name ...in smaller type in the corner... Yes, it is by them right enough, 'Rabid Revenge'.

From the moment he recognised the album, it became difficult to listen and concentrate on what she was saying. This elderly couple surely wouldn't have that type of music in their house because they liked it. It couldn't be their choice. It had to be because of the son, surely? At least he was at the correct house. As parents they would be pretending to think the music was wonderful – that's what good parents do.

Mrs Jones sat down again. There was a long silence while she wrestled with the thoughts in her head, and then she starting telling Derek a little of the family background. There had been a family split, he was told. Jonathan did well at his school studies, so, for his birthday, his sixteenth, he received a drum kit and he was delighted – and that was why their garden was the envy of the neighbours.

Derek didn't quite see the connection.

The son's incessant drumming had driven his mother out of the house – into the garden, but she had made good use of the time, and then couldn't stop. Now she was addicted, but struggled due to arthritis, lumbago, and exhaustion, at times.

She told Derek how their son would rush home from school, complete his homework, and then practise his drumming all evening. He had a good sense of rhythm – there was no question of that – but the drums could not be played quietly. When the radio was on, he played along; when the television was on, he played along; if his mother or father tried playing their own music on the record player...etc... And he didn't always use the drum kit. The kitchen table bore witness to that, she said.

Sadly, Jonathan never realised that he'd driven his mother into the garden, in all weathers, and that she had been reluctant to say to him, her only son.

His dad didn't suffer as much as his mother, because he used ear plugs, or put on the earphones and listened to his audio books, but eventually he was the one who decided to ask Jonathan to give up the drumming. If he didn't he would drive his mother crazy, he was informed. Unfortunately, the father, in standing up for the wife, suffered the reaction – and the son didn't stop.

To Mrs Jones, the giving of the drum kit as a present was a

decision she regretted, not immediately, but very soon after. Though she didn't know it at the time, she would regret it even more, a few years later.

He joined with others at the school and a band was started. Being allowed the school premises to use for practising gave some relief to his mother and father and, no doubt, to the parents of the other band members as well, although to a lesser extent.

Little by little the playing became important, then very important, then the be-all and end-all, and, in no time they'd lost him. He'd gone, not physically, but he'd grown up and was making his own decisions without recourse to them. He wasn't interested in what they had to say any more. They were forgotten; ignored; history...

He was into music.

The band was the centre of his life, and he became a dedicated member; still at school, as were the others in the band, and, to give him his due he was not allowing playing in the band to affect his studies. Surprisingly, each member of the group continued to study successfully and pass their exams.

Then collectively, they reached a conclusion – school was over – they were going to be famous. The opportunity to turn professional came along. That was to mean them leaving home and country, and going to America; and sadly for the Jones family, saying goodbye to each other. Their son's departure for the States was to be the last occasion they would stand close.

The sparsest of communications came from their son from that day on, and, for what did appear, it stated the barest of facts and was totally lacking emotion. It didn't stop his mother from putting kisses at the end of her letters though...

Reluctantly, at that juncture, Derek made mention of the time. Maybe he should come back another day, he suggested, there must be a whole lot more to be told.

"I'll get your jacket. It should be dry by now," she said, and went to fetch it.

He glanced again at the stack of discs sitting beside him. She came back, and the jacket was warm and dry. She handed it to him but he didn't put it on.

"There is one thing more I could show you," she said, and left the room once again.

Afterwards, Derek couldn't understand what came over him. He couldn't tell anyone either because he felt ashamed, but it was too late. When she left the room, he reached over and lifted the top album in its sleeve, from the stack of records at his side, and slipped it under his jacket out of sight. He did this in front of Mr Jones too, but he wouldn't notice...

The piece of paper she returned with was given to him to read; it was a handwritten letter she'd fetched. She was being too kind to him. Knowing he'd filched something from them only seconds before made him feel a real lowdown no-good son of a bitch – and he blushed accordingly as he read it silently.

'Dear Mum and Dad,

It's been a long time, I know, and I feel really bad about it, but I'll make it up to you some day. Please do me a favour and look after my record collection. The package will be delivered by special carrier to you. Could you store them for me, please? Try not to break any. They could become valuable in the future.

Your loving son, Jonathan.'

'Your loving son' was the most affectionate phrase he'd stated in all the years he'd been away, Derek was told, and all because he needed a favour!

"It was two years ago that we received the letter, and then his record collection arrived. Nothing has been heard from him since, and we don't know where he is," she informed him. "That's them sitting there – his albums. So, if any of them would be useful to you, and you wanted to listen to his music, you are welcome to have them – on loan, of course."

Derek wanted to crawl under the chair and cry. She was offering them to him, and he had already stolen one from right under her nose. How low could a person sink?

"I'd love to – but I don't have a record player," he bluffed. "All my stuff is on CD, or DVD, but if you can leave your kind offer open, I may take it up later."

He said his goodbyes and left, and walked home again feeling a tad uncomfortable about it all.

Slimy toad...

31

Boy, did his conscience give him hell...

"How'd it go?" asked Sally when he returned to the cottage.

"OK..." he mumbled, with his head lowered, and feeling guilty as he carried his folded jacket into the other room.

"Oh, was it that bad...?" she said, and thought it better not to enquire any further.

He hid the stolen album under the bed.

Visiting the Jones' house had left him quite disturbed. It wasn't just due to his blatant and regrettable theft from under the nose of a blind man, or his lack of progress in locating any members of the band. He felt bad for the elderly couple. They had lost a son, through no real fault of their own, and all due to giving him a drum kit for his birthday? Not a bad present though, he thought...

'Growler' was a fierce sounding name, but after spending time with the Jones, somehow that nickname seemed too informal, too friendly even, for Derek to be using, knowing now how he'd treated his parents but, when scribbling notes, Jonathan T Jones was a bit long winded – so 'Growler' he'd stay.

Wonder what the 'T' stands for? Could be just a showy affectation – that's what you do in show-business. When he spoke to the mother and father, he'd meant to ask that question, but forgot. Had they given their son a middle name, or was it his choice to add the letter? Did it stand for anything?

The parents of Jonathan T Jones would have had nothing to do with his nickname – Derek could be sure of that. It's not a name you'd call your son, is it, 'Growler', but, he reflected, after what he did this afternoon what name did he deserve to be called? If anyone found out about it, it wouldn't be complimentary! What made him let the side down like that? If he hadn't helped himself to that one blooming record he could legitimately have had access to the whole set of albums.

Going back soon and returning it would be best. He could slip it back onto the stack without them even knowing. Yes, that would ease his mind – and he'd get access to the rest.

Mr and Mrs Jones had no idea currently where their son could be. They presumed he was still in America ...somewhere. His last letter, two years old now, was from Chicago according to the postmark, but he hadn't given them an address. They promised to let Derek know if they found out his whereabouts in the future.

A direct contact for Growler had been Derek's hope, but, unfulfilled...

It wasn't a total time wasting exercise though. He came away with some clues. They'd known something about one of the others, Twister – shown in Wikipedia as the bass guitarist. According to Mrs Jones, he apparently was now an agent in London, organising concerts and appearances for singers and musicians. She knew that much, but didn't know how he could be contacted.

She seemed to have a dislike for him. One of those guys who made money from other people's hard work, she said, and probably creaming off ten per cent of their earnings from every job – living off them. As Mrs Jones said that to Derek, she had given a slight shudder. The way she explained it made the job sound so sleazy.

Derek suspected that she was confusing Agents, and Pimps.

Another thing she told Derek, linked to 'Sailor' but, unfortunately of only limited use, was about the man's father. It meant the name of that parent could almost certainly be crossed off the 'to do' list.

Sailor's real name was Theobald Walters. Old Mr Walters, was definitely in Slatterfoot, but couldn't possibly help. He was in a nursing home, and would be of little assistance – with Alzheimer's, and a fairly advanced condition too.

However, it occurred to Derek, wouldn't the hospital know the next-of-kin...? Could a contact number be wheedled out of the staff? Hmm ...confidential details; could be difficult; not information to be passed out willingly, Derek guessed, but worth the effort if it was Sailor's name and address they had.

If he went there, what should his cover story be? Could he pose as a long lost relative? He had already made himself a thief, hadn't he? No, not a good idea really, and would make things worse, but it could be borne in mind, and if all else fails it might be worth a try....

Another fact he'd learned, was that when they left school, a veil of secrecy was deliberately created around the band members, or so it seemed to those outside the group. Would the mystery have been a means of making them appear different from other bands, perhaps? They would have had to beat a lot of competition in those days, and back then, to be noticed, a band would have had to stand out like a sore thumb...

Now he was home, sitting at his PC, Derek recorded some notes from today's foray, hoping Sally wouldn't be too inquisitive. If she did ask, and she might since she was taking more interest, he considered he would claim he'd moved forward with his research. How much could he tell her though? Had he really made any progress? There was something she mustn't find out, and that was what a fool he'd been by becoming a thief today.

The information obtained so far, although somewhat scant, would have to be made to sound positive. He knew the proper names and nicknames for the fellows, Growler, Sailor, and Twister, but not for the girl. Mr and Mrs Jones had known it, but couldn't remember. There was a nickname only for her – or maybe it was her real name: she was just Millie.

And, the fifth one, Steven Thwaite, he had no nickname, but he'd left them after a very short career. This was the boy who chose to stay at home and refused the American move. Hopefully he would be traceable; could still be around – in Britain maybe? He wasn't local nowadays, or at least he wasn't in the phone book for this area. Maybe some clue would surface from one of the others.

Millie was the only girl in the group – wait, that's not true. She was the first female vocalist. She lasted quite a few years before another took her place – Sadie Truman was the replacement – there were no leads for Millie at all. He had nothing on Sadie, the second girl, either but, if the swop of girl singers happened in the States as seemed likely, Sadie Truman probably wasn't from Newingsworth anyway, she would most likely be American.

So, if he was to move further forward, he would have to find the London Agent – his best lead. Should he search the London telephone directory? That would be a big task – better avoided.

Though, if Twister is supposed to be an Agent for musicians, he is bound to have a web site. Now, that would be easier to access than the London telephone directory. It would just mean sitting at the computer again.

Easy-peasy...

Sally admired Derek's approach to his research. A bit bad tempered tonight maybe, but it was all positive so far, and he had not become disheartened. So much better than on previous tries but clearly, to her eyes, any success he was having this time was with thanks to having a supportive wife.

Would he succeed in completing this book? She hoped he would. His last try had been a total failure. "How a male can be affected by wearing female clothes." That was the original title attempt – not exactly snappy, though it was changed to: "He dressed to thrill".

Then he had to spoil it by thinking personal experience was an essential. That's where he'd gone wrong – big style, squeezing into her stuff – the cheek of him, her clothes; she'd put an abrupt stop to that. His project went no further after he ruined both her clothes and her best shoes.

So, her silent wish this time was – Derek, please do nothing silly, and no foolish attempts either to get together with that vixen, Sophie Clerkenwell-Brown. That would really open up old wounds.

Sally wouldn't put it past him to try to set up an advance publishing deal. The need to interest a publisher in this story was already something he'd mentioned but, as far as Sally knew, he had one contact only in the book publishing world, the wrong one –

Sophie Clerkenwell-Brown. Sally vowed, as she gazed lovingly across at her Derek, typing away enthusiastically on the computer keyboard, that she would flay him alive if she found he'd been back in touch with her.

He couldn't be trusted near that one. Whereas Derek's problem had been the putting-on of female clothes, that vixen was an expert at taking them off. However, the most annoying part for Sally: Sophie Clerkenwell-Brown – without clothes – looked absolutely fantastic.

32

To reduce the boredom of Angie's day, they invested in a new laptop. It would be specifically Angie's but if Sam required it for some schoolwork he would be permitted to use it. They also took out a telephone and internet package, and though it seemed expensive to Sam, this access to the Web was to be the answer to Angie's unhappiness.

She was skilled with computers. To her it was simply another communication tool. Part of her school curriculum, of course, so she had learned early, but it had also been an essential work-tool when she'd been managing the restaurant. It was such an easy way to order items and such a simple method of payment, inputting a card number – painless...

Unfortunately, she developed some bad habits. Therefore it had also been agreed with Sam, before the actual purchase of this new laptop, that she would resist the temptation to be constantly buying stuff for herself on line – a failing back in Detroit. It had given overly easy access to almost anything she wanted and, at that time, could afford, and all obtainable from the comfort of home.

Back then she had money from her own earnings, money to spend. That was what it was for; otherwise it would be sitting in a bank somewhere gathering dust, wouldn't it? Being on her own, when Sam crossed over the big pond to Newingsworth, the brakes came off for Angelina. In Detroit he was the one who'd had to discourage her spending so, for many months, with Sam far away, her skill at doing just that became so much slicker.

Buttercup Avenue, Newingsworth, was different. This is where she lived now, with one wage only; Sam's, paid into the bank once a month and mostly needed for daily living. Of course she would rather be working and earning as well. More cash would be nice, but the right job obviously was not there for her. Or, was it? If pressured, she would probably have to admit as far as job-hunting was concerned she was being overly choosy.

She was outside, on her way home. It was late morning and beautiful in Buttercup Avenue, and in the sky only a few sparse clouds could be seen, high and fluffy and presenting no threat to the day, but rather than walk about in the fresh air, or sit out in the park in the pleasant sunshine, Angie was hurrying back indoors to switch on the computer.

Who could blame her? She had hardly used the new internet service properly yet, and this was her chance. Anyway, today's visit to Bisko's was completed in record time, and surprisingly, without incident. All that needed to be done had been done, so she was free to sit inside, in front of a computer monitor if she wanted to, and surely without criticism.

Shopping every day for her was not necessary but it was easy to pop into Bisko's when passing because, whether she wanted to or not, she was walking everywhere and exercising in the fresh air. Who needs a car anyhow, she thought. She didn't mind walking; she had a trim figure and wanted to retain it, but without tedious visits to a gym. That had been tried back in Detroit and written it off. She found them to be boring places ...machine-driven hellholes, populated by fanatical, crazy people, where the smell of stale sweat permeated the air. So, her current fitness regime had to be better.

She walked to town by different routes every day, there and back – well, a varied route would be a better description. There were limitations to how far she could stray to reach her destination, so there had to be some repetition, but with minor variations. Something, however, was now more regular in her behaviour. She had developed the habit of glancing over her shoulder, often, on the return journey.

It was hard to forget how she'd been stalked in the supermarket, although it hadn't been so bad recently. The old guy was almost always there and when she glared at him he took the hint, disappearing from view, but she couldn't get rid of the suspicion that one of these times he would tail her all the way home. Anyway, the glancing around was good for her neck muscles!

Now, sitting at home with her laptop open and deciding which shopping site to visit, she was pretending she didn't feel guilty, trying hard to forget her promise to Sam, but failing, which seriously annoyed her. He was controlling her, and that wasn't acceptable. What could take her mind off shopping-on-line? Aaaaah, yes... She could e-mail Mom...

'To: millicent@good.sort From: Angie&Sam@Bt-deal.co.uk
Hi MOM, I've been meaning to contact you this way for a long time but we've only just gotten round to getting the laptop. It's so much easier writing real words instead of text-speak – I've never been very good at that. You're able to beat me every time. Oh, how I miss you Mom, and all my friends and the old place. I wish now I'd never left. I shouldn't have listened to Sam. I can't find a good job here, I've not much money, I've made no new friends and I'm really miserable, but, how are you keeping? How's business and how is Maggie succeeding? She is probably filling the gap I left very admirably. I'm sure I made a very good choice and that she's doing absolutely wonderfully, and you don't even miss me, (but deep down I desperately hope you do).
I must tell you about my STALKER, my very own, godawful, old man STALKER. Every time I go out shopping, there he is I tell you, gawping out at me from behind the shelves. He even brought his wife along to look. Sam tried to chase them off but they are stubborn.
We were going to try to get a little video to take to the local police showing them tailing me, as you suggested, but instead Sam gotten nearly blinded when the old guy set off a flash in his face and took Sam's photo instead. I can imagine he goes round doing that with all the visitors to this country, and has a special room where he goes and sits and gazes at the frightened looks he captures on film – THE PERVERT.

He leapt out the other day, and said hello and frightened the goddam life out of me. If he'd said, or done anything else, I would have screamed for the manager, but I couldn't when he'd just said hello, could I? He just walked off with a stupid grin on his ugly face.

Sam sends his love. I am not certain I'll stay here, Mom. Sam likes it but I feel I don't belong. You might find me, in the not too distant future, knocking on your door. I didn't know what being homesick felt like – but I do now. Please reply as soon as you can. I need to feel your love, even if it is only through this machine.

Your ever luvvin daughter, Angelina xxxxxxxxxx'

33

Andy Woodstock was feeling smug, and no wonder. He was now doing the job he was born to do in the Metropolitan Police Force, and he was a best-selling author, and he had a cracker of a girl-friend, so why shouldn't he be feeling smug?

Yes, he may still only be a constable, happily pounding the beat, but one who was recognising the unsavoury happenings in the higher echelons, and one who knew there would be gaps to be filled in the organisation very soon. Promotion would come...

Inside his smug head, he has the capability of writing another great novel, he knew, and it would be just a matter of timing – of his choosing of course... A 'free spirit' was the way he liked to think of himself, drifting wherever his fancy took him; in truth, he was a follow-the-rules sort of guy.

Being given clear instructions and forced to adhere to strict routines with a partner to keep him on the straight and narrow was definitely the best thing for Andy's police duties. He liked meeting people, and in his job he was meeting new people all the time. What could be better than the freedom of wandering the streets legitimately every day in the fresh air – even though it was London's fresh air.

Being on the beat, the free football matches were a little extra he could enjoy, except that he had to attend in uniform, and be on duty, and have to wade into the usual supporters' fracas afterwards but only when it got serious. When it happened he vigorously advocated bringing in the water cannon. That was the answer and he would volunteer to drive it – a speedy solution. Luckily for the football supporters, the choice of the water-cannon was way beyond his responsibilities, but it was that sort of stuff that made him feel his job was always fun. Ups and downs, life was full of them.

There was definitely more action in London and every new day was exciting. He was a relatively new boy here in the big city, but not without previous experience, and certainly no new boy to the force. He had seen duty back in his home town. His many years in the Newingsworth and Slatterfoot District Police Force should eventually stand him in good stead for promotion here in the Met, surely?

His record card in HQ.HR files showed he'd done his bit as a Uniformed Police Officer in Newingsworth, and secured promotion to Plain Clothes as a Detective Constable in that division also. That had lasted for several years, and then it was back to Uniforms once again for a short time, before transferring down south, to the big city.

Now, looking at his record sheet, one would assume that he was the one who chose this unusual start/stop career path – not totally correct.

The transfer South was wisely submitted and approved before his boss realised fully the cods-wallop DC Woodstock's last investigation at Newingsworth, had become. The official decision not to pursue the matter of Woodstock's 'failings', was perhaps influenced a little by the bets. Not thinking things through properly first, as usual, Andy Woodstock unwisely made a bet with the small squad of detectives, his mates, that in no time at all he would crack the case he was about to start. Everyone in the team, including his boss, bet heavily against him, and Andy lost!

After his lousy performance of duties, there should have been disciplinary procedures; however, that can be messy, and embarrassing questions tend to be asked of the man who should have been in charge. To an outsider, the facts might look dodgy: a special transfer of personnel; betting on the outcome of a case with money changing hands, even though it was all Andy's; and the question of why the idiot was promoted to Detective in the first place.

All this might have looked a little odd to superior officers; the perception being that the transfer was influenced by blackmail, or bribery, or even simply to dumping dodgy staff on the Met. So Andy

Woodstock's boss, satisfied at having received his share of the winnings promptly, turned a blind eye to his man's inadequacies and gave him a good reference. It was the right thing to do. With so much dirty linen currently being exposed in the force, there was no sense in possibly creating more...

Hence, not only was Andy enjoying his current job, he was now down south enjoying a new lifestyle. There he was, sitting in the luxury of his girl-friend's apartment, which was now his home too. As for his girl-friend, he couldn't believe his luck. She was a beauty called Sophie, Sophie Clerkenwell-Brown, and, being in publishing, had been the one who had made it happen for his book. It was selling like hot-cakes, and even he couldn't understand why?

He certainly wasn't complaining.

Andy had the place all to himself. It was a pleasant feeling knowing he had no working shifts for another forty-eight hours. With a lazy day on his own, Sophie being at work, he could do whatever he fancied. He fancied writing another masterpiece.

He'd done it with his first attempt, 'The Door Creaked', but heaven knows how! His very own detective adventure story had failed to impress even him, but it was selling like mad. So, now was the time for his hero, Andy Pandoletti, to be given another challenge. This time, he would be involved with a Mongolian Princess, rescuing her from a lift that was jammed between floors, in the Hilton Hotel, while being chased along the corridors by Mongolian Warriors. Yes, that would do for starters.

Pandoletti, his personal creation, a fictional heroic private detective, had done him proud so far; and he was about to detect again ...but, before starting on another masterpiece, emails to be checked and surprise – one from Derek, Derek Toozlethwaite – and Derek needed help.

He had come to him!

Wasn't that nice, and from that very first glance he realised that if he was going to aid his good friend, it was his brilliant powers of detection which would require to be revitalised. Forgot about the new book for the moment, concentrate on real stuff...

Andy considered Derek to be his friend. However, why this was had never been clear to Derek. It was only a few years ago that Derek and Sally were considered to have been thieves, wrongly accused by DC Andy 'Pandy' Woodstock. To a great extent they were the cause of his transfer back to Uniforms. Yet, the next time, out of the blue, when Andy met Derek, he was a Constable again, and, for no obvious reason to Derek, he became a 'mate'.

To any sane individual, Andy's reasoning for the friendship might appear somewhat obscure...

Point one: he credited Derek as having been the catalyst causing a return to the job he was most comfortable doing – pounding the beat as a Uniformed Constable. Point two: he gave Derek the credit for causing him to meet and rescue Sophie. His brave action had immediately made PC Woodstock a hero in Sophie's eyes and they soon became close. At the same time her interest in his book was sparked ...all accomplished in the space of one evening, leading to his present comfortable life.

Even if Andy's logic as to the reason for the friendship was explained a second time to Derek, it is likely he would still be baffled. To Derek, it appeared he was being thanked for being lucky to have a mother-in-law who lived in Cloverton, and for making a fool of a police detective along the way which therefore messed up the man's promising career!

Yes, very strange ...

Andy read the email in his hand.

Now, Derek needed help – and had turned to his old mate, Andy – who was touched. So, in his spare time, and maybe during a little of his working time too, he would figuratively don his Sherlock Holmes' cape, borrow a second-hand violin to play forlornly, and search for an elusive male hiding somewhere in this giant metropolis, which was London.

It seemed that Derek had tried his own methods of searching, and found nothing. This man was apparently an Agent, based here in the capital looking after musicians and singers, and Derek had been surprised at finding no website carrying this man's name. Was he in hiding perhaps?

Andy recognised immediately that this man was a Secret Agent... The alternative was that maybe the Agency had its own name, but that was what this ace ex-detective was about to find out...

Having contacts in a situation like this can be a godsend, he realised, and he had quite a few nowadays, particularly in the CID. These were the boys with ears in all the right places. Drugs, prostitution, people trafficking, inter-gang warfare, etc, yes, CID were the guys having even more fun than he was. They knew all the strip joints, real agencies and pseudo agencies, and would have a large file for easy reference.

He hadn't had too many clues to give them. To date, all that Derek had gleaned was on the email. Andy translated the information into his own language, a detective's language...

SUSPECT – adult male; name – James Hoist; 'Rabid Revenge' – a band apparently that this adult male was involved in years ago (never heard of it, Andy thought); 'Twister' – a nickname used by the suspect when he was in said band (a perfect name for a Mr Ten per Cent, Andy also thought); probably owns the bass guitar he played in said band; age about 48 to 50, but being in showbiz, probably claiming to be about six years younger (he may even be wearing a disguise, Andy considered); currently is suspected of running an agency for musicians, singers, and other layabouts.

It took three days for the suspect to be traced. The CID pulled out all the stops under the circumstances, it being an unofficial, 'you scratch my back' type of enquiry to help a colleague in the force. The email was replied to immediately – top priority.

Unfortunately it arrived on the day Andy did absolutely nothing associated with work, which included checking emails. It arrived on his rest day and Andy believed rest to be important. He always avoided keeping up to date with the outside world on these days. This email must have arrived, without him realising, when he was sitting with a beer in his hand enjoying the repeats of 'Columbo' on Sky, two days before; now he was a detective to look up to...

So ...five days later Andy discovered the result, unread, on his lap top.

He would have reacted personally and promptly if he had known earlier because it was a job he was doing for his good pal, but that wasn't to be, and unfortunately, finding it early in the morning, just when he was leaving to go back on shift, caused him mixed emotions.

There was gratitude and pride for the Metropolitan CID to have given it top priority, his team and what a team, and guilt at not having found it earlier for Derek plus frustration at not being able to take the immediate action himself, to send it to his dear friend. If he did, he would be late and in trouble with the sergeant. If only he had checked his laptop before.

As it was, the job would have to be sub-contracted, but would Sophie oblige and send it for him? He would have to ask.

Sophie was still lying spread-eagled in the king-size bed, looking warm and sensual, as only Sophie could. This was distinctly off-putting for a uniformed policeman who had to leave for work. Looking at her almost made him forget why he had returned to the bedroom.

Would she send Derek Toozlethwaite an email – please? All she had to do was type the message on his behalf, giving the name and number Derek needed to enable him to contact the traced 'suspect'.

He realised it was a lot to ask of her, because Derek was his friend and he should be doing it himself – she had never met him. As far as Andy knew, Sophie was only vaguely aware who his friend was; she might even refuse to send this to a stranger ...but he was wrong on several counts.

Of course, Sophie knew Derek – very well in fact – not something she'd mentioned to Andy. Yes, she told him, she would be delighted to do that little task for her lover boy.

So, he left the flat feeling happy to have completed the cycle. This would strengthen his friendship with Derek...

It was late morning when Sophie arose and had a luxurious bath, followed by a relaxing breakfast, determined to make the most of her non-working day.

By early afternoon, she was ready to sort-of work, and the email to be sent came into that category. Andy had scribbled out the facts to be transmitted, so it would be easy to type those, and then she decided she could include her very own nice little message – to Derek.

So, she did ...and in no time the cursor was over the 'send' icon; she simply pressed it, and the deed was done.

Surely Derek would not have forgotten her.

34

The first letter in a plain envelope with the address in large stylised block capitals, when received two days before, was delivered to the Gazette Office marked specifically for Sally Toozlethwaite.

She'd looked at the content, then realising what it actually was, quickly hid it away from the view of those currently in the office, Derek, Spider and Rob. The mild surprise – her initial reaction when she opened it – rapidly changed to incredulity when she thought about it. Who would wish to send her a letter like this?

The capital letters spelled out –

TELL YOUR HUSBAND TO STOP.

Stop what, she asked herself? This is someone having a joke. It wasn't signed. Derek's not being doing anything wrong ...or has he? This sort of nonsense had never happened to her before. Is this a poison pen letter? She was aware of what they were, but only from stories she'd read. Do people really send them? Well, I suppose they must do – I've got one, but why me?

Sally was rattled, but attempted to display only her normal calm unruffled exterior. Who would want to cause trouble? This was implying that Derek was misbehaving. No chance. This was wrong.

Derek wouldn't misbehave again, not Derek. He wouldn't dare...?

That nonsense with Sophie Clerkenwell-Brown was in the past. Derek had explained all about it being a misunderstanding anyway, and was believed – eventually. That was over and done with.

And then the other letter arrived!

Spider sorted out the post in his usual highly efficient manner immediately on delivery shortly after nine. She found it hard to belief that a second letter, recognisable by the writing on the envelope, should be landing on her desk.

"Your boyfriend's written again?" smiled Spider as he placed it in front of her. She hoped he hadn't noticed how she froze at the sight of it, and then turned red. She left it where it was, afraid to open it in case it proved her guess to be correct.

It was – another poison-pen letter, but not initially understandable...

IT'S A DO-IT-YOURSELF VERSION THIS TIME.

Out of the envelope tumbled a lot of small pieces of paper, each with one word in the same large print. She stuffed them back in the envelope. This was her problem. She would have to deal with it herself, particularly if it involved Derek...

She arrived home well before Derek, which was not unusual but tonight she'd made certain. With relief she found the house empty, Hammy hadn't appeared either, so she had the house to herself. The contents of this new letter perturbed her, and the message, whatever it may be, was not yet even known to her. She needed peace and quiet to work it out, she had to know...

The many pieces of paper were spread over the table. She counted them – thirteen. Oh-oh, that's unlucky, but then again receiving a poison-pen letter is not exactly lucky either, especially one which has to be sorted into an order to be understood.

She laid the bits on the table, face up, and studied them.

HE   HUSBAND   YOUR
THINGS   FINGERS   GET

UNWISE   DOING   BURNED

WILL   IS   CONTINUES   IF

Right, here goes. She never had been good at doing this sort of thing and hated jigsaws. She did not consider herself creative or imaginative. Doing as she was told, and following instructions she could do very efficiently, but not much else. But wait... That's not true. When she thought about it, she was the one who did the organising at the office, and when Rob's kids had to be looked after, who thought up the various games and activities to keep them amused? She did.

So, she shouldn't be totally incapable of solving this...

YOUR   UNWISE   FINGERS

GET   THINGS   BURNED

IF   HUSBAND   IS   WILL

HE   CONTINUES   DOING

So, how does that look? Not bad for starters. But where's the poisonous message? Which of these words are supposed to hurt me – I can't cook? Well, that's not news... 'If husband is Will...'

Has it been sent to the wrong person? My husband is Derek...

No, it was clearly addressed to me.

I'll try again...

IF   YOUR   BURNED   HUSBAND

CONTINUES   HE   WILL

GET   UNWISE   FINGERS

DOING   THINGS

She was getting somewhere because that seemed a little more menacing, more what she expected it should be, but she was left with an 'IS'. She had only used twelve words, so, she shuffled them, yet again...

YOUR   HUSBAND   IS

DOING   UNWISE   THINGS

FINGERS   WILL   GET   BURNED

IF   HE   CONTINUES

Well, that is much better ...it makes some sense now, but is it really telling me something, she asked herself.

Is it warning of some danger?

No... Derek doesn't do 'dangerous'. He's going nowhere in a hurry with that book, but that's only frustration, and it may be unwise that he doesn't have any time for anything else – unless this is something to do with the people he's contacting. Is he getting himself into trouble? Surely he would have said.

There was a noise at the front door. Derek was back. She quickly swept the little bits of paper into the open envelope, and back went the envelope into her handbag.

"You look a bit flustered," said Derek, "Is everything all right, Sal?"

"Of course!" was the curt reply.

35

She was first home again. Well, she was nearly first home. She beat Derek, but Hammy had beaten her, and his presence startled her; in fact, everything did at the moment, particularly since she'd starting receiving the 'letters'.

These days Hammy was just appearing for meals as it suited him. He was becoming an irregular visitor now, living more at the caravan than he had been. His 'just appearing' was mildly annoying, but she made no comment to him, and she was probably more aware of the change of pattern because of the letters. The letters were making her irritable, so she mustn't take it out on him...

Milder weather, Sally presumed to be the main reason for him staying away, although, eating out was another suspicion, maybe even eating out – with a friend.

Hammy had said nothing recently about Thelma, or about that Sunday evening visit. It didn't seem right to question him outright, she felt, so she just watched for the signs. It would all become apparent soon enough, but to ask him was sorely tempting ...and anyway, it wasn't something he should be keeping to himself, she considered. He should be sharing good news, so how could she find out some more?

If things became desperate she could always make him talk...

She visualised tying Hammy to a chair and then, slowly, pulling a single hair from his head. It wouldn't take more than about four hairs being removed, and he would spill the beans. She was confident of that. Hammy had a great head of hair, particularly for a man of his advanced years, but he was terrified of losing it. He could not stomach the thought of being bald.

It was a different Hammy tonight though – here he was, and on time and he'd brought back pre-packed meals for the three of them, and a bottle of wine. This could be the announcement, was her immediate thought.

She was dying of curiosity about him and Thelma. Her mum was reluctant to ask her sister-in-law, even though they were living in the same house and she was seeing her every day. Thelma wasn't offering any information of that nature either, in fact, she had not mentioned even meeting Hamish.

Normally, Sally's first task when she arrived home would be to prepare the meal, unless of course it was Derek's turn. It was to have been her turn tonight, but Hammy has beaten her to it and taken over completely, much to her delight. However, his attempt to have the meals hot and ready was failing due to Derek not having arrived yet, so, unfortunately, what were steaming packages some moments ago were sitting getting cold. Still, a little bit of reheating should do them no harm.

There she sat, fidgeting. What to do while they waited for Derek? Hammy fussed about in the kitchen; Sally fidgeted some more...

Should she look at the third letter she'd received? That should have been done when the office had been quiet this afternoon, but she'd missed the chance. It was very difficult to remain calm. Oh, what will it say this time – something nasty, no doubt? This is very upsetting... No, she couldn't look now, not with Hammy in the house.

There must be something she could do while waiting for Derek...

Check for emails!

On went the computer to be informed 'There will be a short delay'. The message appeared 'currently updating your programmes...' so she twiddled her thumbs a little longer.

Derek was getting later and later every night it seemed, or had she been leaving earlier? She wasn't sure on that, so she wouldn't criticise him. It can become a habit, criticising each other, she told herself – not something she or Derek indulged in, thank you very much.

Ah, all updated at last, and into the home page she went; nothing too interesting on that, well, other than war, floods, famine and pestilence, as usual. It's the emails I'm after and there they are – four new ones.

She always felt a tiny flutter of excitement before she opted to open the email file. The anticipation of a really exciting one was always there. She wanted to be surprised by one that said: 'YOU have won the Lottery Millions, you lucky girl.' That would make her forget poison-pen letters for sure. She and Sweaty could squander it together; have a wild time! And Sweaty wouldn't need to write any silly books then. Oh dear, I'm forgetting, she told herself – I promised to stop calling him Sweaty... Now let's see, what is there...? *'Marks and Spencer offer you a 10% reduction on all ladies clothing starting from tomorrow...'*

Duly noted, and very tempting, but the nearest store was miles away and not worth the effort, next...

'Our files tell us that your house insurance is due next month and we are pleased to offer you a new starter deal of 20% less than you are currently paying, whatever it may be...'

Yes, you pay twice as much next year to make up for it, she thought cynically. She had not been thrilled, so far.

'Are you a wine connoisseur? Of course you are, but if you are not, you could be – by buying our wines at the introductory special price offer. You get 10% off all wines over £25 per bottle, together with a free bottle opener, and an opportunity to win...'

Oh yes please, I'll have a lorry load which will be here tomorrow morning, because you have a lightning super delivery service too – and I'll pay using my Lottery Winnings...

Next...

'Dear put-upon-cuddly-wuddly Derek, I hope you haven't forgotten me. Andy asked me to send you the answer you were looking for, and I thought I would include a little message from yours truly, Sophie – your hot little friend – your 'damsel in distress'. Our time together was short but sweet. Couldn't go the distance that day, could you? How I remember seeing you lying there, hot and exhausted... You are still with Sally, I presume; she wouldn't let a good guy like you out of

her clutches, if she's wise – but if she did ...who knows? Anyway, the message was that Mr Twister, or whatever he's called, can be contacted on his telephone number +440205793579 – it's The Fort Knights' Music Agency, apparently. I think that's all he said, but what about your book? Have you finished it yet? Did you see what I did for Andy's? I'm sure I could do a lot for you. You are going to contact me the moment you do finish it, I hope. We could go far together – if you are willing... Lots of love and kisses, Sophie xxx.'

Hammy came back into the room, and looked across to where Sally was seated. He wondered what had caused the pained look on her face ...and she was a funny colour!

36

Sam came home promptly every night.

"Hi Honey," he would call from the hall, "I'm home, Sweetie Pie," in the same way, every night.

Tonight was no different.

"I'm in here, Sam," was the standard reply, but it was said mournfully tonight. It had been another bad day – he could tell.

Mom hasn't replied. It would be early afternoon back in Detroit, plenty of time to have seen the message and to have sent something back. Angie was agitated. Why hadn't her mom replied? Has she forgotten to switch on the machine? Is she not speaking to me? Is she ill? Oh my God, what if she's ill? I am over here and she is over there, we are hundreds of miles apart.

"Mom hasn't come back to me. I sent the message this morning, and she hasn't replied. I think she is unwell," she wailed.

"She wouldn't think to look at the computer. She is a busy woman remember. You were the one who commandeered the computer at her house, if I remember correctly, weren't you?"

He could tell he wasn't reassuring her. When she got something into her head that she thought was correct, there was never anything he could do to change her mind.

"What's for eating, Honey?" he asked gently.

"Food...? Oh! I'd forgotten about your meal..." said in such a sad little voice.

"It's ok, Honey," he replied, "We could eat out tonight. We haven't done that here yet."

"But Mom...?"

"She'll be alright, you'll see. Send her a text. Tell her to look at the computer."

"Sam, you are some guy," she said, immediately brightening up, "Why didn't I think of that?"

They walked arm in arm, in the pleasant early evening air, away from Buttercup Avenue towards the centre of the town. Neither had any idea where they might find an eating place, this had never been a consideration before, so, they were pleased when they reached 'The Old Indian Curry House,' established 1993.

It seemed all right, looking from the outside, though Sam had the sudden and horrid foreboding that they were about to walk in and come face to face with the old guy who had been stalking Angie – maybe even him and his missus ...but that wasn't to be the case.

They entered.

The little bell above the door gave a tinkle which brought a young Indian lady to meet them. The colours used for the decor of strong pink and pale pink on the walls, and pale green carpeting, with white tablecloths, didn't quite gel with Sam's tastes for decoration of a restaurant, but Angie made no comment which he took as a good sign. The place wasn't busy, three or four couples spread about, and a table with seven boys. As he passed the boys' table, he realised with a sinking feeling, that he knew them, and they knew him.

"Good evening, Sir – Mr Walters – Sir," they chorused.

"Evening," he mumbled, and felt himself reddening. They had been here for a while, it appeared, having had a meal, and some beers, and were even less inhibited than when in the classroom.

"Is this your wife, Sir? Are you going to introduce us, Sir?" they goaded.

"Err, no, it's not my wife."

"Ooooooh..." they chorused.

"Who's wife is it then?" shouted one, and they all laughed...

"She's not my wife – and she's not anyone else's wife. She's my partner. We're not married – yet..."

Sam realised that seeing him being made uncomfortable by this crowd was amusing Angie. She was laughing at his squirming, and that made him feel even less capable of dealing with the situation.

"It's been nice to meet you all," Angie interjected, "but my partner has been working hard all day, as you should probably know, and is desperate to eat now, aren't you darling? It has been a pleasure meeting all you sweet boys. We may see you later..." and at that, she blew them a kiss, turned and guided Sam to follow the waitress who had been patiently standing.

As they moved away, Sam heard a stage whisper from one of the lads, which he presumed, due to a few beers having been consumed, to be considerably louder than had been intended.

"Yea.... He made a good choice, didn't he? American too... She would be eminently shaggable, she would..." and the rest of the group were in total agreement with their extremely observant spokesperson.

What should Sam do? He wasn't supposed to have heard that. Does he reprimand them as a conscientious schoolteacher, out of hours, and cause a scene? Maybe Angie hadn't heard... He glanced at her. She had a slight smile on her lips.

They carried on and sat down opposite each other, now out of earshot of the boys. The waitress handed them each a menu. Sam looked down the list, unsure what he should have. Angie was looking at the card in front of her, but she wasn't reading the words. She was thinking...

"Sam, what does eminently shaggable mean?" she asked.

Oh no, she did hear them. They will suffer tomorrow in class, I promise, he said to himself.

"Eminently shaggable? Hmm..." he played for time.

He had been in the UK long enough now to recognise most of the language of the school playground, and toilets, or should that be the gutter?

"It's eh ...a complimentary term used by British schoolboys. It means you are highly desirable."

She looked across at him and smiled. Sam was uncertain of the meaning of that smile. It was sort of like the Mona Lisa one... Yea, that's what it was ...enigmatic. Her menu appeared to become interesting to her again, but that same smile remained.

Eminently shaggable, she was saying to herself, they said I was eminently shaggable. She raised her eyes and looked again at the lovely man sitting in front of her, and smiled to him, a real, almost going to burst out laughing with happiness, smile. She liked these boys. That was one of the nicest things anyone had said about her since she had come to this goddam country.

Suddenly the world seemed a nicer place...

"Let's eat," she said to Sam, and smiled again, as she reached across and squeezed his hand.

37

Opening her e-mails, Angie felt a surge of pleasure to find that Mom at long last had replied. She was the one person who would understand how her favourite, and only, daughter was feeling. Other than the high spot last night, the moment of sheer joy in the Indian restaurant, her mood had been sinking quickly back once more into a pretty miserable state. Yes, the evening out had had a moment to savour when the young guy had said... Uhmmm ... but otherwise...

Mom's wise words would help her out of this deep despair; she cared about people. Her mom was wonderful in that way and now there, the wise words were displayed in front of her.

'To: Angie&Sam@Bt-deal.co.uk
From: millicent@good.sort
Dear Angie babe, I am so sorry that I haven't had a chance to send back an email sooner, but I have been so busy. My Alberto has been takin' up all my time. He is a wonderful guy...'

Who the hell is Alberto?

'You won't know Alberto. We just met last week, but it's the real thing, Honey. You will love him. Get ready to have a new daddy in the not too distant future. I told him that you weren't feeling so hot in your new place, but he says that it'll all blow over in no time at all. He says a big hug from him would make you feel real good – he is that kinda guy. He knows just how bad it is for you because this man

has travelled the country and he has known low times, and he says you just have to shrug your shoulders hard, and shake off the blues... He has seen it all.'

Yea, Mom, you have known him only one week and he knows everything, does he? I don't want to know what he thinks. I want your thoughts on my problem. What do you think Mom? Please tell me you want me back home and I will leave here immediately. I could return and work at your side and never think of leaving again. Sam can lose himself in his work. I can't ...and I do not want to know about your fancy pants, fly-by-night new man-friend...

'Alberto is going to take some of the weight from my shoulders and manage the restaurant for me soon. Maggie is doing ok but she is not management material and, unfortunately, she keeps making mistakes in the orders. She does not get on well with the chef, or the rest of the staff, either, according to Alberto. I'm scared I might lose them, particularly Charlie. Losing such a good chef, for sure, would be a catastrophe and a half. Did you show Maggie how to do the ordering? She says you didn't. Alberto is going to try and help her. He's a genius at that sort of thing, you know, and he knows how to deal with the chef. He says getting tough with him is the only way, and that's what he is gonna do at the weekend. He is a marvel...'

Oh Mom, thought Angie, you are getting carried away. You weren't even interested in guys when I was with you. For all those years you have been happy on your own, and suddenly this jerk appears and he is God's gift... And yes, I did teach her how to order...

'And, I know I shouldn't tell you this, but I can't keep it to myself. When we're in bed... Wow... You know what I mean. Him bein' so young and havin' so much energy, he is unstoppable. At my age, it is fun and a novelty – but a bit tiring... Every night we are at it, so you will know why I haven't had time – or the energy – to reply to your email.'

He is a young man? Oh Mom, what are you doing to yourself? How young is he?

'He may be only in his mid-twenties, but he has a maturity way beyond his years – he has had so much experience. He tells me he will be doubling the takings in a month. He can tackle anything.'

Mom, he's half your age!

Angie was in the wrong place, and in the wrong mood to absorb these revelations without feeling even worse than she had been feeling. Should she phone and tell her mom to quit while she was still winning? No, maybe not a wise idea – it wouldn't be taken as kind advice. Tempers would get riled at both ends of a phone call – Angie knew unfortunately that she suffered exactly the same short fuse her mom did when it came to calm and reasoned discussion.

Suddenly Angie realised that she was no longer wrapped up in her own miseries. The situation had dramatically changed. She was rapidly becoming embroiled in her mother's troubles...

Her mother was describing this guy, Alberto, as being both her saviour in a time of need, and an animal who was exhausting her – fast, and he was about to be handed the control of the restaurant. That wasn't a wise idea.

What should she do to help her mother and, being on other side of the Atlantic, how could it be done? This was a challenge to go at.

Angelina felt invigorated by these new revelations, yet, in the pit of her stomach, she felt decidedly sick...

38

She held her temper and shut off the computer, but it didn't stop her sitting fuming. She glowered at Hammy, who came through from the kitchen only to ask when Derek might be home. Luckily he recognised the warning signs; a time for kid gloves. He smiled and tried to make light conversation to pass the time and brighten her mood as they waited for Derek – but he failed –totally. Thank goodness he was thick skinned!

During the meal, the announcement Sally expected from Hammy didn't materialise, but, the way she was feeling, it would have been an anti-climax if he had mentioned Thelma. Sally now had other things to think about.

When Derek eventually arrived, they sat and ate, and Sally tried not to choke on each mouthful – nothing to do with the quality of the food that Hammy had been thoughtful enough to buy, and reheat – all to do with that cheeky bitch, Sophie Clerkenwell-Brown.

Imagine her making contact like that with my husband, on the pretext of passing on a message... That hussy!

Sally was fuming.

How dare she? Imagine her trying to embroil poor innocent Derek again – especially when he is trying so hard to progress his new story line. The bare-faced cheek of her! He would not want to become involved with someone like that again, not after the last time. Derek knew he was in the wrong because Sally had told him in no uncertain terms – and he hadn't been given the option of arguing.

She continued fuming inside. He knew it would do him no good to get involved with that young blonde female publisher, again, didn't he? He didn't need the help of Sophie what's-her-name. He could succeed in some other way... How dare she contact him again – totally out of the blue!

Or ...was it really unexpected?

Yes – it must have been, mustn't it? He wouldn't have been making secret contact with her, would he? No, of course not ...but, there was still another letter...

It had not been opened it yet. She should have looked at it in the office, because the printing on the envelope had been recognisable. If only she'd taken the plunge there and then it would have been settled. It had remained sealed all day while she hoped she would be proved wrong about the contents. It couldn't possibly be another of 'these', could it?

Trying to convince herself, but failing, she was now sitting there, chewing the same piece of meat for the umpteenth time, not knowing for certain and becoming more and more uptight, and after seeing the message this evening on the computer – it just added more fuel...

"Oh, you have an email, darling," she managed to force herself to tell Derek calmly. "I think it's from a ...from your friend ...Andy ...the policeman? I didn't really have the chance to read it," she lied.

"Oh good, it should be a lead on one of the members of the band," he replied happily. "With luck another step forward..."

Sally looked across at his face. He had never been good at telling lies, at least, not without the signs being obvious to her, but tonight he seemed innocent enough...

After the meal, Sally went into the kitchen; Hammy went to the spare room and Derek sat down eagerly in front of the screen and began to read the good news. It took only a few lines before he began feeling decidedly queasy. Thank goodness Sally hadn't read this. He hadn't had any contact with Sophie in ages, and now this! What was she thinking of?

His mind wandered back to the moment ...that unfortunate moment – very unfortunate! This message and all of it would have to be deleted, hurriedly. Now and again Sally used this computer. If ever she were to see this, he would be dead meat... Reply before deleting though, and tell Sophie that ...but ...just a moment... Oh-oh! Something is not right.

He froze...

He sensed a presence behind him – and he had not yet cleared the screen... The hairs on the back of his neck were rising ...and with a horrible sinking feeling he realised she was reading over his shoulder!

He steeled himself awaiting the inevitable painful fatal blow to his head. Let me just go quickly, he wished, as he turned round slowly to face her...

"You urr sailin' righ' close tae the wind again, Sunshine," Hammy whispered in his ear. "Did ye no' suffer enough the last time?"

"I haven't done anything!" Derek hissed back. "It's Sophie. She's playing silly buggers..."

"Och well, ah suppose we've all got oor wee secrets..." said Hammy, wistfully, shaking his wise old head. "Och aye..."

"...But I've never even..." Derek vainly tried to protest, still hissing, as he began to defend himself – then realised he was wasting his time because Hammy wandered off to the spare room, and left him.

Derek listened. Sally was in the kitchen. He had the impression that she was trying very hard to smash as many dishes as she could. Was something wrong with her? The noise she was making was usually reserved for when she was in a bad mood, but at least she was out of the room.

Now was the time to send a reply, though he may have lost the return address having closed the screen so rapidly when Hammy surprised him. He was breathing rapidly – due to a guilty conscience, or fear? It could be almost certainly both. He opened the email system again, selected 'compose a reply,' and typed quickly...

"Dear Sophie, what a surprise to hear from you again, and thanks for the info. How could I forget you ...and your perfume! So you did it for Andy. ....And you would do it for me too, would you? That sounds good, and I would love to meet you again when I'm ready with

something fresh, but Sally wouldn't be happy. She doesn't like you as much as I do. In fact, she hates you... I must deal only with a male publisher, she has instructed. Maybe you could cross-dress and we could fool her? Only joking! But this seems like an offer I couldn't refuse – and we could maybe have another mud-bath together! I am only joking again! Very kind regards, Derek.'

It was at that moment Sally came out of the kitchen. He rapidly closed the screen, though, he wasn't sure in his panic, had he actually sent the reply or not?

"What are you doing?" she asked, although she guessed what he'd been up to.

"Nothing!" was his not too surprising response.

He was behaving as if he had something to hide this time, she observed. All the signs were there. Derek was not very skilled at being naughty – even worse at hiding the fact. Although she was undecided if the email that she'd read had been a surprise to him, or not, there was clearly no question, at this very moment he looked guilty...

She tried to behave as if she'd not even noticed and went into the bedroom. The letter – it had not yet been opened. She would have to look at it; the envelope was ripped open and the paper removed to see the writing style she'd grown to love....

'HAVE YOU FOUND OUT MORE, YET –
ABOUT HIS OTHER WOMAN?'

Sally chilled as she read it. It had been a bad day for her, a very bad day... The previous letters disturbed her, but they had been ambiguous. The email from that Sophie female, of course had only added to the suspicions, and now this. Yes, the information was quite specific – another woman.

She went back into the living room. Some questions had to be asked.

Where was he? He had gone into the garden, out of the firing line presumably. It had been a certain giveaway, the casual whistling after the lie, and scratching his left ear at the same time. He only did that when he had something to hide, something he was feeling guilty about. She knew him well... The computer, what had he been up to? When she'd come out of the kitchen, what he was typing had been closed suspiciously fast.

Sally selected the emails.

Ah yes, as suspected, there was a reply: '...*your perfume*', '...*you would do it for me too*', '*another mud-bath together*'.

Oh yes, wouldn't that be lovely, with your 'little damsel in distress', who can't forget you lying there 'hot and exhausted'. Well ...my little cuddly-wuddly husband, maybe this is something we should be discussing!

Obviously, there was only one course of action could be taken, and she decided it had to be taken right now.

"DEREK!" she yelled.

39

"This message will self-destruct in five seconds..." That was the well established security procedure which gave good service to the ever-vigilant members of 'Mission Impossible'; if only that facility had existed on his machine...

Derek sat glaring at the screen in front of him as if it was the computer's fault. The reply did go to Sophie, he now knew that for certain, but, having the knowledge that he'd pressed 'send' correctly failed to give him satisfaction – he'd omitted to press 'delete'!

Poor old Derek! She's gone again, back to her mum's – before he'd even had time to take in properly the reasons for her vanishing act. He tried pinching himself.

The tirade had started the moment he returned from the back garden.

"You know fine well what I think of that hussy and yet you're sending little love notes... *'Oh Sophie, what a surprise! Thank you so much for the information...'* I told you never to see her again, and what did you do, after you promised. Eh...?"

Sally barked it all out, giving him the full works, rattling on with arms waving and fingers pointing accusingly, until finally, "...This – in addition to all those letters! You have done it now, I'm off..."

She'd just exploded – as if this was the final straw! It was a ruddy email, nothing more and nothing less: not even a physical thing. The Sophie issue was ages ago with no contact in between and yet, a silly little email from her, and Sally goes bang!

On the previous occasions, he grudgingly admitted that he just might have deserved it, but not this time, and these letters, how could he be involved? This was the first she'd said of them. It was all so sudden – and wrong in his humble opinion. Life did not seem fair.

"Dinna worry, laddie," Hammy said, after she went. "Ye still huvv me."

Now why did Derek not feel cheered by these warm sentiments?

"Onywey, whit huvv ye been up tae this time, ya silly gowk? Ye can tell auld Hammy. Ah could dae wi' a guid laugh."

"It is not funny...!"

"Wharr ah'm standin' it is hullarious... but ah think ah know as much as you do, yerrsel'. Ah could hear a' the shoutin' that Sally wis doin'. Whit did ye expect? If ye'll no' behave yersel' that's whit happens, ye ken."

"Look I know nothing about these poison-pen letters, and as for Andy Woodstock, I contacted him, not Sophie. He should have replied. How Sophie got involved, I do not understand and she is his publisher, it said in the email? I didn't know that. Oh well, Andy ...thanks for landing me in it! And it's not fair blaming Sophie; she was only being kind – offering to help with the book!"

Hammy was struggling to suppress a grin as Derek rattled on...

"And then Sally would have to find my reply, wouldn't she?"

"Och weel, ye're goin' tae huvv tae live wi' it. Onewey, will ye be comin' back here at lunchtime? Ah can guess that Sally'll no' be back. Will ah hae the hoose tae mahsel the day?"

It was only a sort of grunting, and a 'not very happy with the world' noise that came from Derek, but Hammy interpreted the sounds as a "No..." and a "Yes..." respectively, which suited him admirably.

The two of them left the cottage at the same time, Hammy, to go along to supervise, expertly but lazily, the building work as usual, and Derek, to go to the office.

Derek was not looking forward to facing Sally's wrath again, particularly when he felt it was undeserved. It was a small consolation when it occurred to him, Spider would be suffering too.

These letters Sally had been sent, where did they come from? He certainly didn't do anything to justify them – other than the other day at the school. He saw Big Brenda, and only her.

It had been nice seeing her again. She was the one who helped him through these formative adolescent years. She taught him all about it, but then again, she had been very willing – and popular – with all the boys. The back of the bike shed was well used when he was at school, mainly for Big Brenda's tuition.

She was the only female recently he'd had any close contact with, and anyway, no one saw her snogging him, did they? Ah, wait a minute, no-one ...except the headmaster! ...But he wouldn't have... Surely Beakie would not have gone to the bother of getting his own back in this way, not after all those years, but, who knows? There was a roguish look in his eyes, Derek recalled, when he thought back to being seated in front of him.

I will ask Brenda, he decided, and dialled the school number.

"Hello," said the voice he now recognised, "This is Newingsworth High School Administration Department, Brenda speaking, and how can I be of assistance?"

"Hello," was all he needed to say.

"Sweaty..." was the immediate response, "It's you again. You can't keep away from me, can you? I hadn't seen you for years, and now I have to fight you off. So, what do you want from your Auntie Brenda this time?"

"Brenda, has the headmaster been sending poison-pen letters?"

"What?" and she laughed. "And you think I would know? Would he have asked me to type them out for him?"

"Well, he was the only one who saw us canoodling the other day, and my Sally has been sent several letters since then, each one implying that I was having an affair with someone."

"Weren't we about to have one then?" she said, with just a hint of disappointment in her voice. "Wasn't that the real reason you appeared here?"

"Stop having me on, Brenda. I'm in big trouble. My wife has left me because she believes these letters are true. If it is the headmaster who sent them after seeing us in a clinch as I suspect, I will report him, but I haven't any evidence to prove that he is the one. I hoped you could help."

"Does this mean you don't love me anymore...?"

"BRENDA!"

"All right, I'm sure it's not him, but because you've asked so nicely I'll try and help you."

At the end of the call Derek felt relieved. At least he had made an attempt, and he knew, deep down, he could rely on Brenda. Big Brenda had never let him down in the past...

Brenda sat looking at her nails. Bright red, blood red in fact and almost like claws which had sunk deep into flesh. She should have known it. That stuck-up little madam Sally was not able to take a joke – still the same as at school, wasn't she? No reason for her to have changed, but it wasn't fair to be taking it out on poor Sweaty...

"Brenda dear ...dear Brenda..."

The headmaster had come silently out of his office and was standing behind her. His hand slipped under her blouse, and she made no attempt to stop him.

"Same time tonight then?" he whispered in her ear, close enough for her to feel his hot breath.

"Yes," she replied, wary that one of the stupid school kids could walk straight in at any time, and catch them. It hadn't happened yet, but she always felt on edge that it might.

"My wife returns tomorrow but I am pleased to say that, as long as her mother stays ill, Elizabeth will be off again soon. Someone has to look after the dear old soul. I do hope the old dear doesn't die. That could spoil it for us..."

That is funny, Brenda thought, exactly my fear when he is in bed with me – the possibility of him popping his clogs when we are at it. He is no spring chicken himself. How embarrassing that would be...

40

It was a bad night for Spider. Yesterday he promised Rob that he would sleep on it but, he didn't dream of the winner of the 3.30 flat race at Epsom as hoped. He woke with a feeling of foreboding. Things felt wrong. It took longer than usual to prepare for work. Cutting himself while shaving only happened occasionally – today was an occasion. The milk was turned – now that was unusual, and he had to do without cornflakes and his milky tea for breakfast. It was dry burnt toast – on its own – he'd run out of butter.

Derek and Sally almost always cycled to work together. As soon as Sally appeared, without Derek, Spider knew – there had been another fall-out, and that meant he was about to become piggy-in-the-middle again. Did this happen in all offices, he wondered?

At his last job, Saddanbroke's Betting Shop, it had been every man for himself. No mollycoddling was allowed there. Of course, they didn't employ females, and the ones who came in personally to place bets knew what they were about.

She wasn't tearful this morning – she was raging, and they had to be told. Spider and Rob would rather not to have known, but she gave them no choice, and by the time Derek arrived they were well aware just how much of a rogue he was, and how many women were involved in his love life, and how much she was suffering since discovering this. As a consequence, Derek was met with silence and shifty looks from the two males, and daggers from the one female.

Spider in particular, found all of this a bit hard to believe. Derek seemed so docile, and not at all as described by Sally, or how he pictured a 'philandering no-good-down-and-out-womaniser' should look. However, that is exactly what Sally had said – so who was he to argue? She should know...

As usual, Spider's day began with the sorting of the mail.

Not too much this morning, but that writing was familiar. It was addressed to Sally in large block printing; another one of the several he'd handed to her recently. The last one he even joked about being another letter from her secret boyfriend, he recalled, and received a fearful look. He would be making no chirpy comments like that this morning – he could get stabbed severely, with a biro...

Spider looked over at her desk. There sat the previous letters, all together stacked neatly with the glass paperweight holding them down, placed there aggressively when she'd arrived. He hesitated. With the way she was behaving, maybe she didn't need this additional one just at the moment. He waited. She left the office to go along the corridor to powder her nose and that was when he slipped it onto the corner of her desk. When she returned, his head was well down. He didn't want to know...

The office was silent.

Derek was seated at his desk, as far from his wife as possible because that seemed best when they were working normally – at times like this, it was essential.

Sally looked at the new letter sitting there, then at the three males, but heads were down and all three were studiously concentrating on their work. No-one was looking in her direction. Reaching for the envelope was done reluctantly. Should she put it in her bag to look at it later or should she be really brave and look at it now? If she looked at it now, and it turned out to further confirm Derek's disgusting behaviour, the other two would be witnesses of the paperweight being used to smack the back of his head!

The letter was lifted. She had to blink several times to clear her eyes. There it was, in front of her – and now opened – the usual large printing that, since the first one, she couldn't stomach to look at, but forced herself to...

'DEAR MRS SALLY TOOZLETHWAITE,
IT IS WITH GREAT REGRET THAT WE HAVE TO INFORM
YOU THAT A CLERICAL ERROR OCCURRED IN OUR FILING
SYSTEM. IT WOULD APPEAR THAT THE LETTERS YOU
HAVE BEEN RECEIVING ABOUT YOUR HUSBAND SHOULD
HAVE BEEN SENT TO A DIFFERENT PERSON.
IT WAS NOT YOUR HUSBAND WHO WAS HAVING A GOOD
TIME. WE KNOW OF COURSE, BEING MARRIED TO YOU,
HAVING A GOOD TIME IS NOT A POSSIBILITY FOR THE
POOR FELLOW.
HOWEVER, WE HOPE THIS HAS NOT INCONVENIENCED
YOU IN ANY WAY AND THAT YOU WILL FORGIVE DEREK
FOR BEHAVING LIKE THE COWED GENTLEMAN HE IS'

What a load of rubbish ...and not very inventive. She looked over at the back of his head. She was rather disappointed in her husband. He could have at least conjured up a smarter way to beg forgiveness, surely... And worse still, how could he be so stupid as to think she would fall for this infantile attempt to excuse his behaviour? Who does he think he is – trying to make out he was innocent? He will not get off lightly this time.

The office was still silent. The eyes of the three males were still concentrating on the paperwork in front of them. How could they just sit there when her mind was in such turmoil? Did no one care? How dare they...?

Then it came to her, they were males, and all males are the same – males have no feelings.

41

He had no plans for lunchtime and going out with the other three today was very obviously not on. Whatever Sally told them earlier was making them treat him like a pariah. Having asked Spider what it was had resulted in his colleague looking at him coldly, and saying, "Derek, you have disappointed me; how could you be so cruel?"

Rob was curt and pushy about some new ideas for next week, and Rob being pushy was not the Rob he was used to. So, Derek was on his tod – so what? Let them all huff, he decided. They would regret it one day – when the truth came out – about the headmaster.

That thought caused him to wonder if Brenda had discovered anything yet. He couldn't be sure, but there might have been another of those letters. He'd been scared to look, but he did think that earlier this morning Sally could have been reading a piece of paper from an envelope like the letters she received before – but no – that wouldn't be likely. If it had been another letter, and even if it had been all lies, she would have tackled him again about it, surely. She would definitely have said something.

Leaving the office was a wise decision, but cycling home didn't make him feel any less gloomy. He was making his way back home on his bike to have lunch, alone. There might be less chance of indigestion if he ate at the cottage, away from the current stifling atmosphere of the office, and the silent criticism.

Crossing over the main road pushing the bike at a gap in the traffic was safer than riding it; most times it was more like a racetrack than the main road into Newingsworth. He was now walking along the quiet farm road, well away from the busy main thoroughfare, and it seemed a good chance to phone the school.

"Brenda...?"

He stopped walking for a moment.

"...Is that you, Brenda?"

"Hello again, Lover Boy," she answered chirpily.

"I wish you wouldn't talk that way, Brenda. I'm in enough trouble as it is. If Beakie were to hear you talking to me that way, it would give him more ammunition for the letters."

"What's wrong? Has she not forgiven you yet? She did get the letter, did she not?"

"What letter?"

"She should have received it today. It was to get you off the hook. I said I'd help didn't I?"

"Brenda, I don't understand. What letter? How have you helped?" he asked anxiously.

"Didn't you realise, Sweetie Pie, it wasn't the Headmaster who sent the letters – it was me. It was going to be a joke. I didn't think it would get you in trouble. Please don't be angry."

Derek couldn't think what to say. Big Brenda sent them, and now he was in big trouble thanks to her...

"Oh..." he squeaked, "No, of course I'm not angry. I... I... I..."

"Derek, do you still fancy me?" she said in a cute baby voice.

"DO NOT START AGAIN!" he yelled into the phone, and hung up.

He wanted to strike out at something but there was nothing to strike out at in the lane. The big world was infuriatingly normal. The sun was still shining. The birds chirped and twittered away in the shrubs as if nothing mattered in the world, except to sing happily.

It was only his little world which was collapsing...

He felt wobbly. Some food was needed and maybe some alcohol wouldn't go amiss if there was any left in the cottage. He picked up his bike and pushed it for the last fifty yards, and began to feel a little more at ease.

The source of the letters was now settled, but had it helped?

Earlier in the office, that must have been Brenda's last letter Sally had received. The one to sort it all out and "Get you off the hook," as she'd said but, it was blatantly obvious – it had not. What lies were told this time? Whatever it was had made not the slightest difference in Sally's attitude towards him. What could he do? His being wrongly accused was a difficult one, and at this moment he could think of nothing believable to help.

As he laid his bike against the back wall, beside the living room window, a movement caught his eye. It was Hammy, inside.

Of course – he had said he would be back at lunchtime.

He looked happier than Derek was feeling at this moment, and still enjoying the benefits of the hot shower he'd obviously just vacated. He was looking refreshed and relaxed, and smiling as he continued to dry himself. Derek was happy to note the second towel, modestly wrapped around his lower extremities. For his age, he looked remarkably fit, except around the middle...

Unusual for Hammy to work so hard to warrant a shower in the middle of the day – that was Derek's uncharitable thought. He was about to knock on the window and surprise him, but stopped – another figure appeared from the direction of the shower room. It was Sally's Aunt Thelma...

Derek dodged back from the window, afraid to be seen. She had obviously been showering too. She was drying her hair as she entered the living room, but she only had the use of one medium sized towel and that was for her head. She was starkers...

It was with extreme caution that he peeped through the window again. The bath towel was now demurely covering her body, as she sat down on the sofa, looking very happy as she reached up to take one of the two glasses of the bubbly stuff Hammy had poured.

Derek's throat felt dry. Was it thirst on seeing the champagne, or shock at the other vision? One thing was obvious. At this moment, the inside of his home was not a place he'd be welcome. In these circumstances, he realised regrettably, he would be remaining hungry and thirsty – and outside. He backed away. Carefully lifting his bike again, attempting to make no noise, he pushed it part-way down the lane before pedalling back towards town.

Today had been a definite downhill struggle – up to now. At least, he could smile about this – catching Thelma and Hammy together again. Obviously, by the minute, life was becoming more serious for them. How much longer can they possibly keep it under wraps?

He couldn't mention this to anyone, could he? Was there an easy way of suggesting to Hammy that perhaps next time he should close the curtains?

When Derek thought back, the signals were there this morning – the questions Hammy asked about his plans for lunch; would he be having the house to himself? Oh yes, the signals had been there all right, but he hadn't noticed them, not having been in the best of humours himself.

Wouldn't Sally be mad if she found out he knew something that she didn't, and he could imagine how she would go absolutely ballistic if she ever found out how he'd learned – by peeking! Could turn out worse than the Sophie episode...! Anyway, he couldn't tell anyone, even though it did have the makings of a good story.

At least he was smiling again. He might be feeling hungry and thirsty and missing his wife but, as he pedalled along just thinking about the pair in the cottage, his smile gradually developed into a wide grin, and his eyes twinkled. He was visualising Sally back home with him again, her sitting at the opposite side of the table having breakfast with him tomorrow morning, enjoying the casual chat.

"It's nice to see that Hammy and Thelma are getting on so well now, isn't it, Darling?" he would tell her, and before she could reply, he would add, "Be a pet and pass the butter please and ...are you having that last piece of toast? Oh, I meant to say – saw Thelma yesterday – she suits the full Brazilian..."

42

He sounds a wonderful guy, indeed, she said in the next email to her mom, though it was typed with tongue in cheek. It seemed a shame to be critical of a woman who had suddenly found so much love – even though it was doomed, and of that Angie was certain. She did not want to hurt any feelings but, for heaven's sake, this guy was half Mom's age.

This time, Angie was more upbeat in what she said about herself, telling her mom that she was about to start a new job and it hurt being so pleased about it, but that was a sham – there was no progress on that front at all – still no job to go to, and still no friends.

She and Sam had discussed it together. Maybe the call-centre would be better than nothing? Others would be working there in the same situation, and it would mean money. Maybe it wouldn't be such a lousy job. Should she give it a try? Sam was all for it. He wanted her out of the house and mixing with people because she was on a short road to depression, he feared. If she didn't fancy the call-centre, he suggested that she might try the supermarket. It was a big store and Bisko's must always be looking for staff – but Angie didn't fancy that either. Neither was to know that another opportunity was waiting for her.

Wandering aimlessly along Newingsworth High Street was better than sitting moping at home and being criticised later by Sam, but today, she stopped in the middle of the pavement and made a decision

– no aimless wandering. She would play a game – of mind-blowing activity.

Newingsworth shop-window displays – get ready for inspection – by me. Come to think of it, this could be worth developing ...and not just as a game.

Why stop at just inspecting? I could give the result to the shopkeepers, who would receive it with delight and thank me, and immediately correct the points made and that would be just the start. As soon as they realised the benefits of my visual critical skills, they'd come back to me. Free consultation initially, and then they'd pay for more of my help. Then giving each shop owner the opportunity of my expert advice would improve the town's image at the same time, and how this town needs help. What a smart idea, Angelina! Right, let's go...

This window will be first then – a newsagent's, right...

Oh, oh, bad start. Background, old wallpaper – a common fault and disliked intensely. Sorry, minus score already! Looks neglected and has been given little thought – very disappointing – needs more effort please. Space, filled with badly positioned 'rubbish'. Anyway, why are these things in the window? Items for sale should entice. Everything is dusty too, and generally lacking tender loving care...

That was when she realised, the comments being made – it was how she felt about herself – sadly out of place, serving no useful purpose, not trying hard enough, and hanging about collecting dust. Oh dear ...but enough of this demoralising, silly game – why did I think of it?

She straightened her body, pushed back her shoulders, and smiled at her reflection in the glass. That is much better, she told herself, now keep smiling...

Suddenly, she was startled by the realisation that there was a face glaring back at her from inside. The look conveyed a message, 'I do not know why you are standing there grinning at me, but I don't like you, so get lost!' and brought today's game to a rapid conclusion.

Angie smiled once again, this time obviously to the woman placing another item in the window, but received only a blank stare in return.

Angie moved on.

There were no more shop windows to look at on this side as she walked farther along, and anyway, she had given up on that. She was approaching the local Bingo Hall. As there was little of interest for a while on this side, only business premises and houses, she crossed the road.

For a High Street, it was remarkably quiet today, considering it was mid-morning. Perhaps, with the grey clouds, people were reluctant to come out shopping. Then why was she out, she thought? She was inspecting window displays, or rather had been...

She was fed up, bored, and now her game seemed so silly. On top of that, she was thirsty; and that is why she entered Anton's Old Astoria Cafe – for the first time.

There were no other customers, it must be the weather again, she decided. Inside she stood and looked around. A decision was called for; she had access to any table she fancied so, which one? The choice was eventually to be beside the window.

Seating herself, she looked at the decor, but only semi-consciously assessing it; sort of continuing the earlier game. It was inviting, not too modern, but not too old fashioned either, and sort of what she expected in this town. It was obviously not one of the large chains of coffee shops so prevalent back home, and was nowhere as modern as the cafe in the supermarket, either; the supermarket obviously upgraded theirs every year.

This was all right though. It had a comfortable, welcoming feel.

From out of the back shop area a man with a round smiling face appeared. He was rather plump, but he did not look the sort who would become flustered, or bothered by anything demanded by a customer. He had probably been doing it for years. He displayed a lazy competence that matched the mood of the surroundings. It appeared to be only him and her in the cafe.

"Goodamorning, younga lady. I no seena you before. Whatta today you wanta for yourra pleasure?" was his welcome.

Anton was second generation Italian. His mother and father emigrated from their homeland to Britain before the start of the Second World War and stayed, so, having been born and brought up in Newingsworth, Anton was therefore a local and should have had a local accent. The only occasions he'd been out of the UK were his three visits to Barga, Italy, to visit relatives who had difficulty understanding him each time – 'I couldna speaka the language', he would tell you. No matter, he always liked his customers to think of him as 'Anton – the Beega Italian'.

"Something to drinka, yea?" he asked, and she nodded. "Whatta you besta like? Americano? Cappuccino? Espresso? Or maybe you wanna cuppa Earla Grey tea? We havva them all."

"Americano, please," Angie answered.

"Ah, ha-ha, an Americano for an Americana," he laughed.

She smiled back. The man was an idiot...

"Ah, you new here, eh?" said Anton.

"Sure am. All the way from Detroit, Michigan," she replied delighted to be actually talking easily with someone who wasn't Sam.

"Detroita Tigers..." Anton said, immediately trying to impress.

"You know about Detroit Tigers?" she smiled again.

"I sometimes on telly watcha da baseball," he replied with a laugh, "...I no' understand eet! Butta you wanna coffee, I getta you coffee."

How fortunate to stumble into this place. She gazed out the large window – still very few people walking around. While she waited, a new game, giving marks out of ten for style to each person passing outside. Five people passed by. No-one got more than a three...

In no time, Anton was back with coffee and some complimentary biscuits for his new customer.

"Do you minda eef I sitta down for a moment, and talka?"

She certainly did not mind. It seemed ages since she felt comfortable and relaxed like this. He was like her father had been, totally unthreatening, and so unlike the old guy who had been stalking her.

"No customers today?" she enquired.

"Anda no-one to serve them iffa they comma in, either," he responded. "My son, he is ill, and the other two, huh, who knowsa? So, today ...I worka ...by myself. You no looka to worka, by any chance, no?"

"Hmmm, perhaps..." she coyly replied, enjoying the company. It was pleasant chatting to him. "Well, yea, I could be interested, very interested..." she followed up.

Suddenly, they'd become old buddies. She explained how she had searched, but found nothing that appealed to her, and anything so far was well below her capabilities. There were no jobs paying good money either, but...

"Money ...oh, no, no... Forra you thatta issa important? Whatsa wronga weeth 'appiness, no?"

"Well..."

"You worka here, younga lady, you be happy. You betta my cotton socks..."

That was why at Buttercup Avenue, when Sam came home after school, a happy, loving Angie rushed at him and dragged him into the bedroom. He didn't find out the reason until later...

43

Without creating bigger problems, he still could not think of any way to convince Sally that the last letter was not from him, and that there was no truth in anything which may have been said in the others. So, he had to settle for life as it was, and carry on. That was not good at all, but on the bright side, he now had a telephone number for Mr James Hoist, thanks to you-know-who.

'Twister' was one of the 'Rabid Revenge' members that he was looking for, and this could be a big step forward if this London number was really his. He dialled. This would be his first chance to call himself by his new pen-name 'Derek Tee'. All authors have one, he decided, and it would hide his real identity – sensible, in case of any come-backs. Toozlethwaite, being the only one in the UK, would be too easy to find.

"Hello, this is The Fort Knights' Music Agency, how can we help you – musically..."

It was a pleasant female voice which was singing in his ear. He thought he had gone straight onto a recording machine, and hesitated.

The voice suddenly changed...

"If you've phoned me yet again, you dirty rascal, just to breath down the phone and say naughty words, I am in touch with the police and..." was hissing menacingly at him.

"Sorry," Derek said, "I would like to speak to Twister, I mean Mr James Hoist, please. Is he in?"

"Are you from the Inland Revenue?"

"No... I..."

"Are you from Customs and Excise?"

"No... I..."

"Are you from the Child Support Agency?"

"No..."

"Right... I have to make sure about these things. What do you want then?"

"I'd like to speak personally to Mr Hoist."

"He's not in."

"Oh. Can you tell me when will he be back?"

"You could try in an hour. Mr James might be back by then – bye."

So, almost exactly one hour later, he tried again...

"Hello, this is The Fort Knights' Music Agency, how can we help you – musically..." her voice sang out again.

Derek wasn't so surprised this time and managed to continue the conversation.

"Hello, I'd like to speak to Mr Hoist, please, I..."

"Are you from the Inland Revenue?"

"No... I..."

"Are you from the...?"

Derek butted in this time.

"Excuse me, I'm not, and I think you will find that the 'Inland Revenue' and 'Customs and Excise' are now a combined organisation called 'Her Majesty's Revenue and Customs'." Derek was inclined to become supercilious in situations like this, so, he had to be careful to remember that he was at her mercy. She could be his only link to 'Rabid Revenge'.

"Oh, is that so..." she responded sarcastically, "...Child Support?"

"NO!"

"Mr James will speak to you now..."

No, that's not who I want, he was about to say.

"Hello," said a gruff male voice. "What are you after?"

"Mr Hoist? Sorry to bother you. My name is Derek Tee, and I would like your help..."

"Yea, a lovely name I'm sure... What instrument?"

"Pardon?"

"What instrument d'you play?"

"I don't play an instrument..."

"Just vocals, is it? Sorry, no gaps for singers at present, Mr Tee. Try again next month."

At that, the phone was disconnected.

As Derek learned in the newspaper business, perseverance was required in some instances. He tried once more.

"Hello, this is The Fort Knights' Music Agency, how can we help you – musically..." her voice sang out yet again.

Surely she gets fed up singing that, thought Derek.

"I was speaking to Mr Hoist and we were disconnected..." he said.

"Are you from Her Majesty's Revenue and Custom?"

"NO... MR HOIST PLEASE!"

"Hello, you are a persistent bugger..." Mr Hoist answered irritably.

"Mr Hoist, you seem to have misunderstood why I wanted to speak to you. It's been very difficult tracing you. It was only through my policeman friend that I was able to obtain your number. I would like to ask you a few questions about... Hello – hello! Are you still there?"

Derek, to give him full credit, did not give up. It required him to once more run the gauntlet of the very protective secretary to eventually be reconnected to a rather annoyed Mr Hoist. Derek took no chances when he reached his destination this time. He blurted it out quickly.

"RABID REVENGE..."

There was a silence at the end of the line. Derek thought again that he had failed, and that he was to be summarily dismissed, but no. This time it was only a stunned silence.

"Yes...?" was said very cautiously. "So...?"

"I am endeavouring to write a book..."

"If it's a publisher you want, son, I can't help you..."

"No, don't hang up, please. I know you were one of the band members. All I would like is some information from you about your days with them. Getting contact with the others is another thing I am trying to do, and it would be great, if you could help me – even a little – please."

"Ok," was said with resignation in the voice, "...What do you want to know?"

44

Once Derek secured the agent's attention, he worked hard not to lose it again. It was obvious that this man's tolerance factor was on the low side but Derek persisted and, to his relief, the man even seemed to mellow slightly.

Being a quieter day than usual for the business, Mr James Hoist decided it was time for a break, he would talk a bit, but he was suspicious... Does this guy at the other end have something on me?

Derek, at the other end, was visualising who he was speaking to: probably someone who led an extremely hectic but sedentary office life, and was never off the phone; old enough to have been his father, he presumed; and in his sumptuous office, would be stretching out on his swivel seat and putting his feet up on a large desk, using only one of his many telephones; relaxing for a change.

Would a cigar be involved? That usually went with the image. Derek considered he could be doing this fellow a favour by forcing him to slow down. It must be nice for him not to have to be doing deals for a little while. Haggling with everyone all the time for the best outcome for his clients, and for himself no doubt; it must be tough on a person and it would not be good for this man's health.

Just talking pleasantly, sharing thoughts and not negotiating for once must be a true relaxation, but it occurred to Derek that this man's old nickname from the band, Twister, was probably even more suitable to him in the job he now did.

"What's in it for me?" punched out Mr James Hoist.

This question was not in the least surprising to Derek. What did he expect? The man is an agent. At least at this point they'd been talking for almost ten minutes, so Derek considered he'd done very well to get so far into the conversation before being asked. He realised he would have to play smart, or the little earnings he might obtain from the project could finish in this expert negotiator's pocket.

"We'd have to see how successful the project turns out to be, wouldn't we?" was Derek's cautious response, and was surprised when his reply was accepted without argument.

With some gentle persuasion on Derek's part, the talk was steered back along the line it was moving in before it became mercenary.

What was more promising was when a vast record of newspaper cuttings was mentioned, retained in Mr James Hoist's scrapbook, but these were not being offered for his use – yet. This was useful knowledge – but he played cautiously. Getting his hands on these would be perfect for Derek but he guessed it would be hard work persuading this gent to hand them over.

His guess was wrong.

It was unusual for anyone to experience a magnanimous gesture by James Hoist; that wasn't his style, so Derek must have been doing something right; he was actually offered several samples of these newspaper articles – at no charge.

When asked about the other members of the band, the agent was reluctant to say too much to begin with, but Derek gradually coaxed him into telling a little more as the call progressed. It was interesting stuff; just what Derek required as a boost to his word count, and his morale. He was doing well, until there was an interruption on the other line.

"Sorry, have to go," Mr Hoist said, "Another agent on the other phone, needs a good lead guitarist – urgently. Panic, panic, panic...! You don't play the... No, no, of course you don't. So do call again Derek – but only if you feel you really have to."

That last comment was a let-down for Derek. He thought they were chatting away happily and willingly, and almost establishing a relationship for the future – not so obvious now he thought about it; probably misread the signals.

Disappointingly, it seemed this gent knew nothing of the whereabouts of any of the other band members, though he made quite a few snide comments about them. From the way he talked, it didn't sound as if they had been overly happy together.

So, Derek's knowledge moved forward, but only a little. Up to now, there was barely enough to fill a few chapters of the book, but these newspaper clippings, they could be really useful. He might chance another call in a few days and see if he meant what he said. Maybe this man could be encouraged to supply more?

At least he could look forward to receiving the ones promised, provided Mr James Hoist did not forget; but would they really turn out to be freebies, he wondered?

It was shortly after he ended that call, another idea occurred. Maybe he should contact the fans? If 'Rabid Revenge' has been a successful band in the States, there was bound to be a veritable army of people who'd have known the group in their heyday and have tales to tell, even though they would now be part of an older generation. He could use their stories, but that would be fruitful only if a message could be conveyed to them.

How could he make contact?

Newspaper articles or adverts, a television spot, radio interviews, all would be excellent, especially if they covered the whole of USA, but...

Who was he kidding? He didn't have any contacts in the newspaper industry in the States, and though getting a story into the national press, would be one way of approaching it, or having a two minute news item on national TV or radio was another, the reality was, he knew no-one in those fields at all. So, unfortunately, none of these ideas could be achievable – but there could maybe be another way... YouTube!

Reputations could be created on that computerised channel. It was a fact, or so he understood, that anyone could easily add a video. He had seen some really crazy ones – guys self-destructing on skate boards and such like and pretending they hadn't hurt themselves, or animals caught on video looking overly-cute or stupid. People couldn't help but look at the results of that sort of crazy footage.

People could become famous almost overnight, an instantaneous pop sensation singing self-penned songs. Just create a short video to display your talent, and anything becomes possible after that. Sit in your own favourite armchair, input it on YouTube, and achieve instant world-wide fame.

It had been done many times to his knowledge – though admittedly, talent did play a part. Could he do something like that? Maybe create a little video asking for help from the loyal fans, and see what happens?

'Rabid Revenge' fans probably have computers, but being of an older generation are they likely to be able to use them? Some of them could even be into Zimmers – but nothing ventured. So, Silver Surfers – I want a few words with you, he decided.

Yes, that is what he would do – he would make a video.

45

Sally had partially forgiven him; the 'Sophie email' still smouldered and he was desperately having to try to explain away Brenda – a happy-go-lucky person from way back at school who'd tried to play a joke on the pair of them, and failed miserably. She meant no harm and was greatly upset on learning that she'd caused their happy family to break-up. She wanted to apologise personally, if only Sally would just give her the chance. The poor girl was distraught about her dreadful mistake.

"Poor Brenda ...really ...you can only feel pity for a person like that," he confided in his wife...

Sally did not seem wholly convinced.

"Phone her yourself then," he blustered out, and then regretted it.

It had been a difficult task convincing Sally that Brenda was the real culprit and that the letters had nothing at all to do with him. He knew he was blameless, but as most of what Derek latterly told Sally about Brenda was conjured out of his head on the spot, his fear was the possibility that Sally might actually phone – and hear Brenda deny it.

"What? You want her number? I ...eh..."

Derek's heart stopped when Sally said she rang today; the school had been contacted. He was prepared to make a bee-line for the door as she started talking. "I had a chat with your friend, Brenda," she told him.

Oh no, what did she say? Did she confess? Tell me quickly, his brain was demanding.

"...And she confirmed your story."

As there was no apparent recrimination in Sally's tone, his heart considered restarting, then the way Sally began to relate the conversation it sounded as if she and Brenda had been best pals forever. They had even arranged a time to meet for a coffee.

His heart was now beating almost normally.

"Of course you are forgiven, Brenda, I told her," recounted Sally. "It was really funny, and I said to her that I didn't know why you, Derek, were getting so upset – and she became all tearful. Now don't be silly, I told her, there never was any problem... Oh, and Derek – she sent you her love."

Having gone through all that procedure, Sally was now reassured. At long last, the truth was out in the open. She knew it all. He, Derek, her faithful husband, had been innocent all along.

It was nice to be told that he was forgiven.

Forgiven, my foot. He could tell by the way she said it, she did not believe a single word, because, even after telling him he was absolved of all blame, she still came out with the final throwaway comment.

"...Of course, there is never smoke without fire," but at least Sally had come back to live at the cottage.

Alexander was as much relieved as Derek, about Sally returning to Toozlethwaite Manor. Being in the company of his wife and his twin sister was bad enough; a daughter, in addition, who always argued with him, was too much. He could cope for a few days, but anything longer...!

Life moved on. Sally was going to assist in the making of Derek's video, but only provided that it was all above board, and that it wouldn't be a naughty one, she told him.

"What do you want me to wear, something provocative?" she asked, and was disappointed to be told that he was the one to be filmed. She was only to be his little helper; she could wear what she liked. As usual, he could have phrased it better, and avoided her scowl.

To ensure it would work like clockwork, he had done some planning. It would be filmed at home, in the evening, so as not to interfere with their work at the Gazette. That was a novelty in itself. He would not be Derek Toozlethwaite; he would use his new pseudonym, Derek Tee, and, as he would rather not be identifiable for humiliation at a later date as the pillock on the screen, he would be disguised.

In the local newsagents, he'd found black plastic glasses with an attached plastic nose and black moustache to hide behind. It had been a spur of the moment purchase. He would combine that with his old baseball cap worn backwards and the disguise would be complete. He might even use that on the cover of the book, a book which was still a figment of his imagination.

The dialogue was to be scripted. He began on that two days ago, and since then had rewritten it four times, mostly during Gazette office hours. The borrowed record album cover was intended to be used also. (He used the word 'borrowed'. It sounded so much better than 'stolen', and helped his conscience a little.) The cover would be recognisable to fans and it would immediately invoke pleasant memory associations, and encourage them to contact him – he hoped.

Sally would operate the camera and hold up the large idiot boards and, because he wouldn't be using his normal spectacles, the boards were being printed using large letters, so that he could read them. It was important that he did not mix up the very important sequence of the prepared script.

So, get the camera ready for action.

We are about to roll...

46

Angie said it would happen and it looked like it was going that way, that is, if she was correctly reading the recent communication from Mom.

'To: Angie&Sam@Bt-deal.co.uk From: millicent@good.sort
Hi Angie honey, I'm not sure I was wise letting Alberto speak tough to the Chef. Good old Charlie, the best chef in the district – and he's gone. He'd been with me for ten years, that guy, since we opened the friggin' place. I told Alberto that he'd gone over the top, that he shouldn't have fired him, and that he'd said he was only going to talk to him, but he says the guy had it comin' to him. There's a new chef stepped in right away, someone Alberto knew, a young fella, 'bout the same age as Alberto. Now, wasn't that lucky. I hope that Alberto firing Charlie wasn't just to make a place for a buddy. If I find out that was the case I'll kill him, I will, and that aint no joke either.
But how are you now, babe? Happiness was shinin' out of the last email, and you said you were working, but you didn't say what at. I hope it isn't a Call Centre. These places will suck you dry. And the old guy, the one that was stalking you, have you hit him yet, because that's what you may have to do to put him off.
Maggie's still struggling with the ordering. Alberto has started to spend more time with her to try to get everything sorted out properly. I've hardly seen either of them all week. I've been keeping things moving myself, like I used to – you'll remember.
I can't think of any more news, other than, you'll be pleased to learn,

that I've banished Alberto to the spare bedroom since he sacked poor old Charlie. And do you know what? I don't feel nearly so tired... Love and kisses Mom.'

It pleased Angie to see that her mom had taken some action to control Alberto a little – but imagine him sacking Charlie. He shouldn't have done that...

Charlie and Angie had been great friends when she was back there. He was the one she went to when she needed some advice or reassurance – if her mom wasn't available at the time, of course – and he'd never let her down. Poor Charlie...

'To: millicent@good.sort From: Angie&Sam@Bt-deal.co.uk
Hi MOM, I was really sorry to hear you'd lost Charlie. Alberto sounds a bully-boy to me. Charlie was a great pal of mine. Did he find another job, do you know? I hope he did. His wife doesn't work and they have three kids to support. He may not be entitled to benefit if he can't get a job. It would be nice if you could help him, Mom, in some way.
I've made a friend, Anton, and got a job in his cafe, but it's not going to stay as a cafe for much longer. He's given me a real humdinger of a task. He wants me to estimate and organise what is required to convert his cafe. He wants to change it to become an eating place, a small restaurant. The town sure could use a nice one. I'm working with his son and he's a real caring guy too. He's married and his wife has just had another little baby. They have a four-year-old boy already. It's great working with Anton and Peter. Anton talks funny. I have to really concentrate to understand him.
Sam has made a new friend, too, met him at the school and we've to go to have a meal at his house some time soon. That'll be great. The world feels a much nicer place now – at least, here in good old Newingsworth the sun shines. You'd like it here too, Mom. That should bring us up to date with the news. Don't stand any nonsense from Alberto. He doesn't sound the right sort of guy for you in my opinion, but you will know best – you always do. Your ever luvvin daughter, Angelina xxxxxxxxx'

Right that's done, now, what time is it? Eleven o'clock already. Where are you, Sam? Sweetie, do you want some hot chocolate? You surely can't be sleeping already are you? Oh, yes you are...

47

Hammy was not sure how he managed to get involved, but involved he was. Derek said he'd volunteered – Hammy was sure he'd been conned. The idiot boards were to be his responsibility; he'd be holding them when Derek was doing the singing, or rather – the rapping.

"Yoh man, y'all go?" asked the director.

The director was Sally – a task she'd assumed. The other two had not objected. Derek couldn't do it, obviously, being in front of the camera. Could Hammy have done it, or did he even want to? No, because he was quite happy doing the minimum; he had the boards, and the backing raps; all of this carefully planned by Derek, of course, over several days, and rehearsed by all three until, in their opinions, it could be improved no more.

All that remained was to do it. He was ready, and she was ready, and Hammy was ready.

So, the director called "ACTION!"

The camera was started by Sally, there was a silent count to five, and they were off...

"Well, a great big 'Hi' to all you lovely folks out there in the United States of good old America – from little ol' me."

He sounded rather like Elvis. Derek was talking in what he considered to be an American mid-west accent, and he was ready to rap, planning to get the intonation and rhythm of it absolutely right. It was laid out on the idiot boards for him to read carefully – because he wanted it to sound refreshingly unrehearsed.

"My <u>name</u> is Derek, <u>D</u>erek Tee,
An' <u>I</u> want you to <u>cont</u>act me.
It's <u>all</u> about a group that <u>you</u> all knew,
The <u>songs</u> they sang were <u>good</u> for you
At the <u>time</u>... (two, three, and four.)
At the <u>time</u>... (two, three, and...)
Rabid <u>R</u>evenge... (two, three, and...)
Rabid <u>R</u>evenge... (two, three, and...)"

Sally and Hammy were off-camera. For extra effect they were rapping the chorus, those last two very important lines, repeating the band's name with Derek, each nodding and counting silently in their heads at the end of these last lines, exactly as rehearsed. It was not easy fitting in the band's name the way Derek wanted it, and the trickles of sweat were already on Hammy's forehead. Could he reach the end without making a mistake? He didnae want tae let Derek doon...

"They'd <u>stuck</u> together for a <u>long</u>, long, time.
<u>In</u> it for the money and the <u>money</u> was fine.
Four <u>guys</u> and a gal singin' <u>rock</u>'n'roll,
But did the <u>rock</u>'n'roll lifestyle <u>take</u> its toll?
At the <u>time</u>...
At the <u>time</u>...
Rabid <u>R</u>evenge...
Rabid <u>R</u>evenge..."

There was a slick, hip, nasal quality to the sound Derek was emitting – caused by the plastic nose being a little too tight for his own.

"I'm <u>sure</u> you remember when <u>you</u> were there,
<u>All</u> your own teeth and <u>all</u> your own hair.
<u>Not</u> a care in the <u>world</u> you had.
<u>They</u> were good – <u>you</u> were bad.
At the <u>time</u>...
At the <u>time</u>...
Rabid <u>R</u>evenge...
Rabid <u>R</u>evenge..."

The next part was spoken by Derek, direct to camera, still with an Americanised nasal voice; still off-camera, Sally and Hammy were providing the backing sound.

"Oooowa-ha (breathe) Oooowa-ha," (breathe)

"Oooowa-ha (breathe) Oooowa-ha," (breathe etc...)

Sally and Hammy were doing the 'Oooowa-ha's' exactly the same way as that dear old Australian with a didgeridoo would have done donkey's ages ago. It was providing a great rhythmic backing track, even though Hammy was struggling for breath. This had been Hammy's very own idea. They had practiced for nearly two hours on this little portion, and had it off perfect...

"Dear friends, friends of 'Rabid Revenge', how would you like to be the very first to supply me with the best memory of this won'erful group? Their very last album cover looked like this. Does that jog your memory?"

He held up the album cover in front of him, the one he had stolen (sorry), borrowed, from the Jones' house, hoping the focus would automatically adjust on the camera.

"Your fond memory could be one of many that will be recorded in a superb book which will tell of the life and times of those won'erful rockers, 'Rabid Revenge'.

You can e-mail your story to me, Derek Tee, right away..."

Derek held up a card that showed the e-mail address in large letters.

der.sal@bt-deal.co.uk

"Soon the book will be on sale and you will be able to purchase it for yourself, and read your very own won'erful anecdotes within its magnificent pages."

He held up the email address once again.

"So, don't delay, email today – der.sal@bt-deal.co.uk."

"Oooowa-ha, Oooowa-ha, Oooowa-ha, Oooowa-ha..."

They stopped at that, on cue, and froze, counted to five, and...

"CUT!" yelled the Director.

That was it, in the bag they hoped. Sally heaved a sigh of relief and flopped down in the chair, Hammy had to sit down as well, exhausted by the experience, while Derek pulled the overly-tight nose away from his own. The skin around his nose now marked with a strangely shaped red ring, which he sincerely hoped would not be permanent.

"Well?" asked Derek of the other two, "Did we crack it?"

Sally smiled and nodded, yes. She had enjoyed playing the part of 'Director', even though she had taken it off her own bat, delighted that she had proved to herself that she could do more than just take orders.

"Weel, ah'd say it wis different, laddie," Hammy contributed. "Aye, a wee bittie different..."

"Let's look at it on the computer then," said Derek. He was feeling fairly confident that they had succeeded, and in one take. Now that was something the professionals couldn't do...

The camera was connected, and the short video downloaded. The process took no time at all and they were pleasantly surprised by what they saw. Hammy's voice came through with a bit of a Scottish accent, admittedly; no matter how hard he tried it could never be anything else. Derek's voice had enough of an American accent to sound authentic – to someone who didn't speak English – but it was clear enough, and the message seemed to get through.

It was as Hammy had said – different, but that is what they had been wanting. It had to be noticed. It had to stand out from the others. More importantly it would have to be seen by people, by the fans, or even the critics, all would be quite acceptable. They were agreed – there could be no reaction, unless it was viewed.

It wasn't difficult adding it to the thousands that existed already on YouTube, and at least it didn't appear upside down when they called it up to see and admire it themselves...

The three performers crossed their fingers.

Now, please ...somebody ...LOOK AT IT!

48

The next evening after work, trying to avoid over-anticipation, the three of them rushed back to the cottage to see the worldwide reaction to their video. In truth, each was highly pessimistic about the possible result, with Derek's confidence wavering as usual. He had doubts on how he'd categorised it; if he had done that part wrongly, how would anyone find the video? Perhaps the box-ticking part should have been considered a little more carefully? The rush had been to download it and view it themselves; maybe done in too much of a hurry...

It was unusual for them all to arrive home at the same time but each was desperate to learn how many had found the video, but their worst fears were justified – no one looked at it. They'd had no hits at all...

Twenty-four hours later and it was the same rush home by each, and again – total and utter disappointment. What had they done wrong? More to the point, had they done anything right?

The same rush the following night, and this time – a result – one person had looked. He had even left a response...

'What a geek – I know where you could get a good cheap nose job done, because, boy, do you need it. Buddy, for your hooter, they'd probably do it for free.'

Yes, someone looked: obviously an admirer.

For the three of them by the next night the enthusiasm to search for results had waned somewhat, but they brightened when another comment appeared.

'Where'd you learn to rap, man – with Eminem, or M&S? Sad man – really sad...'

It just wasn't happening for them, but it had been viewed – by two people now, though the second one probably knew nothing about the band anyway, or the USA: M&S? A dead giveaway...

Next night, it was only Derek who bothered, and...

Hello, what's this – about twenty responses in the form of emails? He started to open each, delighted to have had so many hits, finding them mainly from older females but each with a surprising amount of detail, being apparently recalled and quoted, that made him doubt that they were all genuine.

After all the years these ladies were vividly describing special moments. The words of songs were recalled by many, but most seemed to want to share more delicate details, like how intimate they had been with the boys of the band? A few memories were overly graphical in detail.

"Surely not..." was Derek's slightly embarrassed comment, out loud, a few times.

Dates and venues, very specifically identifying the 'where' and 'when' of particularly tender and sensual moments, were being stated with amazingly precise detail; facts which must have been lovingly locked away in a diary somewhere, for the amount they were able to quote.

A pattern was quick to emerge as he worked his way through the list of emails. Although it was mentioned that the band played well at particular gigs, the facts being stated most fondly were of the fun each fan had had with one of the boys afterwards.

The pattern was simple and straightforward, it was not just the music that had made them popular – it was the sex.

Derek wondered how these guys had managed to lift their guitars some nights. In many cases, dates quoted by different females coincided with the same guys' names, several times. He tried to imagine how they had coped, several times a night, and after playing a gig? Oh my God... He could manage once a week!

The next night, when Derek checked, there were even more replies, and the pattern continued. Sex, sex, and more sex ...and the replies were coming from all over the States. This group of males, for every single venue, very obviously had been far travelled, highly potent, and well satisfied.

Then there was the one saying, 'Confidential – for Derek Tee only'.

Private and confidential doesn't work in this house, he thought ruefully, as his ears burned thinking how easily Sally found Sophie's message, but this one appeared to be very special.

It was more officious than the others – from the American Tax Authority. It was formal, and even had the Eagles Insignia at the top.

'HIGHLY CONFIDENTIAL
THE UNITED STATES OF AMERICA, FEDERAL TAX AGENCY

To: Mr Derek Tee

We, the Agency, are aware that, based on your recent actions on YouTube, there is a likelihood that contact will occur between you and ex-members of the band 'Rabid Revenge'. The members of this band are registered citizens of USA, and, as citizens of this great country they are required by statute to pay taxes based on earnings etc. The group members of this organisation have been evading the taxes that the law demands, and therefore it is imperative that we, The Agency, trace their whereabouts. This would permit us to discuss the matter with them and arrange means to achieve clearance of their outstanding debt. We therefore request that you inform us, confidentially of course, when this liaison occurs, and that you supply us with any contact telephone numbers or addresses you obtain, so that justice may be done.
As an upright citizen of the United Kingdom, it is your civic duty to help us obtain the taxes owed to our dear country. You, personally, will not go unrewarded if you are willing to do this for us. To enable

us to pay you the reward that you will so rightly deserve, directly and confidentially, please inform us, by immediate return, of your address and the bank, into which you would wish the reward to be paid. Of course to permit this to happen, we will also require your bank account details.

The reward, which will be substantial, will be paid into the said account the moment you contact us with the required information.

Yours in anticipation: Frederick J Openheimer,

Tax Evasion, State Department, United States of America.'

"Sally, would you look at this!"

Sally, at that moment, was clearing the dishes after tonight's evening meal, a meal that Hammy missed again. She stopped and went over.

"This band, it looks as though they haven't been paying their taxes, could be for years, and now the tax department is looking for them, and they are offering a reward for information. I wonder how much? Could be a large sum, I guess. These guys will have made millions."

Sally was reading over his shoulder, and it didn't take long...

"Derek... They are asking for your bank details," she pointed out.

"Yes, to pay me a reward..." he reminded her, with a smirk.

"...Derek, your bank details?" and it was said a little slower and clearer this time, "...To maybe remove the little money you have...? It's a SCAM!" and having put him right, back into the kitchen she went.

There is nothing worse than being told by your wife how stupid you are, he thought. The foolish feeling and annoyance at himself almost caused him to miss the next one...

'To: der.sal@bt-deal.co.uk From: millicent@good.sort

I don't know if this will be much help, but I thought I'd contact you anyway. Old news sometimes isn't all that interesting, is it? Once upon a time long ago, I knew a lot about 'Rabid Revenge'. As you might have noted already, my name is Millie, Millie Schwarz, to be precise...'

Yet another, Derek thought. All right then Millie Schwarz – as you are eagerly wishing to inform us, tell us all please on which night one of these highly sexed rockers satisfied you, and which bloke it was... We need to know...

This sex repetition was turning out to be anything but exciting. What he was being told by all those love-sick old women was a repeat of the same tale of conquest, over, and over. He could use that type of story in the book, yes, but only once. Some facts, or tales, told from a different viewpoint, that's what he wanted and needed. Even the odd concocted fantasy would make a change. However, I must not take out my frustration on this latest reply, he told himself. I might as well let Millie Schwarz have her moment. So, to continue... Millie the floor is yours... Now, where was I? Ah, yes...

'...my name is Millie, Millie Schwarz ...and I was part of the band in the early days when all of us were young and full of enthusiasm. As the lead singer, life for me could not have been any better...'

Millie...?

MILLIE...

It's THAT Millie... Oh my great heavens! He had to stop and take a deep breath. This was what he had hoped and dreamed about. Here was actual contact with one of the original members of the band. He could not believe it had happened.

"SAL-LY..." he yelled out, really loudly in his excitement.

Sally's scream of surprise was louder than the unmistakable crash of breaking crockery – but only just...

"What is it? What's wrong?"

She rushed through from the wreckage in the kitchen.

"No, there's nothing wrong," he said, "what are you getting worked up about? Just calm down, it's all good news."

Not what she was expecting at all, it was a crisis he had created, and the casserole was dropped because of him, so, in her agitated state she could not prevent herself reacting as any normal woman would...

She lashed out.

"Ow! What was that for?" he said, rubbing the painful part of his head where the tea towel made contact.

"Sorry," was the best she could do, but why should she be sorry? He had shouted – very loudly, and the casserole had been smashed – all because of him. It was his fault. She didn't have to feel guilty at all and anyway, Derek was well used to blame.

49

'Hi Angie honey, I've just gotta tell somebody about it, get it off my chest like. They said at the hospital it wasn't life threatening, but at least it was mighty painful for him, I'm glad to be able to say. Stabbing him in the hand for what he'd been getting up to, in my book, was being very generous to the pig, although emptying the swill over him, as well, was maybe a bit over the top, I suppose.

Yea, you did say at some time how that guy was not the right one for me, honey. I know, so, please do not rub my nose in it. Catching dear Alberto with his hand in the till was one thing but then catching him and your so-called friend Maggie, having it off in the kitchen, out of hours, was much worse, I can assure you.

"I was just trying to help the girl get the stock right" he bleated when I found them, but I came back at him with, "Her missing briefs ain't part of my stock, mister," and I told him, "You can get your things and get the hell outa my life – and fast."

I'll say this for him, he didn't back down, my cocky Alberto. "You can't fire me, Millie, honey, you need me too much – for all sorts of things," and it was the way he said it. He leaned across the chopping block with his hands in front of him, leering at me – and that's when I did it. It all happened so quickly. I was really wild at him after all those weeks of 'sweetheart', and 'baby', and 'honey', and he turns out to be two timin' me. Unlucky for him, I was holding the big sharp kitchen knife. I found it was so easy to stab the back of his hand. Works best when the knife is real sharp. Mine was – it went right through to the wood, yea... So, how are you honey?'

Angie's mouth opened when she started reading the latest email, and it was still wide open nearly two minutes after she finished. This was her mom and she was recounting this as if it had been just another day at work. Where did she send this from? Was she at home, or was she in gaol?

"Sam, I think Mom's in trouble..."

Sam came and read over Angie's shoulder. It was about the third sentence, before it hit him what was being said, and the seriousness of it, and the further he read, the paler his face became. What had she done?

'... I'm glad you've found something that interests you now. Anton's place sounds great, always was, and you are the one who is going to ring the changes, are you? Good luck with that.

You were worried about Charlie. He hadn't gotten another job, and was finding it hard even for the short time he had been out of work. He was worrying himself sick about his wife and the kids. So, lucky for me, he is restarting here tomorrow and we'll be back to the old team, him and me, because I'm going back to doing the job on the floor, where I belong. So, rest easy, Honey, Charlie's gonna be fine. Oh, by the way, I'm not in gaol. The officer that came, when I called emergency services, was on my side. He knew Alberto of old and told me he'd been swindling widows in the area for years and getting away with it, young though he is, and he got a bit tough with him, so, no charges against me.

And just so you know, me and Officer Hernando, we are going out tomorrow. I feel I owe him and we'll go somewhere for a good meal, and maybe the theatre afterwards, unless we come back to my place, and, who knows what might happen. I think I'm in love again – with a cop.

Love and kisses, Mom.'

50

What an enormous leap forward in his knowledge. Being contacted by the original Millie was wonderful news, and although spoiled a bit by being smacked around the head by Sally, it was still a beautiful feeling.

He read the rest of the message, when Sally left to clean up the casserole mess.

'I was part of the band in the early days having started with them when we were home in Newingsworth, a small town in the UK. We had all been at the High School together and played as amateurs around the area. If you want any more detail, please let me know and tell me the type of things you are looking for. Enjoy your search – Millicent Schwarz.'

What type of things do I want to know? She asks me! Was she just taunting him? He wanted to say – everything, absolutely everything and anything, please...

Her reply must have been as a result of looking at the video. He couldn't imagine what she looked like, but she would have seen him on the video of course, and somehow he doubted that she would have been impressed...

YouTube was opened again for another play of the video. The plastic nose, it did look as if it was real – not in the least attractive – just unpleasantly real. The joint could not be seen and it was flesh coloured plastic so, unfortunately, it did look like his nose.

Hmmm, no, of course Millie would not be impressed, but the disguise was serving its purpose all the same, and at least the video was getting hits. Admittedly, he was not the spitting image of Brad Pitt, but he could relax – he would not be recognised.

A reply to Millie had not yet been sent, because he was still pondering on what he would say. He didn't want to frighten her off by writing like a geek as well as looking like one. Tomorrow night I'll reply, he decided.

At work the next day, Derek was faced with the task of deciding which competition next to run. The Little Mr Muscles theme was successfully used a few weeks back, and the prize by now should have been received by the little lad who won.

The current competition was Little Miss Pink, and the difficult decision of choosing the winner from the eighty-two photographs received, would have to be faced next week at the latest.

So, what theme could he use next? 'My potato looks like...' would not be suitable until early autumn. How about, 'Our Town's Fattest Granny'?

No, maybe not – there would be too many entrants, wouldn't there? It might be better if it was, 'Isn't my Granny Great?' Yes, that's the way to go. If a grand-child takes the photo of a gran, it would be a competition for the young and the old; the standard of the photo and the glamour of the gran. You are firing on all cylinders today, Derek, he told himself, it being apparently not a day for feeling modest.

Then Rob arrived with a trophy.

The presentation he attended last night was a shock to his system – the Gazette won a prize! A Silver Trophy, although Derek was sure it was only plated, but the winners name was engraved on it – their newspaper – so the plating mattered not. They had never won anything before. 'The Newingsworth Weekly Gazette – Best New Features,' it showed. Derek was quite proud of himself. He was the one who had done the donkey work, conjuring up the various special features during the past year.

The bottle of champagne Rob brought out at the morning break was much appreciated. It was not the expensive stuff but Sally, Derek, and Spider agreed that it was a nice gesture, and in no time at all, the bottle was empty, the plastic glasses thrown in the bin, and everyone was feeling considerably happier. It was fortunate that the main work for this week's edition had already been put to bed, and that the pressure was off, because the four of them did sweet Fanny Adams for the rest of the morning.

For a breath of fresh air, Sally went out with Derek at lunchtime. They rarely went together at this time in the day, normally due to the staggered lunch-breaks, or because Derek was out wandering on his own.

The Old Astoria Cafe was the choice for a drink and a sandwich. Many others had chosen that venue today, and they were lucky to find a seat together. Anton and his son, Peter, were bustling around with the orders and seemed to be keeping everyone happy. There was obviously someone else in the back doing the preparation for them to be able to maintain the pace of supply they were achieving. Sally and Derek sat patiently and eventually Anton saw them.

"Hello, mya friends. It issa good to see you today. Very busy, no? Whatta you wanna I getta you?" he asked, his eyes darting around the rest of the cafe as he listened.

They ordered the sandwiches...

"I talka you later, yea?" and he rushed off again.

It was his son who delivered their order very soon after, as he and his father continued buzzing about. Eventually, rush hour subsided and a normal pace began to return to the room. Anton came back out, looking a little less harassed and sat down beside them.

"Anda how it goes for you botha?" he smiled. "For you Derek, especially, I see it all. It ees all agoing verra good, yea?"

He gave a nod and a wink, showing he was into the secret.

"Yes...?" Derek responded, not sure what secret Anton was into.

"The video... yea?" he continued. "You looka verra handsome onna the YouToob, no, no? Your lovely wife agrees witha me, yea?" and he looked at Sally, who happily did agree. "We verra mucha likea your nose!"

Derek gave a weak smile. So much for the disguise...

Someone came out of the back area just then, and started to wipe the tables and remove dishes. Derek had not noticed who it was, but Anton called her over.

"I wanna introduce thissa younga lady – my special assistant – she ees Angelina. She worka here now and she gonna change this place to something mucha better, yea?"

"Hello, I'm Sally," and Sally held out her hand.

Angelina smiled and shook the outstretched hand, and Derek stood up and held out his hand too. "...And I'm Derek."

"I am really pleased to meet you both. I don't know many people in this town yet. Sally and Derek... Derek? Say, you aren't the Derek who was up at the school are you – met my partner, Sam?"

"Yes, I am," Derek replied.

"Oh, so, it's you ...and you have a ...grandad?"

As she said that, she looked straight at Derek, slightly fearfully and as if dreading the answer.

"Yes..." he said tentatively.

"Wow... I know him too..."

That was said in a shocked voice by Angelina, and she stood a few moments, wide eyed and still, without breaking her gaze of Derek. Then the conversation was terminated as she turned on her heel, and hurried back to the kitchen.

51

Ok, so their YouTube video was not going to become a world favourite, but, it wasn't meant to be – as long as it was being found. That was the main thing, and found by the right people. New email replies were appearing every day. Some were of no consequence, some deliberately abusive, but each had to be read to determine the content. Usable material was carefully sifted out and filed separately.

The one from Mr James Hoist of The Fort Knights' Music Agency was different. It was not in answer to the YouTube appeal. His was the fulfilling of a promise. His offer of the old news articles had been remembered and he had sent something, or more likely, his singing secretary had.

There was a smile of anticipation for this one. This looked good, very good. There, on the screen was the email – with fifteen attachments. Even though Derek had no idea what was included in the attachments, the quantity fired him up. Anything was better than nothing to get the book off the ground, and this could mean moving forward again. Maybe Twister was a better bloke than the initial impression. His aggressive attitude could just be a front he used to scare off the weak.

Each attachment was opened ...and ...wonderful!

Newspaper scraps from a variety of performances had been scanned, and now were displayed in front of him. These were gazed at – lovingly. The newspaper banners were with the articles too, so each cutting also showed the origin and the date. And the photographs, oh excellent...

Derek allowed his mind to wander. He could see the finished item – the published book – sitting proudly in the little bubble floating above his head, already on the bookshelves – his name in print as the renowned author. He was delighted that in his imaginary world it was selling fast, and even more pleasingly – it was a hard-back at an extortionate price!

These newspaper cuttings were very important. This was probably the best stuff acquired so far. He printed them, something physical to place in his file for the future. Just how unreliable an electronic memory could be was a lesson learned a while ago; everything went that last time and it had shaken him, his old computer dying at the moment he decided on a career change. It had not broken his spirit – but it had been mighty close.

No reply received yet from Millie Schwarz, the recently discovered female ex-member of the group. Several days ago he thanked her for making contact and posed a few simple questions to see if she was really willing, and if she would follow up her offer of information.

Would she be homing in for money, as Twister's motives initially indicated? Having left the group a long time ago, being strapped for cash would not be at all surprising.

Her surname was Schwarz. Knowing that could be another leap forward perhaps, though it may not be the name she was born with. The phone book was checked again but without success. He might as well wait to see what she tells him. Of course, it would be a new name if she'd got married, wouldn't it?

What had she been doing with herself in the meantime? Female singers from bands tended to attempt a solo career if they'd gained a following, but an on-line search for that gave nothing to indicate she had been along that path. Why did she give up when the band's career prospects were so good? Had there been a fall out? What is she doing now?

Anyway, why the speculation? In a short time he should be receiving the answers from her. Having to be patient until she replied was going to be hard...

He looked at the prints of the newspaper cuttings to see what she looked like, and in each picture he saw the same lovely looking girl. He went back to the computer version and was able to enlarge the image, and up closer she looked even nicer, and then he realised something – this was Sadie.

The cuttings were for the period from 1986 onwards; when Sadie Truman took over from Millie. There was no information for the earlier concerts, neither was there a picture of Millie.

Not to worry – must have been an oversight on Twister's part. The information sent had probably just been lifted at random from his scrapbook, and by coincidence... All it would take would be another email to that gent and the gaps would be filled. He would only have to ask...

Unfortunately, when he received a reply from Mr James Hoist, he was sadly disappointed. In short, the reply simply stated: 'Sorry, no can do...'

52

When sent, Derek's request seemed totally innocuous.

The thank-you email to The Fort Knights' Music Agency only said: 'If you have any cuttings for before 1986, when Millie was with you, I would appreciate having copies'. He was not to know that in asking that, he was accidentally opening a wound that Mr James Hoist considered totally healed – but wasn't.

Mr James was how she referred to him for all of the eight years the Agency had been in operation. It functioned effectively with just the two of them, Mr James and her. Only two weeks after James Hoist established the office, Mabel joined him, and they split the work two ways: he did the selecting of all the clients, negotiating with concert organisers and entertainment managers on their behalf, and obtaining the work and payments; she did everything else.

She acted as his devoted hand-maiden, though this was just a figure of speech – she was actually a married woman, and her husband was an ex-professional boxer. Though she was very good looking – about ten years younger than her boss – and a bit of a temptation in his head occasionally, nothing improper had ever taken place, or had been suggested by Mr James. The boxer in the background would have been a deterrent to any male, no doubt, even one who had fading memories of a riotous life as a rock star and self-centred sex god.

It may have been Mr James Hoist's business, but she was in control. For any outsider to be successful with this agency and to have dealings with Mr James, a phone-caller would first have to get passed her. She was the sentinel, the telephone communications security guard. That is the way he liked it. He had enough on his plate doing what he did. Very few were given his mobile number, so there were no short cuts – the only way was via Mabel.

Mail arriving for The Fort Knights' Music Agency – be it electronic or snail – arrived at her desk. Mabel was his filter. Mr James could not cope with opening letters and certainly wasn't 'into' computers, so the dealing with paperwork, finicky technological detail, and electronic bits and pieces, was left totally to her.

Only paperwork that she deemed worthy of his attention was handed into his office. Those pieces of mail which she considered to be junk – begging letters, or letters from someone who was becoming a nuisance – would be destined for the dustbin.

On the computer it was easy to simply delete messages which were undesirable or unsolicited, otherwise they would be selected to become print-outs for the recipient, her boss – he was not into this paperless nonsense.

Derek didn't realise his luck. His email passed the test, and a hard copy was currently in the process of being printed for the boss.

More newspaper cuttings were being requested by Mr Tee but for a period in time that she didn't seem to have; she had already checked. To have found what was wanted herself would have made her happier. Sample cuttings, right back to the earliest date in the scrapbook that she could access, had already been sent, so, as far as she could see, unfortunately Mr James would have to become involved again.

Mabel understood this information was intended as a contribution towards a book about her boss's younger days, when he was in America, something he rarely talked to her about. She knew he had been the leader of a very popular rock band. The agency was started when he stopped performing and was continuing because he needed the money, or so she was told a long time ago. He was doing this job for simple financial necessity, he claimed. She found that hard to believe.

His donkey work was done by her, willingly. The other day,

when Mr James handed her the old scrapbook, it was she who selected which items to scan and send. She was a little more generous to Mr Tee in what she sent than her boss instructed. If there had been any cuttings in that book for the earlier period he now wanted, they would have been sent. She presumed earlier stuff must have been stored somewhere else by Mr James. She would obtain them from him and send them later.

He was on the phone when she went in. The photocopy of Mr Tee's email was placed in front of him. He automatically lifted the piece of paper, scanning what it said as he talked on.

"No, no, that's not good enough. My boys will need the main dressing room and..."

He stopped in mid sentence, and seemed to go into a day dream, only for a moment, but his train of thought was broken.

"...Oh ...eh ...Steve, could I call you back. Something very important has just come up..."

He hung up the phone.

Mabel felt a little uncomfortable. He was looking at her, but not seeing her, it seemed, and, except for a faint buzz of traffic, there was silence in the room, which was most unusual. The sounds from the busy street outside were rarely noticeable. Normally there was noise in this office, noise being generated usually by Mr James himself. Oh-oh, this was not the boss Mabel was used to.

His head was in his hands now. He was gazing at the sheet of paper before him, having come to a grinding halt for some reason.

"Are you all right? Can I get you a coffee? A glass of water?" she asked anxiously.

He looked up at her. He seemed saddened, and when he spoke it was not the normal harsh driving voice she was used to.

"Yea, I'm all right. It's just... Tell that guy – no, we don't have any, Mabel. No more photographs..."

She had a puzzled look on her face as she left his office.

He sat back in his chair, slightly dazed, gazing at nothing.

So long ago – why should it have suddenly jarred like that? Over the years, he had become a hardened ex-musician who was well versed in lying and pressurising others to achieve his own ends – for the betterment of the clients, of course. The life he'd led hadn't been perfect and he knew that better than anyone but he couldn't change it.

Anyway, he had shrugged it off, and given up feeling guilty many years ago. He had done the dirty on her, but then he'd had the same done to him; a painful experience he remembered. Afterwards, he considered it only fair for him to suffer because he deserved it and it almost balanced up the score. Therefore dues had been paid, surely.

He should not have to feel guilty ...so, why did he?

She should have taken precautions, and it wasn't his fault she got pregnant. The band had to continue whatever happened – she knew that very well, but he shouldn't have left her – and the child. He should have supported them, shouldn't he?

If only he had gone back – at least to make sure things worked out all right for her and the baby...

It had been partly Sadie's fault, she'd seduced him – but he had been willing. She was a lovely girl, and conveniently she could sing as well, appearing just at the right time to take Millie's place. Replacing Millie in the band was all that should have happened. It shouldn't have changed his life, but Sadie was good – in so many ways, made him forget about Millie very quickly, that was until now...

That damn phone call from the young author, Tee; that's what started it off again, wanting to write a stupid book, and now wanting facts about the time she was with them. This was stirring up the past, a past best forgotten. If Tee hadn't made contact, Millie would never even have crossed his mind.

What happened to her? Where could she be? At least when he last saw her, she had arranged a comfortable home for herself and the child; and money couldn't be a problem. She had her share of the cash they made, nearly five years worth of earnings, probably all stashed away in a bank vault; and there would have been a lot. Millie was more careful with her money than the rest of them were. So, why should he be worrying about her now?

Gradually he relaxed. This time he enjoyed the silence. It was a momentary lapse, but upsetting all the same. He leaned back in the chair and put his feet on the desk. Life hadn't been all bad. The fame and the excitement were great at the time, and as for the after-gig parties – WOW – all those adoring fans, but that stamina was gone...

He lifted the telephone again.

"Sorry about that Steve. My secretary – got a little excited about something that only I could fix. Now ...where were we?"

53

It was disappointing to receive the 'going nowhere' reply from James Hoist, and it took a few days to recover enthusiasm and regain momentum. Optimistically he had been seeing himself roaring forward in the project, until that simple 'no'. It brought him back to reality with a thump. Derek comforted himself with the fact that he had already received more than he should have expected, but still...

He had another source now, but what if it turned out to be a nil return from Millie Schwarz? If a negative reaction came from her as well, he would ...he would ...he would throw himself in the stream! It wouldn't be unsafe, but it would tell the world of his disappointment ...and make him rather muddy. No, he wouldn't do that at all! That was just silly talk...

Something positive was being achieved. He had hundreds of responses from mature females all claiming to have made mad passionate love with the 'Rabid Revenge' males and many, if they were to be believed but which was doubtful, had enjoyed the experience at least three times per gig.

He was now pretty certain that there was more than a little exaggeration creeping in. Some even claimed to have become celibate after those concerts, because no other man afterwards was ever able to provide the real satisfaction that these guys did.

There were also a few from males who had fancied the boys too – and still felt the pain of rejection.

So, he wasn't without material; many of these stories were usable for development. In addition of course, the newspaper articles already received from Twister were perfect. He would also use the background knowledge obtained from Mr and Mrs Jones about Growler, (oh, and he still had a purloined record album he'd almost forgotten about); and what about the school? He could use his visit to Old Duckett in some way too, but Brenda would not be allowed a starring role in this version, thank you very much!

And then a reply came from Millie...

'To: der.sal@bt-deal.co.uk   From: millicent@good.sort
Glad to learn that someone is still interested in an old has-been performer, after all the years. Yea, I'd be happy to give you some help with your book, but, and this might be too big a 'but' for you to follow up with, before I tell you anything I'd have to be sure I wasn't bein' hoodwinked by another guy, as happened to me recently, so, how about you spilling the dirt and telling me about you? Then we'll see where it leads us... Millie.'

Spilling the dirt? What sort of gory detail was she looking for? Should he tell the truth – that there wasn't very much dirt to spill, although, there was the episode with Sophie, and what about snogging with Brenda at the school? Should he tell her that his wife had been upset and abandoned him for a spell because of those things; and that he missed her a lot when she did that...?

Whoa! That wasn't spilling the dirt – that was simply a wimp's confession. That would not impress anyone unfortunately.

Oh, what the hell...!

To: millicent@good.sort   From: der.sal@bt-deal.co.uk
Nothing very exciting or titillating to tell you I'm afraid. I'm a pretty ordinary guy, married to a girl that I probably don't deserve, called Sally. I'm in my early-thirties and work for a newspaper organisation as my day job. I have dreamed of writing a book for years, but never managed to home in on a suitable subject. I gave up trying to write fiction after a bad start, and thought I'd try factual, so, last year I dressed in my wife's clothing and went out with my father-in-law, also in female garb, for a meal in town. That nearly ruined my

marriage, so, the idea of researching the truth about cross-dressing by males proved to be a bad one. When Anton started reminiscing about your school band, and how you made it big in the States, it suddenly seemed the one for me, and one which my better half could not criticise. I was planning to find out about you all, and record how your success came about, but it has been difficult finding any of you to talk to. I've located James Hoist and received some help from him just recently. If you can supply anything, it would be appreciated, and if you can direct me towards the other members of your group, I'd be eternally grateful. Thanks in anticipation – Derek Tee.

Derek hesitated before sending this off. The cursor hovered over the 'send'. Had he said the correct things? From what he had written, did he sound strong, intelligent, and capable of producing the goods but without distorting the truth too much in a book? Hmmm, maybe not...

Should he have made himself out to be more macho? Should he have mentioned the shapely Sophie, and tried to impress this woman in the States, claiming perhaps that he had a tame publisher at his beck and call, one that was desperate for his book, and his body, and not necessarily in that order?

Or should he mention that he had never known his mother, and had felt insecure about that, and about life in general – go for the sympathy vote? He'd always presumed his mother would have come from Newingsworth. This woman did too. They might have known each other?

Stop, stop, stop... This was being very silly.

He should not, at this stage, be divulging too much about himself, not yet. As far as this woman was concerned, he was Derek Tee, not Toozlethwaite. She didn't know where he lived either. He didn't want to say he came from Newingsworth, in case that put her off. Luckily on the internet, the person's address wasn't stated, although she would see he came from the UK.

Once again, he read what was typed – and he wasn't impressed. If it didn't inspire him, why should it inspire her? He hummed and he hawed, and then decided the simplest solution would probably be to delete it all and start again as the cursor hovered on 'SEND'...

No, don't send... A second try was bound to improve it.

That's what he would have done – if he'd realised a moment sooner that Hammy had come quietly into the cottage and entered the room behind him.

"Boo!" was all Hammy said.

Derek reacted, the cursor still riding over the 'send', was activated – and that, whether he wanted it, or not, put paid to a second try...

54

The newly designed Farmhouse Hotel, as it was planned to be called, was progressing fast, faster than Hammy anticipated. The building's structure was now complete and ready for the painting and decorating, and Hammy could happily absorb the praise being given by Alexander for a speedy, and 'within budget' project. Maintaining the budget target was an unusual and admirable feat, and something about which to be proud, but, perhaps some of the praise being showered on him was being misdirected.

It is true that he was displaying a natural skill for making it happen, a skill he hadn't realised he possessed although he probably used it for most of his life. He'd always tried to do a job in the most sensible way.

The difference this time was his secret helper, Thelma. She was doing everything the project required, associated with the colour schemes, furniture and soft furnishings, and thoroughly enjoying herself in the process, and without Alexander knowing. Part of her enjoyment came from that secrecy – avoiding her brother learning of her involvement.

There were consequences to her spending so much of her time with Hamish. At 40 Cloverton Avenue, the stock of food and other essential goods was diminishing. Food items were running out, and the timing and preparation of the meals, one of Thelma duties, was becoming haphazard – and it had been noticed...

The general housekeeping at Cloverton had been her task since joining them. This was her form of recompense. Though not earning any cash, she was contributing in her own way, though of course, what she did at Cloverton was entirely voluntary. Muriel and Alexander were well aware of that fact, but it didn't stop them feeling somewhat aggrieved. She was failing to maintain her established routine.

Muriel was resorting to rolling up her sleeves now and then when Thelma didn't appear, and Alexander was forced occasionally to boil the kettle, though only if pushed, being totally useless in housekeeping matters; he always had been – and preferred it that way.

For Thelma, working with Hamish was great. She could have her own way for almost anything asked of him. Occasionally she felt she'd gone a little over the top with some of her ideas for the design of the rooms, but no, when she explained what it would be, Hamish had been delighted every time. He was such a gentleman, and there weren't many of them about these days. It was a bit of a downer when she realised the reason – they had all died off...

That encouraged thoughts of the age difference. It was nearly twenty years but she refused to let it faze her. Now, if they were teenagers, it would be termed baby-snatching, or something equally illegal, but they were both older. As it was, their difference in years could be easily justified, and put down to maturity.

"Hamish, what about publicity?" she asked one day, "...and business cards? How are you going to attract the visitors?"

The blank look on his face, and the silence which followed were good indicators. He hadn't even thought of that.

"Is that something I could assist you with?"

"Oh aye, Lassie, that would be a fine wee bit of a help, ah'm sure," he responded. "Whit dae ye huvv in mind, then?"

Did he sound a little too eager perhaps?

She rhymed off the various possibilities as he sat in awe of her magnificence. He even silently thanked the Good Lord for allocating her to be his very best friend, but, what could anyone, as smart as she was, find to like in an old duffer like me, he wondered? It surely couldn't go on forever, could it?

"Derek would be delighted to help, I would think, for the local publicity. Maybe we could do it cheaply through him. The Gazette is popular nowadays, and I'm sure he could always use a special feature."

Hammy's eyes brightened. He was always eager to secure a bargain...

"...And I could contact the various tourist agencies around about the country," she continued.

This wumman is fantastic, he thought; it's nae wunner ah luvv 'urr...

Contact was made by Hammy with his other boss, Alexander, to ensure that he, as owner, was aware that he would be footing the bill for publicity. Along the way Hammy was quite proud to explain the various other things he had in mind to make the business a commercial success.

"Why don't you get Thelma to help you with that sort of thing," Alexander suggested.

"Whit?" spluttered Hammy.

"It would give her something useful to do, instead of sitting at home all day twiddling her thumbs. You know her well enough to ask her yourself, don't you?"

"Weel...?" Hammy hesitated.

"Go on, man. You can do it. She might even get to like you. You are a likeable rogue, I would say, especially as far as women are concerned, I'm sure."

Hammy stood there, tongue-tied and embarrassed.

"Tell you what. I'll ask her for you. It would be more proper if we did it that way. Anyway, it is ages since I spoke to my dear sister about what she's being wasting her time with anyway. She might even inform me why our meals are never ready on time, these days."

"Aye, weel, if you say so," Hammy accepted.

Alexander took great delight later that evening telling Muriel all about his meeting with his project manager and friend, emphasising his enjoyment in making Hammy feel very uncomfortable.

"And they think we suspect nothing. I believe their little romance could become public very soon," said Alexander confidently.

"About what you told Hammy – getting Thelma to help – are you really going to speak to her?" asked Muriel.

"Oh yes ...and I'm going to make a meal of that... And anyway, when we were at school, she used to be the Girl's Amateur Golfing Champion. She'll design the golf course."

55

Another week had gone by and it was great that the fans were still making contact but with no reply from the important one, Millie, Derek was becoming anxious. What he said in his email to her was totally wrong; it had chased her off; she'd lost interest. If only Hammy had not scared the life out of him something more substantial could have been created, and the correspondence would have continued.

There was also another matter...

Concentration was difficult these days with something pricking his conscience – the 'borrowed' record album. Should he return it to the Jones' house? If so, how could he smuggle the LP back in without them knowing? What if he was caught doing it? He could not afford that to happen. That would be another source of information ruined, as well as being incredibly embarrassing.

Sally was seeing the signs of frustration, and resignation, appearing in his behaviour again, and because she had sworn to help him this time, she tried boosting his morale – at night, in bed. It did not work. Her making the first moves, by removing her silk pyjamas in a highly seductive manner before swinging them above her head, and then purring sexily as she crawled into bed, nakedly nestling into his back, failed to waken 'his little man', or prevent him falling asleep.

So eventually, when a reply did appear from Millie the following week, Sally was more delighted than Derek. Maybe this would get him going again.

It did...

To: der.sal@bt-deal.co.uk From: Millicent@good.sort
*Sorry to be so long in replying but I have been very busy. Thanks for your info. You seem a nice boy, so different from some of the males in my life recently, but none of them have been into dressing in my clothes – so good on you, Buster. Could be, your good lady, Sally, was only pretending that you were a naughty boy. That would have turned me on... You said you got your idea for the book from someone called Anton, but you didn't tell me anything about him. How did he know us? Is he an American? And you successfully located James did you, lucky you? I hope he treated you better than he ever treated me. Worms don't turn, as far as I know. Isn't communicating like this a pain? It would sure be easier if we were sitting in the same room. Although my gut tells me to trust you, it's gonna take a little time before I tell you any really intimate stuff. Ok? And you would like to know where the others are? So would I. The last I heard was that Bonzo and Sadie ran off together and are rolling about in the hay somewhere, laughing their heads off at putting one over on good old Twister, because he and Sadie were paired for a long time. I've no idea where they might be though, but good luck to them. Growler, the drummer, dear old Jonathan, is no longer with us. He got hit by a truck somewhere in Minnesota. Killed instantly, God rest his soul. Truck driver got gaoled for drunk driving. It was ironic – that had been one of the few occasions Growler was sober. I sure hope this is helping you. Could you use any newspaper cuttings? I have a few, so let me know, yours, Millie.
PS. Is that really your own nose?*

That night Derek was like an animal – but Sally didn't complain...

To: Millicent@good.sort From: der.sal@bt-deal.co.uk
Thanks Millie, it was great to hear from you again. It made Sally very happy too. Sad about Growler, but you have to go sometime, I suppose. I guess you are not too pleased about something that happened between you and Twister. He seemed alright to me, maybe

a little bit gruff and short tempered to begin with, but I thought it might just be an act. He sent me some cuttings about the band but he only seems to have those from 1986 and later, and nothing for the time you were in the group, which seems odd. Sadie and Bonzo can't be YouTube fans. I had hoped they'd see our video, the way you did, and make contact. Of course, they may have more important things in their lives if they are together now. Do you want to have a phone number for Twister? You are welcome to it, but you'd have to get passed his secretary first, and she is something else. And yes, I'd love to have any cuttings you have. There's been lots of mail from fans. I'd be interested to know if the male members of the group were really all sex maniacs. To an outsider like me, who didn't know you when you were performing, but going on the way the fans are talking, it seems highly likely. No-one has said anything like that about you though. Anyway, I don't think I'd tell you if they had. I do hope we meet some day, and no, the hooter was plastic! Kindest regards, Derek.

What a difference. He felt good now, much more relaxed. The information was starting to flow the way it should. He was going to be successful this time, but Growler – no longer with us. That's sad, so there would be no information from that quarter then.

The thought came suddenly – Mr and Mrs Jones – it was their son. They could not be aware he had been killed. Should he be the one to tell them?

With difficulty he succeeded in remaining focused on the Gazette work at the office, mainly because it was very necessary. He was looking at photographs, masses of them taken by youngsters of assorted ages, and grandmothers – grannies in focus, grannies out of focus, big grannies, little grannies, old and not so old, and so many of them...

Derek had removed one of the photos which did not correctly fit the pattern. The clothes she was wearing seemed inappropriate and perhaps intended for another purpose? If she was a granny she was a very young one, and it looked as if it had been a boyfriend, rather than a grandchild, who took the photo. No, no, no, this one could not be allowed: high heels, a red bra, and red knickers? It was not in the spirit of the competition and put aside...

There had to be a winner. Which one would it be?

Spider was commandeered to assist, and then Sally joined in. When Rob passed and noticed the one in bra and knickers, he took some interest too, but soon lost it when he saw that the rest of the photographs had not achieved the same standard. He left the three of them to it.

The happy atmosphere was back in the office. They were all mucking in, and that way it didn't seem like work at all, and soon a winning granny was selected in the time-honoured fashion – by picking one out of the hat...

56

The following week, when he was trawling the internet, looking for some fresh ideas he could adapt for the Gazette, Derek thought he stumbled on another of the original members of the band, but he could not be certain. His eye caught the name Thwaite: in reports of court proceedings. A Steven Thwaite had been involved, with others, in a scheme to buy land and property which was then used for growing cannabis, in a grand scale. He was also the brains behind a money-laundering scheme, and various other unsavoury scams involving elderly people. Newingsworth, Slatterfoot and surrounding districts, was mentioned in the report as one of the areas the gang operated.

Thwaite...? Now Derek may have been wrong, of course, and this could be a pure coincidence. Could be another bloke! It was not a unique name, but it was uncommon, so, it might be him – but if it was and, if he was from Newingsworth, how terrible – the shame of it. Imagine someone from Newingsworth being caught doing naughty things. People from around here pride themselves in not being caught...

Derek also remembered, when he was preparing the story about the ruckus up at the farm, he came across the name of the solicitor dealing with the sale. If his memory was correct, that was Thwaite, wasn't it? His father-in-law would know.

When he checked, he was able to confirm a Mr Steven Thwaite had been the lawyer who sold him the farm; Alexander added that he could be a local he knew vaguely from the past. A guy with that name was at school at the same time as him, a couple of years above. Thwaite had made it as a lawyer and opened a business down south about the time Alexander joined the bank, as far as he could remember. Alexander also recalled a Thwaite as being part of a rock band in the last years at school.

Because the sale was conducted by letter and phone with Thwaite's office in London, there was no face to face contact, so he could not be certain it was the same fellow. After the farm sale and the associated scandal, there was no other contact.

"...Unusual though, it was almost as if he wanted rid of the farm," Alexander was pleased to tell him, "...Selling it to me for a snip, as if I was doing him a favour taking it, but I didn't complain..."

Of course, Derek couldn't be absolutely certain but it looked as if he could be onto another lead, but he wasn't too eager to follow-up on this; making contact through HM Prisons? No, thank you. What if it turned out to be a different thug called Thwaite? He would put it on the back burner, he decided.

Anyway, there was delight at the responses from Millie though she had been unable to send all she'd intended. 'Can't get the goddam scanner to work' her email said.

So, there were no photographs, yet, but several emails passed back and forth, questions being asked and answers being given. Anton's cafe she remembered, but not Anton, but she had met a lot of people in the intervening thirty plus years. She did say that in the early days in her home town, Newingsworth, his cafe had been the centre of the world.

Derek had not yet told her where his home was, that he was here in Newingsworth, but that didn't seem relevant to her. She certainly hadn't asked him the question directly, even if she was curious, though maybe she'd guessed.

The right things were being said by him, it appeared, generating some more confidence on her part. Talk had become a little deeper and more intimate about the relationships she had with the others in the band.

Before leaving school she'd had a girly crush on Steven Thwaite, and that he was keen on her too, she told Derek, but it didn't last, even though Steven had wanted it to.

When the chance came for the group to move up into the big time, Steven decided, no. Her rejection of him was part of the reason but it was also affected by James Hoist. Millie was vague in the detail, but whatever the true reason, Steven clearly did not want to remain with the group.

They'd all tried to persuade him to go to America with them. He had been a founder member of the group, and a great singer and guitarist, and deserved the rewards of the hard work they put in together. All those charity concerts, and the club circuits, being paid either nothing, or a pittance: back then they were just grateful of having the opportunity to perform in public. Steven should have been benefiting with the rest of them in the chance for fame.

Although he gave in and went across to the States with them and signed the contract, the visit was short-lived. He changed his mind, and returned to Britain. He told them he had decided to become a lawyer, and was giving up music all together. He would be making headlines in his own way.

Millie was shocked when Derek told her what he had found – that her old flame may now be a crooked lawyer. She was convinced it would not be the guy she had liked, or at least hoped it wasn't him, but people change, she admitted.

Derek pinched himself every so often because she was beginning to tell him, in the emails, the sort of things which would give some heart and feeling to his story, including her bitter memories of having to end being part of 'Rabid Revenge'. Sometimes she was supplying only hints of big events in her life, many still too painful to recall it seemed to him and therefore he was very careful in how he elicited the details.

Coming face to face with this woman was not likely to happen, he knew, but he recognised a strange sensation developing between them. He was feeling very close to her, hundreds of miles away though she was.

When she told him the real reason why Steven gave up the group, he knew that she was truly starting to trust him...

57

The laptop had been a great buy, but he never was given the chance to use it. It was always being commandeered by Angie. Sam wasn't complaining, in fact he was delighted that his girl had perked up. Her good spirits were partly due to the laptop, and regular contact with her mother. This had been great for her, and she was resisting the temptation to spend money on the web sites to which she had been addicted – as far as he knew.

The other main factor to brighten her outlook of life was having a job to do. He had met her boss, Anton, only once. There was difficulty initially in understanding what the old man was saying, but he managed to tune in eventually, and thought him to be a nice guy.

However, it worried Sam a little, Anton having given Angie the task of converting his cafe into an eating house. This guy was taking a big chance, surely. She'd never done anything like that before. Yea, great at organising and managing people, but planning a project like this could be pushing it a bit.

He couldn't interfere, could he? She would do it her way, whether he commented, or not. If he did she would tell him: "It is my baby..."

Oh, shouldn't have used the baby word though, still gets her upset...

The laptop was in use right this minute. Some research in progress, as far as he could see over her shoulder; looking for a particular type of table and seating for the cafe, or should we say The New Astoria Eating House. The lettering and colouring for the name-board, intended for outside, was already laid out. She was clever with spreadsheets.

"Any likelihood of having a chance on the...?" he asked. "No rush, of course!" he added hastily, when he received what he thought was a dirty look.

"I'll just check if Mom has replied to my last email first, Sweetie Pie, if you don't mind waiting," she smiled.

So, maybe it hadn't been a scowl after all...

And Mom had replied.

To: Angie&Sam@BT-deal.co.uk   From: millicent@good.sort
Dear ANGIE babe, I'm so happy I could cry. You know the way it is, don't you. It's my big beautiful cop, Hernando; he's the tops and no mistake. Even your dear old Pop would have approved of him taking his place. He is so gentle for a big guy, but so strong; only uses his strength on the bad guys. We've been out to some shows together. We've done opera, ballet, and Shrek the Musical, and he never fell asleep once, for goodness sake – so different from your Pop. I've been to his house and met his Momma. Nearly eighty-years-old she is, and what a woman. Could she talk, and talk, and talk? She wanted to know if my intentions were honourable towards her son. If he is a mummy's boy, is that such a bad thing? She may be getting a trifle wandered I fear, kept asking me my name, so many times. And he's so good with her, never gets annoyed, but her talking might drive me insane if she was in the same house as me all the time. But what about you, Honey? Still redesigning that cafe? And how's dear Sam, still asking you to marry him and have his babies, or has he given up trying to convince that stubborn mule of a daughter of mine that he really loves her? I'd say that you shouldn't let him go. He's one of the good guys, I can tell, but it ain't no use me trying to convince you of something. You've gotten your head screwed on tight. You'll know when the time is right, I'm sure, Honey. Loveya – Mom xxx
PS. Charlie's doing fine and sends his regards. He knows that you had something to do with him getting back his old job and says he loves you for it. He's definitely the best chef in the business.

"Another five minutes, Sweetie Pie. Just gonna send the reply to Mom. She seems to really like you, but there's no accounting for taste is there. Anyway, you haven't asked me recently to marry you. Do you not love me, anymore, Sweetie?"

But Sweetie had given up, and had vanished off to bed...

To: millicent@good.sort   From: Angie&Sam@Bt-deal.co.uk
Hi Mom, What a wonderful guy your new policeman, Hernando, must be. At least, he'll be nice to know next time you get your usual parking ticket, but his Momma sounds a real handful, and that would make me a little wary. Was she always running after him hand and foot? I know you always liked to do that for Pop, but he was special, and for me no one will ever take his place. I miss him a lot, same as I miss you, but at least I'll see you again sometime soon, I hope. Have you thought of coming over here for a holiday, maybe? You could stay with us, there's room enough for another, if you breathe in. It would be nice to see you, and you could afford to splash out and take a break. You could come for the opening of the New Astoria Eating House, when we get it finished. We'll be having a special party that night. I'm sorry to have to tell you that your future son-in-law seems to have given up asking me to marry him. I'm in the mood now, but it seems he's not. What should I do Mom? Become more lovin' or tougher? But it is late here and time I went off to bed. Give Charlie a big hug from me. Your ever luvvin daughter, Angelina xxxxxxxxxx

She closed the laptop. Obviously Sam had not needed it for anything important...

58

Derek was delighted to learn that for twenty-three years she had been a faithful wife to a devoted husband – who was no longer of this world unfortunately – Pop Schwarz, as he was known for all that time by Millie and her lovely daughter. At work he was called Mickey, but going home, he would look forward to hearing one of them call out, "Hi Pop," whenever he went in the door. He loved the name, because it was his wife, and daughter, using it...

In all his years he had been a really good father and a caring husband. They married not long after she left 'Rabid Revenge', almost on the rebound, you could say. He owned a small restaurant. He nurtured it and with Millie helping, very soon it became a popular place in the neighbourhood.

Everybody knew, 'Mickey's Joint'.

Maybe he worked a bit too hard as he got older, and as happens so often to overly hard workers, the hot favourite killer got him – a heart attack. He was driving on his way home from the restaurant, and crashed the car into a delicatessen. Luckily, no one else was affected, the shop being shut at that time of night, but he died eighteen hours later in hospital, with a grieving wife and daughter by his bed.

The true confessions continued, to Derek's delight...

Sorry to tell a lie earlier, about how Steven departed from the band. It was not the whole truth he'd been told before, she admitted to him, because Steven had been the love of her life before the formation of the group.

What she was telling him now was in greater depth than the

earlier things she'd written...

It had been very serious with Steven. She could have been Mrs Millie Thwaite if she'd said 'yes' to him. He had been desperate to marry her, but she was young and he was her first serious boyfriend. She liked him – a lot – but James had been in the wings, making the right signals.

She'd no wish to play the field – she wasn't that type of girl – still a virgin, and had intended to remain so until there was a ring was on the third finger of her left hand, but there was a date with James – and she took a chance. He'd been very persuasive, and she'd given in. Enjoyable at the time but quickly regretted, especially when finding she was pregnant.

It was only once – just a lucky chance? No, not for her, it had been extremely unlucky.

Derek learned that the baby was not kept. She couldn't have done that, could she? Look after a child, when it was the big chance? They'd been offered a deal to leave Britain and go to America.

She would have lost everything she'd been working towards: the fame, the big money, the recognition that she could write and sing songs that the public liked, and she would have missed performing them in front of vast numbers of people. Anyway, James hadn't wanted any children. He wanted nothing to tie him down, nor did he want a wife.

The real reason for Steven leaving the band was a broken heart, not the future of a steady, well paid career as a lawyer; this was truly why he left. He'd still loved her and offered marriage, but only if she kept the child and stayed with him in the house his parents would have bought for them. Millie had been torn between the two: fame or motherhood.

She chose fame and sadly, Newingsworth was left behind...

James had won and he knew it, but it didn't change anything regarding marriage, he made that clear; there was no chance. He was the leader of the group, and she could go with them, or be left behind. They were already going to have to replace a good guitarist, so replacing a very talented girl singer/songwriter might be difficult, but not impossible, he'd told her coldly.

She went to the States, and never returned. America became home.

On the move constantly with the group wasn't such a bad life. She got on well with all of them. It was a professional arrangement that existed for her most of the time in the newly structured band, and she was treated with respect.

As their fame grew, she observed the boys beginning to appreciate the benefits of having adoring fans hanging around, very willing fans... While she had the occasional polite and chaste date with admirers, the boys had fans begging for it in each of the towns they visited.

The boys never refused...

What they did in their own time was not liked by her, in fact she abhorred the thought that almost every night they were with a different girl. She often asked herself, was she just jealous? She wasn't sure...

There had been a special celebration party in nineteen-eighty-six. The band was in action that night, with a stage performance in addition to collecting an award. They then retired to a restaurant kept open for the band and entourage only. She'd had too much to drink and succumbed to James' advances again, in much the same way as four or five years before, and much to her disgust, with exactly the same bloody result...

Millie apologised for swearing in her email, but it obviously still riled her. Getting pregnant again had not been in the plan, but this time she felt quite differently about the whole affair. She looked at life a little more maturely than at the last unfortunate occasion. This time she wanted to be a mother and look after her child, but that did not suit James' plans at all.

"You fool, you should have been more careful, shouldn't you?" was his comment.

Any magical allure that James might still have had in Millie's eyes went – totally. An 'arrogant, unsympathetic pig' was precisely how Millie described him to Derek, and Derek thought she had been restrained in her description.

What a despicable character, he told himself ...but James is the only other person I have who can supply me with inside information for the book, so, it seemed sensible keeping these comments under wraps.

The happier news that Derek was pleased to read, was that along the way she met Mickey Schwarz, and not long after James abandoned her. Mickey knew that she was already pregnant, but he told her that he loved her and wanted to marry her no matter, and that's what they did, and together they brought up their lovely daughter.

James never made contact again, but, over the years, Millie followed the goings on of 'Rabid Revenge', cutting out each newspaper article, and imagining she was still the one the loyal fans came to see. She could still summon up that dream, when she relaxed.

Their daughter grew up, not knowing that Mickey was not her real father. She called him 'Pop' all her life, because she knew he liked it, and because he was her dad...

59

"Howzitta going, my younga friend? You notta gotta more funny videos, eh?"

Anton's comment was being directed at Derek, who had popped in for a coffee before a return visit to the Jones' household.

Derek was carrying a square plastic bag which contained a record album – the 'borrowed' record album. Hopefully, by returning it to its rightful owners, it would permit him to think about 'Rabid Revenge' without a pang of conscience hitting him every time, but what he was about to do was making Derek feel very nervous.

The big pseudo-Italian was feeling cheery and pleased to be working today, and for him and the cafe, things were going well, and a very big plus was Angie. She was proving to be a wonderful asset.

Not only was she redesigning the place – and seemed to be progressing well with it – with her also working in the place, fresh customers were being attracted through the doors. More males were making an effort to visit, especially the sixth formers from the High School. They would sit and ogle, as well as buying the food and drinks.

As long as they bought the food and drinks, Anton said they were very welcome to ogle. Angie certainly did not seem to mind...

For Anton, today was a wonderful day, except for one tiny little factor – Angie's big changeover plan: a confidence collapse!

She was afraid that, personally, she couldn't actually make it happen. It was the practical part that was scaring her – she had never done that before. As a matter of fact, she had never done design before either, but any mistakes she made with that were known only to her, and easily rectified in private when she realised a better way.

Playing around with ideas had been fun, but the physical work would have to be done correctly from the start or the daily business would suffer, and she did not want that. That would be letting this nice man down. So, she'd been up-front this morning, and told Anton: sorry but she could not handle the actual changeover.

In his conversation today, with Derek, Anton happened to mention that tiny disturbing factor.

"Who coulda do thatta job forra me? ...Angie issa really worried," he told Derek. "I no' likea her to worry..."

"I know a man," Derek smiled, glad to help a friend.

Derek did know someone, someone who was reaching the end of his present task, and who'd recently displayed a remarkable ability to make things happen; someone he was confident could be coaxed by him to do this job for Anton: the perfect person.

"You know Hamish Macintosh don't you, Anton?"

Anton had heard of him; a local chicken farm owner, who had gone bust. He nodded.

"He's the one for this job," said Derek with confidence, "and I'll speak to him. Leave it with me..."

Derek had another task to face before sorting out Anton's little problem, but as he went on his way towards Mr and Mrs Jones, he felt that at least he had done something good today. Maybe it would go towards balancing out his previous stupid wrongdoing.

He looked forward to being rid of this album. Once he replaced it where it came from, the slate should be clean. He still couldn't believe he had done it. Stealing this LP record was most out of character – he was basically a good guy, he tried to convince himself

Was he really though?

Hiding things from Sally? Things like the recent contact he'd had with Sophie about the book? He had to find a publisher, yes, but doing it behind his wife's back was not the behaviour of a good guy, now was it?

When he'd phoned her, Sophie agreed that she would arrange for the publishing, although the promise was based optimistically on him completing what he was explaining to her, and which in no way could be considered even a nearly-finished book. He was extremely grateful to her, but he was being underhand with Sally – for the best of intentions maybe, but underhand all the same.

Today he walked briskly, glad that this time it was not raining and that he would be arriving dry, and here he was, back at 42 Custard Crescent. He rang the doorbell, and the door was opened by Mrs Jones.

"Ah, Derek, it's nice to see you again," she enthused, and looked at the shape of the plastic bag in his hand, which he'd meant to hide under his jacket, like the last time.

"He's come back, Dad," she called out to her husband, "And he's brought it back with him. I told you he would. Come in, won't you."

The red face followed her into the living room, where Mr Jones was sitting. At least he can't see my embarrassment, Derek remembered thankfully.

"Hello, lad, how are you?" said Mr Jones, as he stood up. "I couldn't even speak the last time you were here, could I? But at least, I could hear you."

"Look, I'm very sorry, I..." Derek tried to stumble out an apology.

"Don't worry, lad," said Mr J. "We understand and we're glad you are bringing it back."

"Cup of tea?" his wife asked.

"How did you...?" Derek started out again.

"Oh ... the dust, the dust..." she said. "That pile of records should have been wiped ages ago, but I just never got round to it. The one underneath was all shiny and clean. Your jacket must have been filthy when you got home."

Derek wanted to crawl into a hole.

"So, you are trying to write a book, you were saying," Mr J commented, as his wife left the room to make the tea.

Why were they being nice about this, surely they should be angry...

"Yes..." Derek replied, choking a little, and uncertain how to continue.

"You might like to know there was some other information we remembered about, after you'd gone. Are you interested in any more information?"

"Oh yes, please," Derek perked up.

"There was a pile of magazines Jonathan sent with the records. They were in a cupboard. Mary will bring them through in a moment. She tells me there are articles in there about the bands performances."

This shouldn't be happening, he said to himself. I don't deserve this. They should be getting annoyed with me.

"There you are, Pet. One spoonful of sugar enough?" and she passed over a cup of tea and biscuits.

"It's been good for us, you being here like this. Before you came, we couldn't talk about Jonathan. He was a dark secret that we were angry about. You've changed all that for us. Thank you."

At that point he told them, about Growler, 'being no more'. It just seemed the correct moment, so he explained to Mr and Mrs Jones, what he had learned from Millie. Their wayward son, Jonathan, would not be returning – he had been killed in an accident.

They seemed to be able to handle the information remarkably well, maybe because of the long period of absence, he thought. Deep down, it seemed to Derek, almost as if it was expected. He was glad to have it over with.

He felt humble and grateful as he left the house over an hour later, with a heavy stack of musical journals, each with a long article about 'Rabid Revenge', and this time, they had not been pinched...

He hurried back to the office and cleared up a lot of outstanding bits and pieces, hoping that Rob wouldn't react too badly about the time he was spending on the book, but Rob hardly noticed. A winner a day can make a betting man so happy...

The day ended in a great way too, because when Derek got home, there, on the computer, waiting to be printed out, were the photos Millie had promised. Her scanner was back in action.

It had been a fantastic day ...though he felt he had not deserved it.

60

He now possessed a huge library of information, and was having to edit out the least useful parts. The photos Millie sent were good, and printed well, showing him his first glimpse of the female rock star when she was only twenty – and she looked lovely, a slim trim figure, clad in a glittery mini-skirted outfit – and just look at those legs – wow.

Wonder what she looks like now? He looked again at her face. She seemed familiar...

He wanted to try making contact with Twister again, that is, if the man would be willing to talk to him. The last response had been somewhat curt and tense – meant to discourage perhaps? He rang the number.

"Hello, this is The Fort Knights' Music Agency, how can we help you – musically..." the female voice sang in his ear.

Goodness, he was caught short again, gulp...

"Ehm, hello, could I speak to..."

"Are you from Her Majesty's Revenue and Customs?"

"Hello, I am Derek Tee, We have spoken before..."

"Do I know you?"

"Yes, you sent Mr Hoist's scrapbook information to me. I presume it was you, and I would like the chance to thank you."

"Ooooh – sorry, I didn't recognise your name right away. It's nice of you to have phoned, Mr Tee, I mean, Derek, and it is a pity there weren't any more cuttings or photos."

"That's ok. I've managed in other ways, but is he in, Mr Hoist, that is? Could I speak to him please?"

He was using his 'could you possibly help me, because I'm a useless male' tone of voice, and it worked.

"Of course you can, Derek. Just one moment and I'll put you through."

There was a distinct pause. Maybe Twister really did not want to speak to him.

"Hello, so you've come back to bother me. What do you want now?"

"I'd like some more information, if you are willing, but something else as well – a favour."

"I don't do favours, Sunshine."

"Well, a little assistance then. How would you like a trip back to Newingsworth? I'd pay your expenses, and arrange accommodation in one of the new local hotels."

"What? Why would I want to do that?"

"I thought some pre-sales publicity might help create a market for my book, and it would take you back to one of your old haunts."

"Go on..."

Derek was delighted, at least he hadn't hung up on him yet, but he hadn't said yes to anything either, so he kept going...

"You'll remember the Old Astoria Cafe, the band's old gang hut?"

"Yea, vaguely...?"

"Well it's all being renovated and I thought it would be good for the book, and for Anton the owner, if you were there to help open the place. I'd have the local radio and the local press there too. It would be like being a star again for you. Do you remember that feeling?"

"Mmmmmm..."

Derek was amazed, this guy was still listening, and it looked as if he was going to go along with it.

"Ok, provided the date doesn't clash with anything else. Is that all?"

"No, there was one other thing..."

Holding an interview over a telephone is never easy, Derek had always found. It was always beneficial to see facial expressions, to judge the right moment for a particular question, but he had little choice.

"What were your relationships with the other members of the band?"

"Do you really want to know? I was the leader. They did what they were told, right?"

"I'm sure it wasn't as simple as that."

"If you must know, the females were the problem. You should never have females in a rock band. They cause nothing but trouble and..."

Oh, oh, that's a touchy one. For a guy who had a reputation for being a lad with the ladies it sounded now as if he had become a fully paid-up member of 'The Born Again Misogynists'.

With difficulty, Derek guided him away from the girls to the males. He seemed at little more relaxed discussing them – Growler, he'd been great when he was playing the drums, but a bit of a boozer when he wasn't, especially in later years; Sailor, a brilliant lead guitarist, started showing off during the shows, and he'd had to pull him up about it, and he could get quite huffy; as for Bonzo, he hated him from the bottom of his heart, it seemed.

"A pumped-up no good piece of..."

Derek held the phone away from his ear in case he caught some of the venom.

"And what about the one who didn't make it – Steven Thwaite?"

"I never liked him. He was scum, for sure – became a professional crook."

So, Derek's earlier research was proving correct then.

The talk rambled on for a while longer, but without anything complimentary being said about the others. To Derek, the portrait this man painted of himself was in beautiful shades of perfection, which seemed highly unlikely if Millie's comments were to be believed. Also, the way he put it, having been part of a highly successful band sounded like a terrible experience – and yet they were together for twenty-one years.

"One more question, your two girl singers, they were very attractive. Did you ever consider getting married to either of them, and settling down?"

There was a deathly silence at the other end of the line – and the receiver was replaced.

61

"G-g-g-g-guess who I saw in t-t-t-t-town today?" Hector asked.

"Lady Gaga?" Daisy replied.

"N-n-n-no ...d-d-don't be silly. It was that g-g-girl from B-B-B-B-B-Bisko's. She's never in there now. I've l-l-looked for her. I've m-m-m-m-m-missed her... She was in Ant-t-t-t-tons..."

He sounded really sad not to be tailing her regularly. He brightened up though this morning when he was passing the Old Astoria Cafe and saw her on the other side of the glass. She didn't see him looking at her, or she might have become hysterical; she hoped she was shot of the old guy.

"D-D-D-D-Derek's planning to have a b-b-bit of a d-d-d-do in there. D-d-d-d-d-did you know?"

"No ...what kind of a 'do'?"

"F-f-f-f-for his n-n-n-new b-b-b-book."

"But he doesn't have a book yet, has he? You can't have a 'do' without a book, can you?"

Hector wasn't sure of the legitimacy of having a 'do' without a book.

"...B-b-b-but that's where he's having it. He's invited that b-b-b-b-bloke, James H-H-H-Hoist, he told me, from L-L-L-L-London. It's a l-long way to c-c-c-come."

"No it isn't, not in a big car. He'll have one, I'll bet. It would be a long way if you went on the scooter. Hope there's no trouble..."

"You could do it with your eyes shut," Derek told him.

Hammy was reluctant to take on the responsibility of the conversion of Anton's premises, but a few pints was doing a good job of winning him over.

Wasn't he twiddling his thumbs to pass the time just now, and anyway, the New Farmhouse Hotel was nearly done. Derek was putting on the pressure. Hadn't Hammy already confided that the painting work was completed, and the place was already almost fully fitted out, even though the first guests were not to arrive for several more weeks? Didn't he admit that he hadn't a clue what he'd do with himself when it was finished?

Anyway, it would only be judged successful or not, when the first guests moved in; the hard work would come after that. So, he'd have nothing to do until it opened.

"So, you agree then? You'll do it – the work at Anton's?"

"Och well, ah don't know..." was Hammy's hesitant response.

Derek took that as a "Yes..."

Very soon the hotel would be officially opening its doors, bedrooms, and other assorted facilities, to paying guests, who would be looked after with care by Mr Hamish Macintosh, the manager, and Ms Thelma Davidson, the housekeeper. Both of course would be living-in, to attend to all the needs of their guests, of course.

At long last, he could offer her accommodation which would be more comfortable than the run-down old caravan, and which was available immediately to move into. To Hammy's delight, when he asked this time, Thelma consented to becoming engaged.

Giving their blessing was a pleasure for Alexander and Muriel now that the affair was almost public, because for Alexander in particular, it would mean his twin sister would no longer be living under the same roof as he was.

The engagement was planned for the same night as the opening of the New Astoria Eating House, and that was where they would be celebrating, making the engagement both official, and totally public. It coincided with Derek's plan for publicity for his new book – provided of course that Hammy, and his team, successfully finished the fitting out of Anton's new premises on time.

The sharing of that night by Anton, Hammy and Derek, was a very practical proposal, because they had friends who were shared anyway. They would all know each other, more or less, and it would be a nice cheap way to do it, as far as Hammy was concerned.

Derek and Sally made a list of the people who should be invited to his advance publicity night. Some were very obvious and would be hurt if not asked like Hector and Daisy, and Sally's mum and dad, and of course Aunt Thelma and Hammy.

The mobile phone rang and was traced to the shopping bag in the kitchen, and answered by Sally. Derek heard the giggling noises, obviously some good news.

"Aunt Thelma and Hammy are going to get engaged on the same night as your book launch, Derek. Isn't that great..." Sally excitedly informed him as she came back into the living room.

He was not so carried away. It was old news to him, and news that he should have passed on to Sally perhaps. Hammy told him yesterday, and asked him and Anton if it would be alright if they did the three things together, "...because it would cost less."

In his head Derek had a new name for Hammy but he didn't want to say it out loud. It was meant affectionately, of course, and Hammy did give Scots a bad name...

Sally was delighted for her aunt, and immediately had to make an alteration to the list of invites on the piece of paper. Hammy's entry she changed to – Uncle Hammy. Derek smiled wryly – he would stick with his own choice, 'McCheapskate'. Still, it would be nice for it all to be happening on the same night – a real party.

The special guest, Twister, would be coming up from London specially to introduce Derek's still-to-be-completed book; the two oldies' engagement would be celebrated; and after the formal private reception, Anton's premises would be re-opening to the public the following day.

Derek was going to contact Curly and Carol.

Graham Stockman, Curly, was the head of the local radio station, **'LITTLE RADIO fm'**. Derek was sure that if he asked his old pal nicely, he and Carol would do some recording for a local broadcast.

That way he could gain extra publicity for the book.

Contacting some of his old pals at the Slatterfoot Evening News should guarantee more publicity. Someone would be happy to come along. Free nosh and some wet stuff, were always attractions for these guys. Rob already had agreed to run some articles in the Gazette but that was weekly. These guys would be from the Evening News; they were daily.

Derek reckoned you couldn't beat all that for publicity, especially as it would be free. Now, by any chance, could this be the same young man who had the cheek to call Hammy a cheapskate?

Andy Woodstock would be coming too, and he would be giving a lift to the publisher from London.

"What's his name?" Sally innocently enquired, to make sure Sophie Clerkenwell-Brown was not involved.

"Eh, Mr Brown, err yes, Mr Brown," he'd replied, trying to avoid any body language that he knew Sally could recognise.

There was one small problem in trying to avoid showing the signs, he had never actually found out what the give-aways were ...but Sally accepted Mr Brown.

Derek phoned Sophie. She agreed to come in drag. It had started off as a joke, but she promised to wear a moustache, and a man's suit, and tuck her hair under a baseball cap. Sally would never recognise her, she promised.

Meanwhile, what about the cafe? Angie was panicking. Would it all work out? Sleep was impossible...

She had met Hammy and discovered to her horror that he talked in an even stranger way than Anton, but he seemed to know what was required. It would all be happening over a period of five days, they hoped.

"Dinna fech yersell, ma dearie..." he had said to her at the time.

Angie had absolutely no idea what the man was talking about. His way of talking was the least of her worries though. How could she sleep? There was so much hanging on it going right.

"Cuddle me, Sam. I need hugged."

So, Sam had to wake up and cuddle her, but he didn't find that difficult...

62

The big day arrived for the shiny new hotel to receive the very first guest. This person was due late in the evening, an economy booking at a specially negotiated rate and pre-paid for a Mr James Hoist. He would be travelling up from London and was to be allocated the Hazelnut Room. Thelma had been in to check that everything was in order, and was pleased to congratulate the new maid for an excellent job done.

There was as second visitor, coming over from America, and booked by Angelina, the young lady that Hamish had been working with at Anton's. A very good job had been done for this room also, the Chestnut Room.

Who would be fortunate enough to be awarded the post of Chef was not yet finalised, so, Thelma in the interim would be catering for the breakfast needs in the Hotel, with an understanding having been reached with the New Astoria Eating House for all other meal requirements. Hotel guests would eat there, until a chef was taken on, and the kitchen could come into full use.

If necessary, a shuttle taxi would be laid on by Hamish, if he was available. If not, the local taxi service had been asked to be prepared.

It was all systems, go.

Angie, Hammy, and the men he brought along from the hotel project because he knew he could trust them, had been working extremely hard for four days and half of last night too, and it was all coming nicely together.

The old cafe was doubled in size. Anton had managed to acquire the deserted premises next door, and removed the dividing wall. An unforeseen problem caused by the flooring of the two premises being at slightly differing levels required special attention, but between them, they found a solution, and it had become a feature. Having the step mid-way suited the slightly adjusted layout, together with a ramp for wheelchairs of course, which was almost forgotten...

The tartan carpeting was now being vacuumed.

Hammy said to them all, woe betide anyone who marked it in any way. This warning was issued by him personally, because he was the one using the vacuum cleaner. Everyone was being extremely careful, because due to the Scottish accent the warning sounded so fierce!

The tables and the seating were all looking the part. The lighting had been totally replaced, and was adjustable to suit either daytime brightness, or evening sophistication. The colours of the walls had been carefully chosen and the last coats were being touched up at that very minute. Thank goodness it was fast drying. Everyone would be arriving in only six more hours, but importantly, they had succeeded. The New Astoria Eating House was finished...

Angie and Hammy had met only a few days before starting the work, but it seemed appropriate that, on completion, they should celebrate their combined success with a celebratory hug and a kiss – on the cheek, of course; they were both accounted for.

In the kitchen, the new chef, Tommy, had been preparing the hors d'oeuvre, and pizza, and sandwiches, and many other goodies. Anton and Peter were making sure the glasses were clean and sparkling, that there was more than ample white wine being chilled, and that the pictures were sitting ready to be added to the walls the moment the paint was dry.

Anton had a silly grin on his face. He was finding it hard to believe, his cafe, it was ...modern!

"Who woulda havva believ-ed thees?" he kept repeating...

Derek appeared early to check everything was going to plan, and was amazed. The place now looked so different. Hammy and Angie had done magnificently. What a transformation.

The visitors started arriving sharp at seven o'clock; Hector and Daisy being first, not surprisingly. It is in an older person's genes not to arrive late, Derek decided, and not arriving on time could only mean they were too early.

Next to arrive was his better half. Her parents enjoyed the pleasure of Sally's company this afternoon, because her dad was in the back room on his own with a good book. She came with Muriel and Alexander, and entered the new premises, just shortly after his grandparents, to be impressed just as much as those previously.

Thanks to the Bowling Club, the music of 'Rabid Revenge' could be heard on the Eating House's new loudspeaker system, playing at a lower volume than normal for their music, but creating atmosphere none the less.

The albums from the Jones' household, borrowed specially by Derek, could be played only on the special equipment on loan from the Bowling Club – the modern multi-purpose CD/record/tape machine. Old vinyl LPs responded with music only if you had the right type of needle and a table revolving at 33 rpm, and, lucky for Derek, it was bingo at the Club so they would manage without their wonderful multifaceted machine for one night.

Hammy was pacing about. He'd stayed all day in case anything had been missed and changed into fresh clothes on the premises, but he was watching proceedings with an anxious look on his face. Derek suspected that he was afraid Thelma might have chickened out at the last moment.

There was enormous relief for him when a lovely looking Thelma came in the front door. He rushed over and gave her a very chaste kiss on the cheek. The effect of doing something so intimate in public for the very first time had an exhausting effect, so Thelma helped him to a seat to recover.

Derek expected some mickey-taking to occur when Charlie and Bill arrived. At least they hadn't worn their gardening clothes he was pleased to note; he couldn't trust them though. They saw him and waved.

"Ullo Sweaty, ow are ye mate? Sweaty, Sweaty, Sweaty, go, go, go..." they called out in unison, punching the air in time.

He could tell they'd practised that before they came here tonight.

"Buggers..." he whispered under his breath – the only ones so far to call him 'Sweaty' – but he smiled broadly as he waved back.

Most of the local councillors who were invited were arriving with spouses and had quickly homed in to the liquid refreshments, displaying a particular expertise for this type of occasion.

Mr Jones was led in by Mrs Jones. Derek welcomed them and said how pleased he was that they'd managed, and helped them to the table they chose nearer the back. They already had loaned Derek all of Growler's albums to use tonight. As Derek left them at their table he heard Mrs Jones comment that Jonathan's rock band didn't sound too bad when played quietly...

Rather than change here as Hammy did, Angie had slipped off home the moment she felt the place was finished and ready, and now she looked absolutely radiant. By the looks of her it had been worth it; she was lovely. She came in on Sam's arm, smiling sweetly as she looked around the room, but a little embarrassed viewing her own achievement. She was seeing the changes fully and properly for the first time – that was Derek's impression anyway and he certainly thought she had done a great job.

Then Andy Woodstock came through the front door, but he was alone? What's happened to Sophie? He was supposed to have collected her this afternoon and brought her up here. Did he forget?

Andy was followed in by Rob and Spider, who went straight for the drinks.

Oh, oh ...there is an interloper in the room, he noticed. Derek went over towards him. He would say quietly in his ear that this was a private function and would he kindly leave; and hope he wouldn't be receiving a black eye for his trouble.

As he opened his mouth to say it, a female voice spoke.

"Hello, big boy, is this good enough?" she said softly.

Sophie had done a superb job with her disguise...

"Mr Brown, how are you? Glad you could make it," said Derek loudly. "My publisher..." he turned, making sure everyone could hear, and then whispered to Mr Brown, "I hope you can disguise your voice better, or Sally will flay me alive... "

Anton meanwhile, helped by Peter, was ensuring everyone was being offered a drink, and the food was being placed on the tables for the buffet.

So far, so good, thought Derek.

"Coulda I havva your attention everyone, please because I wanna welcome you all to Anton'sa new place. It'sa gonna be called the New Astoria Eating Housea, and will be open to common peoples tomorrow. Thissa bootifool little lady here, my goodda friend Angelina, has been the one who designas eet, I thanka her, and I thanka my gooda friend Hammy for putting eet nearly alla together... an I hoppa you havva gooda evening, everybody."

There was a round of applause, and it was Hammy's turn.

"Ladies an' gen'lemen, we're aw here the night tae huvv fun, an' ah'm gonnie huvv mair fun than any o' ye, because tonight, this lovely Thelma an' me urr gettin' engaged. So, could ye raise yerr glasses – tae ma luvvly fiancé, Thelma."

There was a loud cheer, and everyone stepped forward to slap Hammy's back and to shake the hand of Thelma, and peck her on the cheek. She was fidgeting and blushing like a young thing. The glasses were refilled, and as soon as they were, there was a loud rapping of a spoon on a table, and an American voice rang out.

"Ladies and gentlemen, could I have your attention for a moment, because I also have something very important to say."

Having secured everyone's attention Sam turned to where Angie was standing, and went down on one knee.

"Angie, my sweet honey, will you marry me?" he said gently.

Angie looked at him, her eyes rolled – and she fainted. This day, for Angelina, had been just a little too much.

63

The evening could have come apart very shortly after that. The usual hullabaloo which occurs when someone faints means some people want to help, but some people have to look away, and others have to visit the toilet. Sophie was in the latter category...

Thankfully, Angie's fainting was not a major problem, and she quickly recovered in Sam's arms. There was a loud cheer as she opened her eyes, and said the magic words.

"I will, Sam, yes, I really will..."

It could have been a problem only minutes later, but wasn't, when Sally decided her toilet visit was required, and she was about to push open the 'Ladies' door. As she reached forward, it opened from inside, and a gentleman exited, a gentleman with a moustache and a baseball cap, and Sally recognised him. It was Derek's publisher, of course.

"Silly man," Sally said out loud, shaking her head sadly.

"Yes," said her mother, who had followed her to powder her nose too, but she did the same as her daughter and double checked the sign on the outside before proceeding.

In the meantime, the Evening News reporter had arrived and made straight for the free drinks. Curly and Carol appeared too, just moments later, carrying their recording equipment.

Derek was nervously wandering around the room. Eight-fifteen was the planned time for the arrival of the star attraction: Twister. Just another five minutes...

He needn't have worried. The next part went like clockwork. As planned at the correct moment, Derek stepped onto the little platform, (the one cleverly designed by Angelina, of course) to make the announcement.

"Ladies and Gentlemen, we have come to the headline reason for you being here tonight. It wasn't just to drink all the wine and eat all the food and dirty the new carpets..."

(Polite tittering from his audience...)

"I would like you all to meet and welcome back to Newingsworth, the local boy who made good as a musician. He was with the world-famous rock group, 'Rabid Revenge', a group renowned for their ear-shattering music, and whose naughty adventures will feature in my future book, on sale shortly... This gentleman has travelled a long distance to entertain us tonight, so please give him a hearty Newingsworth, Slatterfoot and surrounding districts welcome... I bring to you, from 'Rabid Revenge', their ever popular leader – Twister..."

The volume of 'Rabid' music coming through the loudspeakers suddenly increased in intensity, as arranged with Anton, and with a bit of a swagger and right on cue through the front door, in he came to loud applause, although most were saying to themselves...

"What the heck is 'Rabid Revenge'?"

As the star stepped into the room, carrying his favourite acoustic guitar, this forty-nine year old man became twenty again, anticipating the usual rush of adoring, screaming, female fans, and prepared to brush them aside, as he stepped forward, but quickly returned to reality when he saw the faces simply looking at him out of curiosity.

Oh, for the good old days, he thought, stepping onto Angie's platform confidently, because he knew he could still hold an audience. He would talk to them using his good ol' American drawl – they loved that...

"Good evening fans..." he said, smiling at the faces, then realising, "...and all the rest of you, and here ah am again after all these long years, back at Anton's, and ah'm still giving you what you love... What a place this is though... Used to be called our Gang Hut by the band – and ah'm pleased to see it hasn't changed a bit..."

Derek wished that he'd spent more time on the phone with Mr

James Hoist.

"This really feels like comin' home, the lights, the warmth of your welcome, and the generosity with the ...drinks...?"

There was a momentary pause until Anton got the message, rushed forward, and handed him a glass of wine.

"...An' where is good old Anton these days?"

"Heara I ama" said the figure in front of him, who suddenly felt less excited about tonight, and moved back out of the limelight.

"Oh... Yea, hi old fella ...but as ah was sayin', bein' famous, like me, has its disadvantages of course. All sorts of people want to write books about ya, don't ya, Derek? Where are ya, boy? Stand up. Take a bow!"

Derek did this dutifully, bearing in mind that this person had never seen him before – they had only talked on the phone. He hoped that Mr James Hoist would still remember who he was at the end of the performance. He was happy to sit down again, and let the star get on with it. At least, he'd sort-of mentioned the book...

"Now, I brought my geetar with me, ya'll have noticed. I know you wouldn't have wanted me to come here an' not be singin' somethin' special furr ya, one o' my hits, but that's for later. But first, let me tell you some stories about the band..."

After a while, Derek reflected; this fellow arrived on cue and started talking well, the book was mentioned, his stories are funny at times and sad at others, and he is holding people's attention in an effortless style, so it isn't all bad. He relaxed a little more, as the star's tales continued to pour out in an American drawl...

"...But when it comes to havin' females in a band, ah'd advise ya not to have them. They can cause nothin' but trouble in my opinion."

That's when Derek tensed... Oh, oh, he thought, he's about to lose most of the females in the audience if he starts to talk the way he did on the phone...

"Yea, they maybe look good standin' up there in the spotlight, an' they may be pretty good singers, but when it comes to love, and trust, and loyalty, the important things in life – they let ya down every time..."

Now that was the wrong thing to say, Derek told himself.

Suddenly, there was a voice from the back of the room, a voice Derek recognised, but before he could put a face to it, there was a quick turn of events – and a yell!

"You no-good scumbag of a liar!"

And then a whoosh, as a small carving knife, sitting on the buffet table moments before, flew through the air towards the shocked star.

It all happened so quickly.

The knife missed Twister, and plunged into the newly-painted plasterboard behind him.

Everyone stood up in panic, and yells came from all directions.

"Oh my God, not you..." Twister blurted out, standing shaking in shock.

Anton was wailing, hands over face, "Mya wall, mya new wall, looka whatta you doooooo to mya new walla..."

"Mom... what did ya do that for?" came from Angie.

Hector and Daisy were sitting clutching hands.

"D-D-D-D-D-Daisy, I've seen an-n-n-nother g-g-g-g-ghost..." came from Hector as he stared at the figure standing there, and clutched Daisy's hand even tighter.

"Don't be silly, Hector – calm down" said Daisy feeling tense and agitated herself, but not letting it show as she patted his arm gently. "It is your daughter. It's Millicent, She's come back home, at last."

"Nobody move – stay where you are – I am a policeman!" shouted Andy Pandy Woodstock.

"A scoop..." yelled Carol, and Curly, and the Evening News Reporter, in unison, as if they had been rehearsing too.

Bugger, said Derek to himself. It's all gone terribly wrong...

64

It hadn't really been a failure. In fact, if getting publicity was what Derek had been after, he succeeded... The Slatterfoot Evening News had plenty time to prepare for the following evening's edition, and when he read it, Derek had to admit, his friend had been kind.

MUM'S THE WORD
*   By Dave Smart*
Reporting good news is unusual in these troubled times, but, last evening in a new restaurant in Newingsworth, things were happening that could only bring a smile to the saddest face. As a guest at the opening of the New Astoria Eating House, it felt strange for me to be in what had become a favourite gathering place for the local community; a place no-one would have believed could change – Anton's Old Astoria Cafe – but change it had. Now transformed into a delightful restaurant, and bringing new life to what had been becoming a tired old Main Street.
The party was to celebrate the opening of the premises, but, adding to the fun were two couples announcing intentions to be wed. Having a performance by the guitarist who led the highly successful rock group, Rabid Revenge, also brought an extra something to the evening. But it was the appearance of another ex-member of Rabid Revenge, returning to her native town for the first time in thirty-two years which made it so special.
There were tears, but tears of joy, as Millie came face to face with her son, the baby she left behind all these years ago – the local journalist

and author, Derek Toozlethwaite. "Hard to believe" said Derek, "and not what I expected to find while doing research for my book." His new book is called 'Rabid Revenge Revisited' and is due to be published soon. More was in store when he learned he had a sister – now living in town – who'd known nothing of him either.

So, last night, with the good company, loud music, fine wine, happy tears for a family reunion, and the exciting climax to the evening's entertainment, there was no denying – it was great night for good news.

In addition to the blurb there was a group photo showing a happy crowd including Millie and Derek. The photo surprised Derek because all were displaying beaming smiles, including him. He could remember nothing of it. It was unfortunate, but not surprising, that the star performer had not been available for that photo.

Dave had been a good mate when they worked alongside each other before he'd left the News, and he had done what was expected of good mates.

Curly and Carol had been kind too. They ran the story on local radio as a magazine item and expanded it more than the newspaper version, but nothing nasty, maybe poking a little more fun at Derek, emphasising that things had not gone quite to plan.

How could Derek possibly have known before organising that night, that he was about to discover a mother he'd never known, a father he'd thought was someone else, and a sister he hadn't even known existed?

Gran and Grandad had been a bit huffy to begin with, because Millicent had never once made contact with them to even let them know she was alright, but the bad feeling only lasted a little while, and then they all cried in a corner for about ten minutes and cleared the air.

Angie was still in shock at realising the old man she had disliked so much, her stalker, turned out to be her grandad, and was a nice old man after all. She then went into a corner with her newly discovered grandparents, and had a good old cry too.

Sally joined in after a while, to say hello to her new sister-in-law – and guess what they did?

Yes, it was a weepy night... but they giggled a bit as well, especially Sally and Angelina. They got on like a house on fire. They also decided to have a competition to see who would be the first to have a baby...

As for the star guest, Mr James Hoist, he left rapidly, to return to London, even though a room was booked. The Hazelnut Room was ready and waiting for him at the New Farmhouse Hotel, but it appeared he had no use for it. He went off in a foul mood after Millie appeared, and that was a great pity, because Mr James Hoist left without knowing that his son and daughter had been in the same room.

At that point, they hadn't known the relationship either. He had never seen either child, other than for a short time as a baby, and both had changed a little in appearance since then. Of course, he may not have wanted to know them, but no-one had the opportunity to find out.

It appeared to be a very confused and disheartened Derek, who stood inside Anton's place, looking forlornly out of the large front window of the New Astoria Eating House. It looked that way, but inside his head the story for the book was currently reforming.

It was dark outside and Derek was viewing the reflection of the scene behind him. There, in that reflection, he was seeing an entirely new scenario. It had all happened for him tonight. He foresaw that 'Revenge' could be his for the taking as this whole story was opening up in a surprisingly new way. It was now dramatically very personal. In the near future, he could be sharing their fame, provided he tells it well: his mother, and his father, both had been major rock stars – what a discovery!

It was only after James Hoist vanished abruptly and the dust settled that Derek had the chance to sit down with his new-found mum. When he asked her, Millie came clean about it all, and the details came spilling out.

Because Millie had married very soon after her second unplanned pregnancy with Twister, Angie was brought up believing that Mickey

Schwarz was her biological father and she was called Angelina Schwarz. This much, Derek knew from the emails previously, though her name had never been stated.

However – his mother looked a little shameful as she told him this – the surname on his birth certificate had been a concoction. It was a shocking moment when Derek found out that a father called James Toozlethwaite didn't exist. That name had been made up by his mother – thirty-two years ago. No Toozlethwaite had ever existed, as far as his mother knew – until Derek.

It had been done to hide the real father's name, partly due to the shame she felt, but also to save James Hoist from pain. "If I had exposed that the real father was Twister, back then," she explained, "...your grandad, Hector, would have chopped off his bollocks!" These were his new-found mother's very words. Hector still doesn't know, she told Derek. "I hope you can keep this secret from him, and from Angie," she said.

Derek thought of how his grandparents had managed to keep the secret of his mother's identity from him – for thirty-two long years. Yes, he readily agreed, it would be a secret – and then he thought about the book.

That would mean a large chunk being missed out, an interesting and juicy part too – so, he changed his mind. He convinced his mum that Hector wasn't up to that sort of behaviour these days, certainly not without Daisy's permission, and after Millie thought a little more, she decided that Angie was a big girl now. She had loved Mickey Schwarz like a father and would surely continue to do so, even if she learned the truth in the future.

So, the juicy bits would stay in the story...

"But, wait a minute," he said. "You told me, in the email, you hadn't kept the baby."

"But I didn't, did I?" she replied, with a smile. "Your grandparents did."

"All right then, but what about the name? There is no Mr James Toozlethwaite. Why did you use that? And anyway, did you not recognise who I was when you contacted me?"

"How could I recognise you? I couldn't see you – and you used a false name – Derek Tee – and a false nose! You cheated. Anyway, Toozlethwaite was a mixture of the names of the boys in the band. Steven Thwaite, you know about, and then there was Jonathan, dear Jonathan... Jonathan's middle name was Toozle, but for some reason he'd always just used Jonathan T Jones. You'll have to ask his mum and dad about that one, if you want to know more."

"And Derek, where did that come from?"

"A Hoist, that's a derrick, which became Derek, clever eh?"

"Oh yea," he agreed sarcastically, "...landing me with Toozlethwaite – and even worse – the nickname. For all these years, I've been called Sweaty because of it. Thanks a bunch..."

"Sweaty?" and her face broke into a big grin. "I didn't know that. You never mentioned that before. Sweaty, oh yes, I like that, it's different. Do you mind if I call you that – Sweaty?"

"OH... YES... I... DO!" was Derek's determined reply.

Please... Call Me Derek

ISBN 978-1-908135-10-0

Derek travels from child to confused adult, from reporter for the local paper to any job available, doing everything he thinks he should, but doing it his way. Pursuing life and employment leads Derek to fling himself into the sort of sticky situations difficult to explain to his friends or his family. With determination, gritting his teeth, doing everything for the best, how could anything go wrong?

The first in the Derek series, 'Please... Call me Derek' is available in paperback from all major book shops, online through the publisher's book shop www.uppbooks.com and through Amazon.

It is also available on Kindle
ISBN 978-1-908135-21-6

Derek's in Trouble

ISBN 978-1-908135-11-7

As funny as ever and as unlucky as always, Derek is going through another unexpected crisis in his life. A local reporter with the partner of his dreams, his life is all set to be perfect. So, how will he explain his foray out in his wife's dress? Then, there's the leggy lady intent on making a lasting impression ...on top of that, there are everyone else's problems to sort. Is his Gran, the secret Radio agony aunt, capable of helping anyone?

It is also available on Kindle
ISBN 978-1-908135-23-0

If you would like to find out more about Derek and his adventures, please follow Mac Black on www.macblack.info

Derek's Good Relations

is next !